The Wrong Woman To Love . . .

Dan Winthrop had met her just once, and known her only for a night. But that was enough to fall desperately in love.

Now at last he had found her again. Just one thing was wrong. She was his brother's wife.

Until the next morning, that is. Then she was his brother's widow.

And unless Grace Latham and the redoubtable Dr. Birdsong found the murderer, falling in love was going to cost Dan Winthrop his life . . .

"Excellent characterizations, action, verve, and wit. Good reading"
—SATURDAY REVIEW

LESLIE FORD has be-come one of the most widely read mystery writers in America. Her first novel was published in 1928 and since then she has written around forty others.

Miss Ford lives in Annapolis, Maryland.

Among her books are *False To Any Man, Old Lover's Ghost, The Town Cried Murder, The Woman in Black, Trial By Ambush, Ill Met By Moonlight, The Simple Way of Poison* and *The Clue of the Judas Tree*, all published in Popular Library editions.

THREE
BRIGHT
PEBBLES

By LESLIE FORD

WILDSIDE PRESS

Published by Wildside Press LLC
www.wildsidepress.com

1

Dan Winthrop shifted his blond six-feet-two a notch lower in the green and white awning-shaded chair, and stared moodily at the large divot he'd been digging with the heel of his shoe in my blue-grass lawn.

"Oh, I know, Grace. But the thing nobody realizes about Mother is she's never really happy unless she's stirring up a hell's broth for somebody else to stew in."

It was hot and sultry out there in my back garden in Georgetown, the air pungent and heavy like ominous ripe fruit ready to burst. I tried to tell myself—being a sensible woman, mostly —that it was the weather, so appallingly unseasonable for early June, that was making this young man whom I knew very well into somebody I didn't know at all. His jaw was set so that his big good-natured mouth, usually twisted into an infectious and engaging grin, was drawn grimly down at the corners. His blue eyes, ordinarily lighted with an exasperating sort of nothing-sacred twinkle, were as somber and sultry as the leaden clouds gathering behind the summer sky . . . and as disturbing.

I shifted in my own chair, as if moving would dispel the strange uneasiness that had settled between us.

"Actually, of course, darling," I said, "your mother's one of the most utterly charming people in the world.—Isn't she?"

I didn't add, as my colored cook Lilac had done when Dan Winthrop appeared on our doorstep two days before, "And aren't you *just* like her."—"Law, Mis' Grace," Lilac had put it, "ain't Mist' Dan sho' the spit of his Ma?"

He gave me a gloomy grin.

"That's the trouble again, Grace. You see her when she opens Romney for the Garden Pilgrimage, or pours for the Colonial Dames. You don't have the morning mail turned into a slow motion ticker tape to see whether your stock is up or down or just out in the snow—if you know what I mean."

I don't think I'd ever heard quite such unemotionally distilled bitterness before . . . certainly not from Dan Winthrop. I'd got out of the habit of expecting anything else from his brother Rick, whom I used to run across from time to time, or his little sister Mara, whom I see occasionally. But Rick Winthrop is drunk all the time, or most of the time, and Mara . . . well, I just wouldn't know about Mara. I didn't see her often enough even to know whether she was sticking to Alan

5

Keane because she loved him or because it infuriated her mother. And because the children-in-revolt movement always seems rather unreal to me—most parents and children I know getting on more like friends than relatives—I never thought much about it. And if I did, after I'd spent a little time with any of them, I always came comfortably back to the fact that Dan Winthrop, at least, really got on marvelously with his mother. That seemed to make everything all right, some way. Even Mara had a sort of grudging admiration for the way he managed to smooth all the paths.

Rick, so far as I'd known, never managed to get along with anybody, least of all, apparently, with the girl he'd married just before Christmas—against his mother's wishes, of course—and deposited, bag and baggage, in the front hall of Romney while he returned to café society. But Dan hadn't ever gone in for night spots. He'd even had a job that he'd got himself with a shipping company in Paris. He'd been over there three years, and while Mara insisted he only got the job to get on the good side of his mother, he'd certainly kept it, and even gone ahead in it.

I'd seen him once in Paris, two summers before, working like a horse with everybody else off to Iceland fishing, or climbing about in the Tyrol. I'd expected, some way, when Irene Winthrop called me on the phone and said, "My dear Grace, it's too marvelous, Dan's coming home, he's landing tomorrow, and he's going to stop by for you, and you're coming down to Romney with him—it's really important, I'll explain everything!" that he'd have grown up in two years, become more serious and adult. So I'd been surprised, when he first turned up, to find he hadn't changed at all. His ready grin was just as boyish and debonair, and the quick twinkle in his eye just as infectious, and just as many girls phoned him at just as ungodly hours as they had done when he used to be down in Washington during vacations when he was at Williams.

At least I'd thought he hadn't changed, up to this moment. I wasn't so sure, now. Was he, I wondered, like Rick and Mara, a chip off some atavistic block? Because certainly they weren't any of them like Irene, or like their father, who was a cousin of my husband's, and died the same month, eight years ago. Which is how I'd known them all so well during their adolescent and college days. Even then Dan had been the only one who didn't complain constantly about his mother . . . a gay, charming woman, as capricious as an April day, and as lovely, who always seemed much more amused at having produced two great hulking blond sons and a dark elfin daughter than concerned with raising them, or training them for the

6

business of living. I imagine that might explain how, in turn, Dan's attitude toward her took on, as he grew up, an air of affectionate and protective, rather big-brotherish amusement.

"I suppose I'm nothing but a first-class bounder," he said morosely. "Or I'd have stayed over there and said the hell with it."

He sat up abruptly and hunched forward, elbows on his knees, plucking at the cellophane wrapping on a pack of cigarettes.

"But the idea of brother Rick quietly sluicing the family finances down the drain burns me up."

I looked at him.

"It seems to me," I said, "that brother Rick was making practically the same complaint about you, the last time I saw him."

"I know. And the fact is I haven't had a sou, except at Christmas, from Mother for two years. Not since I wouldn't throw up my job and come home."

"I thought she was delighted you'd got a job," I said.

"She was. Only her idea of a job is something you go to Tuesdays, if you feel like it, and knock off for the week end at lunch Thursdays. She couldn't understand why I wouldn't take a couple of weeks off to go to Budapest to a party the new air attaché was giving for his freckle-faced daughter. So she stopped my allowance. Then she heard somebody lecture about Youth and Spring in Paris, and decided I was right to stay there, and started it again. Then she heard another guy on The Pitfalls of Paris, and wired me to come home on the next boat. That practically ended everything."

He lighted a cigarette, a sardonic grin in one corner of his mouth.

"That was O. K. till somebody started advertising all this Frankly Forty stuff. That was when Mother decided it was time she had some grandchildren. She's fifty-five, even if she doesn't look it. So she trots out a whole stable of horse-faced gals and says it's time you and Rick were getting married, and I'll arrange a suitable income for each of you. And Rick does marry, and Mother doesn't like Cheryl, or whatever her name is, so she doesn't arrange the suitable income."

"And now it's your turn?"

He shook his head. "Wrong, darling."

"I thought that was why you'd come back after all these many years," I said. "In fact—"

"I know. She's got her heart set on a gal named Natalie something. But that's not why I came home. I'm not getting married. I came back because . . . Mother's getting married."

I stared at him in the blankest amazement.

"Darling—are you out of your mind?" I gasped.

"No. Mother is."

"Who's she going to marry?"

"Sidney Tillyard."

"Really?"

He nodded.

"I mean, it's all right. Old friend of the family, good-looking, nice fellow."

He shrugged his shoulders.

"It's O. K. with me. I don't *like* it. I don't suppose children ever like seeing somebody else . . . come in. But we aren't children, and Mother has a right to her own life and all that. What I mean is, there's no reason for Rick to chuck his weight about. He's never home. And Mara'll get a break. Mother'll probably give her money enough to go to New York or some place."

"That's not what Mara wants, is it?" I asked.

"Lord knows. It won't help with Alan Keane. It was Tillyard got him out of the mess at the bank, of course. I'd guess that's the sort of thing you can't forgive anybody."

Somewhere in the distance a low deep roll of thunder moved the background of the silence that had fallen between us there in the garden. Dan was right, of course. None of them were children, even if they acted it from time to time. Rick was thirty, Dan twenty-seven, Mara twenty-one, and Irene Winthrop had been a widow for eight years. For seven of them everybody, including me, had wondered why she didn't marry again . . . and now, probably, everybody, including me, would be amazed that she was going to marry.

I glanced at Dan, sitting there, hunched forward, poking the grass back over the hole he'd made in my lawn.

"You're not going to marry Natalie?"

He shook his blond head, almost tow-colored above his sun-bronzed face.

"You've never seen her, have you?"

He looked around at me suddenly, shaking his head, a smile on his lips, but in his eyes something else . . . not pain exactly, but something not far from it.

"You remember those guys at King Arthur's court that spent all their time hunting the Holy Grail?" he asked, pretty casually. "Well . . . that's me."

"Really?" I said. "Who is she?"

He shrugged.

"That's what I don't know."

He got up abruptly, his broad white linen-clad back turned to me. Then he turned around and sat down beside me.

"I've never told anybody this, Grace. It was two summers

8

ago. A couple I knew were going to a chateau down near Dijon. I was going along until it came out there was an eighteen-year-old daughter in the house. I'd had a couple of narrow escapes before I learned that if you dance twice with a nice French girl you're as good as married. So I dropped out, at a place called Vezeley. It's a crazy little sort of hill sticking smack up in the middle of a plain, with a little cathedral on the top of it. They were going to pick me up two days later."

He was silent for a moment, staring down at the grass . . . back there in a cathedral town in Burgundy. The vague distant thunder and the oppressive heat of Washington were no part of his present.

"Only it happened to be the eve of the Fête de l'Assomption, and everybody from the countryside was in the town, and there wasn't any place to stay . . . the little inn at the foot of the hill was jammed. Well, I walked up the cobbled street to the cathedral place. There was a girl there, an American. We got to talking. All of a sudden she looked at her watch. It was half-past seven, and she had to meet two other girls at Avalon.

"She had a rattletrap of a French car. She tried to start it, and couldn't. So I offered to help."

The twinkle came back in his eyes for an instant.

"The trouble was she'd left the ignition on in the first place, so every time she tried to start it she turned it off again. She tried to get a mechanic, but the mechanic had gone to bed and his wife wouldn't get him up."

He grinned at me.

"It wasn't spring in Paris, Grace, but it was August in Vezeley, and the oleanders were in bloom. I had to spend the night there, so . . . well, I didn't start her car. We had dinner at the inn, outside under the oleanders, and we sat up all night on the cathedral steps. The patron offered us his own room, and couldn't understand why we wouldn't take it. We talked all night, and we watched the sun come up. The patron brought us a jug of chocolate and a bag of croissants at half-past four—walked all the way up the hill with them—and at five the mechanic got up and turned on her ignition and started her car.

"I watched her drive down the hill, and waved at her, and she waved back at me. Then she was gone . . . and it wasn't till two days later that I found out I was in love with her. And I didn't know where she lived, or even her name. All I knew was that her hair was the color of wheat in the sun, and her eyes were the color of faded hyacinths."

"Pink, or . . . white?" I said.

"Blue, Grace. Gray-blue with streaks of dark. Well, I

9

couldn't get her voice out of my ears. I went back to Vezeley. I went back to Vezeley fourteen times. Once she'd come, alone, just the day before, the patron said. I stayed a week . . ."

We sat there a long time, saying nothing.

Dan grinned.

"I see her everywhere I go. I'm always getting arrested for following girls about. I see a plane flying, and I think of her . . . or ice on the edge of a pond in the woods, or lilacs in the spring, or a branch of yellow mimosa. In fact, Grace, I'm quietly going nuts. And I never so much as touched her, except when we shook hands saying good-bye."

All effort to be debonair and nonchalant had stopped some time before. I had the curious and rather awed feeling that it was the first time in Dan Winthrop's life that anyone had seen behind that casually cheerful and good-looking façade . . . and that what was seen was good.

He reached out suddenly and took my hand in his big brown paw. "We'd better get going if we're making Romney by dinner," he said—just as Lilac put her black head out of the door and rolled her eyes balefully up at the threatening sky: "You-all bettah get sta'ted if you goin' get down to th' country befo' this here ol' storm break, Mis' Grace."

And because Lilac has dictated my goings out and comings in since I came to the house in Georgetown to live, long before I was left a widow with the two small boys she's practically raised, I got up obediently. Besides, she was right —as always. Dan and I had sat there much longer than either of us had thought, and we were supposed to be at Romney by seven.

Dan looked at his watch, then at me.

"Let's forget it, shall we?"

I nodded.

"I wish to God I could," he added abruptly.

2

So it was already getting on toward seven when we crossed the bridge over the Anacostia by the Naval School of Music, where a lone trumpeter was having tough going with his upper notes, and turned out a road that runs through one of those depressed areas that cluster, drab and undernourished, round the Maryland and Virginia edges of Washington like poor relations below the salt.

Romney—it was called Romney Marsh in the original patent granted by King Charles in 1671—is near Port Tobacco, about forty miles from the District Line on the Maryland side of the Potomac. If you've ever been on a Garden Pilgrimage in the spring, you've seen it, with its white fences covered with miles and miles of scarlet roses and honeysuckle, and its green lawns and long alleys of purple and white lilacs and somber fragrant box stretching down to the river. And you were told there how Washington used to come down from Mount Vernon, moor his barge at its dock and sit on its wide verandah, porticoed like Monticello, talking with his two physicians, whose houses were within a mile or so of Port Tobacco, and the old gentleman who lived at Romney then, childless because his three sons had fallen at Valley Forge. And you've seen, even if you didn't know it was the original, still hanging over the pearwood mantel in the dining room of Romney, the picture of General Washington, in the stern of his boat, waving his slow last good-bye from the river, taken by the old gentleman from memory. Romney has passed through many hands since then, and many changes, but that picture, like the river and the boxwood, has never been moved . . . or the five Corinthian columns where the starlings used to nest before Irene Winthrop took them firmly in delicate iron hand and drove them out, along with the family of land terrapin that shared the smokehouse with the rats.

It was almost eight when we turned at Duke of Gloucester Street in Port Tobacco, by the old Fountain Inn across from the Merchants Bank. We'd scarcely spoken at all since we left Georgetown. I was thinking of when I used to be at Romney a great deal, when my sons were small and my husband was living, and wondering vaguely why it was that I'd never been able to find time to go, these last few years—just once for a

11

week end, in fact, in the three years Dan Winthrop had been away.

I glanced at him, hunched down in the seat beside me, his eyes fixed on the road ahead. I think all that forty miles he must have been taking from memory—like the old gentleman Romney—another picture, the picture of the girl with the wheat-colored hair and hyacinth eyes, waving good-bye from the sunny plain below the little hill of Vezeley. I know at any rate that he was completely unaware of the brassy yellow light that made the road a narrow metallic ribbon through the parched anæmic corn and tobacco fields of Maryland, or the rumble of thunder coming ominously nearer and nearer as we moved through that yellow unreal twilight. And it wasn't till we'd gone through Port Tobacco, and I'd turned in, at the crossroad marker with several of its bright glass eyes missing, between the tall white gate posts with their carved wood pineapple tops and sign saying "Private—The Public are Admitted on Specified Days Only," that he came slowly to life again. It was a curiously unenthusiastic homecoming, some way, and I was a little shocked—or was till I told myself it was clearly none of my business. As far as that went, I myself —knowing Irene Winthrop, and Rick Winthrop, and Mara for that matter, so well—wasn't really looking forward to it with any extraordinary elation.

Ahead of us the narrow oyster-shell road stretched, snow white, between two tall dark lanes of pollarded cedars. The western horizon framed in the narrow windshield was a threatening oblong of inky black and murky yellow, the sheet lightning flashing mutinously behind it and dying in distant rumbles of thunder. It was suddenly as if we'd become part of an El Greco canvas, moving beyond mountains into the vast unknown, portentous and terrifying. And then the storm descended on us. Just as I switched on the lights, a great fork of streaked lightning split the sky, and huge splotches of rain stabbed and broke against the windshield, and it was abruptly pitch-dark, the two long fingers of light stretching out in front of us cut by slanting lines of driving rain. We craned our necks to see through the blinding screen of water that the windshield wipers were powerless against. The sudden wind, whipping and tearing at the boughs of the cedars, contorted them into black mangled arms struggling in the night, and buffeted the car until it lurched drunkenly on the slippery road.

In front of us a terrified rabbit streaked across the path into the frantic grass . . . and suddenly, from somewhere beyond the black screen of cedars, came the most ghastly shriek,

12

rising in the night and the storm, blood-curdling, half-human, half-animal, as eerie as violent death.

I caught my breath sharply and pressed my foot on the gas. "What on earth is that?" I gasped.

Dan shook his head, straining his eyes through the curtain of rain.

I put on the brakes sharply as a small open car, with no lights, shot crazily out from nowhere into the road, without the slightest warning, and careened crazily past, almost ditching itself and us. In the white glare of my headlights I saw a man, bareheaded, his face a ghastly white, his collar turned up, his head bent down, gripping the wheel, driving as if hell and all its black shadows were after him.

Dan sat bolt upright. "Wasn't that Alan Keane?" he shouted above the howling wind. He swung around in the seat.

"It looked like him!" I answered.

"I thought Mother didn't let him come on the place!"

"I didn't get the impression of the ordered departure of an honored guest!" I said.

We slid out of the cedar-lined road into the narrow drive circling the great Romney oak that stands in back of the old house. It's vast leafy arms creaked and groaned, mighty against the storm. A quarter of the way round it we came suddenly in view of the house . . . and we sat there, for an instant, both of us, just staring at it.

It·wasn't the Romney that either of us had thought of coming to—warm and hospitable and lovely in its simple dignity. It lay there in front of us dark and silent, and in some way forbidding. The rain lashed against the old brick, the wind tore desperately at the heavy purple and white wisteria vines until they writhed like whips. The shutters swung crazily, banging and crashing in the night, and the faint shadowy glimmer that came through the elliptical fanlight over the white door only made it eerier, as if something dark and stealthy moved inside there.

And suddenly from close behind us came that scream once more.

I clenched my hands on the wheel involuntarily, and I saw Dan's big hands tighten on his knees.

"What in God's name *is* that, Grace?"

It's silly to say it, but I definitely had to steady my voice. "It sounds like Cassandra," I said.

It's absurd, now, to say that the weird memory I had then of something I hadn't thought of for years and years would have had any significance, if it hadn't been for the incredible things that did happen at Romney. For Cassandra, you remember, was the seeress doomed by the gods to be always right, never to be believed . . . and when she comes back with Agamemnon, after the fall of Troy, she stands before his fated house, screaming, stricken with the fearful vision of the eaves dripping blood and the smoke of blood rising from its walls, and herself and Agamemnon murdered by his queen.

The headlights moved across the porch and the silent bricks and stretched, as I put my foot on the brake, down a long grassy alley between wind-racked lines of somber box. They rested, as I came to a full stop and switched off the engine, on a great blue and red and white target, and picked out, clearly visible to my astonished eyes, a single arrow stuck and left in its golden heart. And with that sight coming as it did, so abruptly on the weird memory of that other far-off homecoming that had raced through my mind, I sat perfectly still, staring at it.

"I must," I thought, "be losing my mind entirely."

Dan's voice, sane and practical, came to my ears with almost a shock of relief.

"I see Mother still plays Robin Hood," he said. "Wonder if she still wears that Lincoln green get-up with the feather in her hat?"

"I wouldn't know," I said. "What I wonder is if the rest of us have to take all the skin off our arms playing Robin Hood too?"

"Certainly," Dan said. "Unless, of course," he added, in his mother's most perfect manner, "you don't *want* to co-operate."

I looked out at the dark house, eerie and forbidding in the violent night.

"I'm not sure there's anybody around to co-operate with," I said. "Are you sure this was the day?"

"Or is this the place, Mrs. Latham?" Dan said. "Wait. I'll get you an umbrella."

"I'll make a dash for it," I said.

I slipped over to the right side of the car and out, and made a bolt for the porch, and drew a deep painful breath of relief when I cleared it.

Dan, following me, tripped and lunged forward, caught himself, swore quietly and gave something a violent kick across the porch. I went on over to the door, put my hand out to open it and stopped, my heart suddenly gone quite still . . . because, as if all this wasn't already too much, the door quietly and slowly opened itself. Or for a moment I thought it did, until I made out, standing beside it in the dim candle-lit hall, Dan's young sister Mara, her dark pointed little face lost

14

in the glow of her great somber eyes and the halo of her dark cloudy hair.

She didn't smile or hold out her hand. She just looked at me, and beyond me at her brother, and said, in that strange, almost poignant voice of hers, "You're late. Mother'll give you holy hell."

She didn't smile or hold out her hand to him . . . and Dan, who'd started toward her to kiss her—after all, I thought, he'd not seen her for three years—stopped abruptly and stood staring at her.

Then he bent down and picked up the long bow, still strung, that he'd tripped over in the dark, and flung it angrily across the porch.

"If this is your bow," he said, "I wish you'd put it in the rack, instead of leaving it around for somebody to break his neck on."

Mara Winthrop's pointed chin went up, her eyes blazed.

"Paris hasn't changed you a bit, has it, darling!"

Her voice was cold and perfectly flat, but her big somber eyes were suddenly filled with tears that she blinked back resolutely.

"Anyway, you'd better come on in just as you are, or the fatted calf'll be all eaten. Everybody's been waiting hours for you . . . including Natalie, the glamour girl."

She turned and started toward a door off the wide elegant hall. I looked around at Dan. His face was set, hurt and angry, and he certainly looked like anything but the returning prodigal. We went on in. I glanced around the familiar long passageway, full of old mahogany, with the strapped leather mail pouch hanging on its hook by the door, and the Sheffield urn full of scarlet roses under the Adam mirror. Dan tossed his hat on a sofa and pushed back his crisp unruly hair with both hands.

"What's come over that girl?" he said. "Would it be this guy Keane?"

I shook my head. It didn't make sense, some way—at least those sudden smarting tears didn't. I found myself wondering about Mara—actually, when I came to think about it, for the first time I'd ever done it. Up to this time I'd always seen her through her mother's eyes, moody and difficult, resisting with the thoroughness of a wilful demon all the efforts made in her behalf. I could see Irene Winthrop, a corsage of yellow orchids pinned on her mink coat, stopping me just outside the British Embassy one afternoon, her eyes raised in amused despair, saying, "Darling, that child will be the death of me!" and the woman I was with saying when she was gone, "You know, Irene's wonderful to that girl. You know, it

15

really hurts her terribly, the way the little wretch acts!" I wasn't, some way, so sure of that, now. I had the sudden definite feeling that Mara hadn't wanted to be so horrid to Dan. Maybe it was because he was late, or because I was there. Then the picture of that bareheaded young man crashing through the storm in his open car came back to me.

"I mean, what the hell have I done?" Dan said.

"She's probably just upset about something," I said. "Come along. Wipe the rain off your face and let's go in. I want to see the glamour girl."

"Yeh?" Dan said. He grinned suddenly and took my arm. "Me, I can hardly wait. Let's go."

Mara Winthrop had stopped at the broad carved pine door at the end of the hyphen that connects the dining room wing with the main house. I saw her push back her cloudy hair from her forehead, almost as if bracing herself for something to come, and then, remembering, hurriedly tie the dangling ends of narrow green velvet ribbons that made the belt of her smart brown cotton dinner frock. We weren't then, I thought, the only ones late for dinner, and I thought again of Alan Keane careening crazily through the rain, and wondered if Dan and I would be the only ones to get holy hell that night.

As we came along Mara threw open the door.

"Lo, the bridgroom cometh!" she announced.

I couldn't hear what Dan said through the sudden blur of excited voices beyond us, but I knew from the grin on his face that Mara was not only forgiven but was even definitely one up. Then I could hear the sound of Irene Winthrop's high-pitched lilting laughter rippling along the top of the dinner table talk and the subdued wellbred clink of silver on fine porcelain that all stopped abruptly as her voice came out to us:

"You *waited* for them, Mara! You sweet angel!"

Behind me Dan made some kind of not too polite noise as we went in. For the instant that we stood there looking down into the room—and I suppose it's because light travels faster than sound, and the eye takes in a whole impression at a glance while the ear has to wait for parts to be transformed into meaning—I saw the long polished mahogany table, with its white lace and crimson flowers, its sparkling crystal and gleaming silver under the soft light from the Georgian candelabra, as an island in the shadowed room, a solid core of beauty and warmth and security that blotted out instantly everything that had gone before . . . the storm-driven sky, the weird racked cedars, the white-faced man tearing through the slanting rain, the shrill cries and the shuttered house, and Mara,

16

dark and elfin and bitter. They were all gone as if they were something I'd imagined, that had never happened at all.

But that was only for one brief instant . . . and I still don't know whether what I saw then was because all of that really wasn't gone at all, was still in my mind, so that I was just fancying things out of a disordered brain, or whether it was a trick of the yellow candle-light that cast long oblique shadows on the people standing round the table . . . or whether in the moment I stood there I had a sudden insight into the characters of people I'd only known pleasantly, as one knows most charming people. But the faces down there, except for two, looked suddenly angular, and predatory . . . and cruel. It was almost terrifyingly uncanny, to see Irene Winthrop's delicate patrician face hard and hawklike, her quick-moving hands with their scarlet-lacquered nails like talons tipped with blood. Rick Winthrop, her elder son, at the far end of the table, was like a brooding bird of prey, too, his thin nose elongated by its own shadows, which deepened the circles under his harassed sullen eyes and gave the tiny mustache above his thin lips an almost sinister look.

The auburn-haired girl next to him—that would be Cheryl, I supposed, whom he'd married and brought to Romney in expectation of an allowance that hadn't materialized—was sharp-beaked, with strange brilliant eyes and high sunken bony cheeks. Major Tillyard, next to Irene, was sleek and round and too well-fed, his bristling eyebrows prominent over his pursy cheeks. Mara and the other girl there, their backs to us in the doorway, seemed small and fragile and drooping. It sounds perfectly fantastic to say it, but for one crazy instant it flashed into my mind that this wasn't real at all, that it was some kind of nightmare, and that in it Dan and I had wandered not into the dining room at Romney but into a den of . . . something . . . and that those two were the sacrifices at a strange altar that was not an altar.

It not only sounds fantastic, of course, it was fantastic; for instantly the whole illusion was dispelled as I stepped down the three steps onto a level with the candle-light that softened and smoothed each of those faces back into faces that were recognizable, and civilized, and even handsome, each in its own way.

As we came, Irene Winthrop rose to her feet, light as thistle-down, and held out her soft bare arms.

"Grace, darling! You've brought me my son! My son! Danny, my sweet!—But you're enormous!"

And he was, beside her fragile Dresden-china figure in crimson chiffon, her white hair piled in Vigée-Lebrun curls on the top of her delicate head. He lifted her gaily off her feet,

17

gave her a resounding kiss, and set her down again, flushed and radiant.

Rick Winthrop had got lazily up and come forward. There was something so grudging and perfunctory about his slow "Hello, how are you?" and his handshake that Dan's good-natured grin froze again, so abruptly that even Irene, who makes a point of never noticing anything that doesn't please her, noticed it. Her purling laugh wavered for just an instant as she turned with Dan to Major Tillyard.

"You remember Dan, Sidney."

"Yes, indeed!" Major Tillyard said. They shook hands cordially. Major Tillyard turned to me. "I haven't seen you for a long time."

"I've been away a lot," I said, thinking it was odd how well I seemed to know him, seeing him as little as I did, and how very well he looked—prosperous and satisfied with himself.

Irene was babbling merrily along. "Dan, darling! I do want you to meet Natalie—"

That was as far as she got. Mara's dark flat little voice interrupted.

"I should think he ought to meet Cheryl, first," she said.

3

In the instant's silence that fell I saw her look across at the auburn-haired girl, who was astonishingly good-looking, now that I was seeing her properly, and in some way exactly the kind of girl I should have expected Rick Winthrop to marry. She smiled, but ever so faintly, her green eyes changing, and I gathered more clearly than if she had spoken that there was no love lost between her and Mara. Then Irene's light laughter gaily wiped the slate.

"Of course. Your sister-in-law . . . Cheryl, dear—this is Dan . . ."

And knowing—because Irene, without saying anything, had managed to say so much about the young woman who had married her elder son expecting a sinecure—what that "dear" was costing her, I looked again at the handsome auburn-haired girl beside him. I saw the smooth but firm set of her jaw, and her hazel-green eyes, and her mouth, not tight-lipped but definitely not soft and yielding; and I found myself wondering, with the first amusement I'd felt since I'd arrived, if it could be possible that Irene had at last met her match, and more than that, had it permanently—like a hair shirt—under her own roof.

The girl still hadn't moved, or changed the faintly smiling curve of her red lips. I realized abruptly that there was something wrong in the room, something more than odd about the deafening silence that had fallen on it as this girl was looking at Dan. I turned and glanced up at him. He was standing, his back a little to his mother, absolutely rooted to the floor, his face quite colorless, his eyes blank, his lips parted stupidly, staring—not at the auburn-haired girl, but at the other girl who stood beside Mara, her back to us.

Irene's voice cut the silence almost sharply.

"*Cheryl*—this is Dan!"

The girl turned, supporting herself lightly against the solid Chippendale chair, her hands gripping the back until her knuckles were like a row of white marbles in her brown hands.

I saw then for the first time that her hair was gold, her eyes as blue as sapphires . . .

I looked back at Dan Winthrop. I wouldn't know how a man looks when he merely finds the Holy Grail . . . but I do know how he looks when he finds it only to know he has

lost it forever, because it belongs to another man. For I realized, with a lurch of my heart and a feeling almost too sick to
bear, that the auburn-haired girl was not Cheryl Winthrop,
that she was Natalie, whom Dan was supposed to marry, and
that Cheryl was the slim fragile girl who stood next to Mara
. . . and that she was the girl of Vezeley, with hair the
color of ripe wheat in the sun and eyes blue as faded hyacinths.

It seemed to me an eternity that they stood there, looking
at each other. I could feel, rather than see, Rick Winthrop's
sullen sleepy eyes moving from one to the other of them,
slowly. They were still motionless, and speechless. Irene
wasn't. She couldn't have fluttered more charmingly, but her
voice had a steelier note than I'd ever heard in it before,
through all the years I'd known her:

"Cheryl . . . why have you never told us you and Dan
were . . . acquainted?"

It must be hard indeed, with a whole golden universe lying
shattered around you, to feel the sudden flick of the lash, on a
spot where your heart is the most vulnerable . . . and neither
of them could have failed to recognize that note in Irene's
voice.

Cheryl stood an instant, stunned and hurt, like a child
struck full in the face by someone quite strange, and turned
slowly around. I didn't know, then, whether she realized there
was nothing she could say to answer her mother-in-law's question, or whether it was the way Rick Winthrop was looking at
her, the expression on his face inexplicable to me. I did know
that it wasn't inexplicable to her. Whether it was a challenge
or an accusation, I couldn't tell; something, certainly, that it
shouldn't have been, probably would not have been if Rick
hadn't been drinking far more than was good for him or
anybody, not only that day but for many many days before.

I saw Cheryl's slim bare back stiffen defensively, and the
color deepen slowly in her high exquisitely modeled cheeks. If
she could have spoken before, she couldn't possibly now. Nor
could Dan. If you dissect the loveliest butterfly it's a mess; the
most delicate and complex frost pattern on a window is a
drop of dirty water in your hand. How could either of them
tell any of these people that they'd sat up all night in front of
a tiny cathedral on a little hill in a plain in France, and that
the patron of a village bistro that had oleanders blooming at
the door had brought them chocolate and croissants at half-
past four in the morning, because they were amusing young
Americans who had declined his own room . . . when everything would have been so entirely discreet?—I could see him

20

shrugging his shoulders—"Ah, les Americains!"—and raising his fat peasant hands.

Or how could either of them say that they'd shaken hands and said good-bye, and waved good-bye again, Cheryl from her rattletrap French car on the sunny plain, Dan from the fence by the door of the little cathedral on the hill, not knowing each other's name, not knowing, yet, that that simple starry night had so changed both their lives? They couldn't have told it. No one in that room would have believed it if they had. No one but Mara, and Mara could believe anything. She still believed that Alan Keane was an innocent man, and he had served thirteen months in a Federal prison because no one else believed it.

Irene's perfect genius of tact in just such moments is a by-word in Washington, in Aiken and Newport, anywhere, in fact, on the Eastern seaboard where there are tables like the one we were at and where it's so easy, these days, to mix inadvertently new deals and old, both foreign and domestic. But Irene, still with that fixed sweet smile of inquiry on her lovely face, was obviously smoothing no paths for her daughter-in-law.

And that increased and deadening silence lengthened almost unbearably, until the auburn-haired girl by my side did her best by putting in—and I don't think she meant it in the least to sound as bad as Mara Winthrop's quick retort made it sound—"I'm sure it was quite all right!"

"Has anybody suggested there was anything *not* all right?" Mara demanded instantly, with positively devastating smoothness. "—And as Mother was saying before Dan went native on us, this is Miss Lane, Dan—Natalie to you—and this is Grace Latham, Cheryl and Natalie . . . for her sins a friend and relative. And now that that's over, Mother, couldn't we eat? Grace and Dan must be starved."

"Oh, of course they must!" Irene cried charmingly, and I thought she gave her daughter a not entirely ungrudging glance of admiration for her rather heavy-handed but effective putting things in place. She drew Dan down in the chair beside her, and I took the one between Natalie Lane and Major Tillyard. I looked at Mara again. Her pointed little face under its cloud of dark hair was perfectly expressionless except for the droop at the corners of her wide unrouged mouth. Was her defense of Cheryl, I wondered, because she liked her—or because she didn't like Natalie Lane? Or did it spring from something deeper than that, some passionate sense of justice that her own moody little soul had invented, and made a cross for all her family to bear? She'd always, I knew, been a sharp thorn in her mother's side, from the day

21

Irene first discovered she had a changeling in the cradle and that all the pretty frilly things made for baby girls made Mara look rather like an Armenian refugee, and act worse. When the boys were brought in and proudly exhibited, little Mara was always left in the nursery. I could still hear Irene's gay careless voice: "Mara? Oh my dear, she's *quite* unpresentable . . . such an odd little creature . . . but I'm sure she'll be awfully interesting when she grows up!"

I looked again at the small pointed face and great somber eyes reflected under the flowers in the candle-lit Empire plateau. There might be something in it, I thought, but next to the lovely golden oval of the face of the girl sitting next to her, her long lashes brushing her flushed cheek, it didn't seem very like it.

I glanced down the table at Rick Winthrop, as big as Dan and with the same blond hair, with broad square shoulders that looked even broader in his perfectly tailored white dinner jacket. He'd always been far handsomer than Dan, I realized with a kind of minor shock that he wasn't now. The thing in Dan's face that made him so attractive and engaging wasn't visible in Rick's; his cheeks were heavy, his dark eyes brooding and sullen and the flesh around them puffy, his full mouth sagged at the corners. The contours that had made him so much better looking than Dan were coarsened and blurred. He had wasted what nature had given him, and wasted it in a short time, I thought. Three years before, when I'd seen the most of him, he hadn't gone quite so much to the fleshpots. I glanced back at Cheryl, wondering vaguely what could have happened to him. He hadn't, obviously, gone completely off, or he'd never have married this girl. Heaven knows there was nothing of the fleshpots about her. She was more like a willow branch tipped with gold in the spring than like the glamour girls one heard vaguely that Rick trained with around 52nd Street. I found myself wondering how it could have happened, this marriage, and what they were thinking now, the two of them, their eyes fixed steadily throughout dinner on the delicate juicy soft crab and water cress, the tender broiled chicken and young asparagus and spiced sweet potato balls, and the tipsy squire pudding that had been a specialty at Romney when General Washington dined there, that old Yarborough's white-gloved hands successively placed in front of them and removed barely touched. Through it all Irene's light chatter rippled, like threaded rose and silver through a dark woof, or sunflecked froth on a portentous sea.

22

4

When Yarborough had brought coffee and closed the pantry doors, Irene put her bare elbows on the polished table and leaned forward, her smooth chin resting on the back of her clasped jeweled fingers. A hush fell over the table, and in the mirror of the Empire plateau I saw the corners of Mara Winthrop's mouth droop and the sides of her nostrils as sensitive as harp strings quiver, and her whole dark little body grow suddenly perfectly still. She had been waiting for this. So had all the rest of them—even the girl next to her. I looked at her, and our eyes met for the first time, just as Irene said, in her most charming voice:

"Grace dear, you must tell us everything you've been doing, you look too fit, really you do! What have you been up to? And Dan, I know you're simply dying to talk Paris! How *was* the trip over? Was it awful?"

A quick smile flickered for an instant behind Cheryl Winthrop's long gold-tipped lashes and was gone, as Irene, without waiting for Dan to speak—and heaven knows he looked less like a man dying to talk Paris than anyone I'd ever seen —went rippling along.

"I did want all of you together tonight! Because Sidney—" she held out one lovely hand to the man at her side—"Sidney has finally persuaded me there's no use of our waiting any longer. We're going to get married!"

She paused brightly and looked around. Good seeds, I'm afraid, never fell on thornier ground. That they had all known it for several weeks didn't seem entirely to account for it. Even Natalie Lane, who tried to look pleased and interested, didn't succeed particularly well. Irene, if she noticed it, didn't mind, and neither, apparently, did Major Tillyard. He looked affectionately pleased, and really quite nice.

"Of course, the real point is that this is a sort of . . . well, a sort of council of war," Irene said.

Dan's eyes caught mine. I looked away quickly, and across at Mara, staring with unseeing eyes into the bottom of her green Worcester coffee cup.

"You see," Irene said—she looked earnestly about at her small brood—"your father was so anxious for you all to have the benefit of the money he worked so hard to make—"

There was a sudden violent motion at the end of the table

23

as Rick Winthrop pushed his chair back and got to his feet so abruptly—and unsteadily—that his chair went crashing to the floor behind him. He turned, smashed his foot violently into it and swung back to us, facing his mother over the candles. I saw that up to that point I hadn't at all realized how definitely he was under the influence—as my grandmother used to put it in the days when no gentleman was ever intoxicated.

"Then why don't you divide it between us, and cut out all this harping about what father wanted!" he said bitterly. "Why don't you let us get the benefit of it, instead of keeping us tied to your apron strings, having to grovel for every penny we get! Then marry Tillyard, if you want to, and the rest of us'll clear out! Then—"

"Oh, shut up, Rick."

It was Dan's voice, quietly matter-of-fact, that interrupted that extraordinary tirade. The rest of us sat, too stunned to do anything but stare at him open-mouthed . . . even Irene, so much more used to Rick's unbridled furies than the rest of us.

Rick turned, his dark eyes bloodshot, his mouth trembling.

"It's all right for you to talk. You don't have to take it— you never have had to. You've always had a way of getting whatever you wanted without the trouble of paying for it."

I still don't know how it was that everybody at that table knew instantly what it was that Rick meant. He didn't look at Cheryl . . . but we did know, just as surely as if he'd said it. Maybe it was because he stopped short himself, as if he too was shocked by it. But there it was, as ugly and revolting as if he'd taken a whip and lashed it across her face.

Dan got slowly to his feet, white with rage, his jaw set like a steel trap. He stood motionless for an instant, turned and walked over to the door.

"Would you mind stepping outside?" he said, his voice so dreadfully quiet that gooseflesh stood suddenly on my arms.

Rick Winthrop moved around the long table.

"We'll settle it right here!" he shouted.

Irene's voice was a low terrible moan. "Boys, *please!* Oh, *please!*" If I'd ever thought her incapable of a very deep emotion—and I had—I'd been wrong. She leaned her head back against her chair, her face white as death. "Please, *please!*"

Cheryl got instantly to her feet, her face pale and set.

"Don't be a fool, Rick," she said quietly. "And please, Dan, come back. He doesn't know what he's saying. He . . . he isn't himself."

She turned quickly to her mother-in-law. "If you'll excuse me, please, Irene—I'd like to go to my room."

Irene nodded without opening her eyes. Major Tillyard,

who'd got up as Rick left his place, stood there looking down at her, his face hard and angry. Then he said, controlling his voice with an effort, "Perhaps if I left too, Irene, this might be a little less . . . difficult."

She held out her hand.

"No, no, Sidney—please stay. Natalie, you go with Cheryl. The rest of you stay here. Come back, Dan. Sit down, Rick."

For a moment no one moved except Natalie Lane, who got up and out like a streak of lightning. Dan closed the door and came back to his place. Rick picked up his chair and sat down, his face mottled, his eyes fixed on the lace mat in front of him. And all the time Mara sat there, motionless, her short thick black lashes shading her dark eyes, two hot dull spots burning in her cheeks, her brown sensitive little hands folded quiescent on the table in front of her. I don't know why that should have surprised me so, and alarmed me too, in a way; for when she finally moved it was to give her mother a look that was utterly disillusioned and at the same time totally inscrutable. That was when Irene, having I suppose so much more survival value than most people—and I still think she had, really, in spite of the way things turned out—moved forward in her chair again, and smiled wanly.

"Now don't you two think you're being pretty silly? You're forgetting you're brothers . . . and Dan's come back after being away so long! And the French look at these things so differently! Now, now, Dan—you mustn't be ridiculous!"

I thought for a moment that Dan was going to invite her outside too, and I'm not sure he wouldn't have if Mara hadn't said quickly, "Wouldn't it be a good plan if Dan would come out and say plainly where he and Cheryl knew each other? That seems to be what's holding up this . . . this council of war, as Mother calls it. We ought at least to try to keep it from becoming a blood purge."

I looked at Dan. He sat there tight-lipped and silent. Before there had been nothing he could say. Now, I knew, there was nothing he would say, even if he could.

Mara looked away quickly. "Then let's skip it. And maybe Rick'll let Mother finish what she was going to say."

Irene raised her arched brows.

"So sweet of you, lamb," she murmured, with a charming smile.

Mara flushed.

"It's of as much interest to me and Dan to hear what you're going to say as it is to Rick," she said. It was almost painfully casual.

Her mother smiled again.

"As a matter of fact, Mara," she said, rather gently,

25

"—whatever disposition of your father's money I may make, I shall certainly have to put definite restrictions on the use you put yours to."

Rick Winthrop's slow voice, angry and also a little blurred, spoke from the end of the table. "—And I'd like to say that if I see that jailbird around here again, I'll fill him full of buckshot."

Mara got up abruptly.

"If somebody doesn't do it to you first," she said. "May I be excused, please, Mother?"

Irene's voice was even a little bored. "Certainly not, Mara. Sit down, and don't be dramatic."

Mara's eyes smouldered with angry resentment.

"I'm not being dramatic—and I won't sit down. I'll not stay around and be treated like a feeble-minded child!"

"Then quit acting like one, darling."

"Everything I want to do you keep me from—you've done it all my life! I'd have run away and married Alan . . . but I've got a right to part of my father's money, and I'm going to have it!"

Irene's voice was composed and pleasant—and impervious.

"Not, darling, if you insist on marrying the unemployed son of a tenant farmer."

"He wouldn't be unemployed if all of you hadn't ganged up on him and kept him from getting a job!" Mara cried. "And what if he is the son of a tenant farmer? Where would Romney be if it weren't for a tenant farmer?"

Major Tillyard spoke with a quiet authority that I thought would calm her. "He could have gone somewhere else and started over, Mara."

She whirled around at him, her dark eyes filled with scalding tears.

"Yes—for how long? Until they found he'd been in prison! But that's not why he didn't go somewhere else—he didn't go because he's innocent . . . and he's not afraid of coming back here where he can prove it!"

"He's had every chance to prove it, Mara," Major Tillyard said wearily. "I admire your loyalty, my dear—but it's badly out of keeping with the facts. We gave—"

Irene put a delicate white hand on his arm.

"Please don't go into that again! Mara's just a silly child. She's hardly likely to marry a penniless boy. She can't even wash out her own stockings.—Sit down, Mara."

Mara stood a moment, choked and irresolute, turned with a stifled sob and groped blindly toward the door.

"Come back to the table, Mara," Irene said—quietly, but the velvet glove sort of thing if I ever heard it.

"Oh, let the kid go, Mother," Dan put in abruptly.

Rick Winthrop leaned forward.

"It's all right with you if she marries a thief, I suppose? You'll always get yours, in spite of jailbirds and . . . fortune hunters."

He looked at Sidney Tillyard, his eyes sullen, his face flushed.

"Now you're being offensive, Rick!" Irene said sharply.

Dan looked at me, his lips twisted in a bitter smile. He got up.

"The council of war doesn't seem to be getting anywhere," he said. "Good night, Mother. I'll . . . see you in the morning.—What about a stroll in the rain, Grace?"

Irene nodded to me, and I went out with him. He opened the big front door with its smooth rubbed pine panels between fluted pilasters, with their carved acanthus capitals and we stepped outside onto the porch. The wind still rocked the branches of the old tulip poplars beyond the lawns, and shivered down the box alleys. The broad waters of the Potomac were dark except for the lights of a single river boat moving slowly on its way to the Chesapeake. The rain came in sharp gusts, wetting our faces. But the air was clean again, not sultry and leaden, as it had been in Georgetown . . . or charged with bitterness as it had been inside those lovely old mauve brick walls.

Neither of us spoke. There seemed after all so pitifully little to say. Dan lighted a cigarette. As he tossed the match on the gravel path he raised his head, listening. I heard a faint sound coming from the dining room end of the house. It stopped then, as abruptly as it had begun, and the figure of a man, dressed in work overalls, a battered gray hat pulled down to keep the rain from his face, came out of the shadows. He was walking on the grass, not moving stealthily, but walking so that his feet were noiseless on the sodden lawn.

He stopped when he saw us, and hesitated. Then he recognized Dan and touched his hat.

"Mr. Dan—certainly mighty glad to see you back."

"Oh hello, Mr. Keane."

Dan strode across the porch and shook hands with the man who had been the tenant farmer of Romney since Dan's father had bought it, when he was still quite a small boy.

"You remember Mr. Keane, don't you, Grace?—This is Mrs. Latham."

"Howdy, Miz' Latham. Ain't seen you down this way for a long time."

Mr. Keane wiped his hand on the seat of his overalls and held it out to me. It was wet, hard and rough, but it was a

27

good hand, with a strong sure grip that had held many a plough to a straight deep furrow. And I don't know why, during all that conversation at the table—even with Mara's outburst over Romney and its tenant farmer—I had never thought of Alan Keane as being Mr. Keane's son. Mr. Keane was as much a part of Romney as the white pillared portico and the boxwood alleys and the pineapples on the gate posts. And Alan had gradually stopped being a part of it, since he'd gone to high school and to college—I'd subscribed to a magazine I'd never heard of, and never got, because Irene was helping him out—and then to the bank in Port Tobacco, and after that to prison.

Mr. Keane glanced uneasily at the dining room windows.

"Is Miz' Winthrop through her supper?" he asked.

"Just about," Dan said. "Anything I could do for you?"

Mr. Keane fumbled with the stumpy pipe in his hands.

"I jus' wanted to see Miz' Winthrop about a little matter, is all. I jus' thought I'd like to see her, if she wasn't too busy."

"You'd better wait till morning, unless it's pretty important," Dan said. "She's just been having a run-in with Rick."

Mr. Keane hesitated. "That ain't hard to do, these days," he said slowly. Then he added, almost painfully, it seemed to me, "I'd mighty like to see Miz' Winthrop, if she ain't too busy."

"O. K." Dan turned and strode across the verandah and inside.

Suddenly out of the wet night came that ghastly eerie shriek again . . . and again. The gooseflesh rose on my arms.

"What is that, for heaven's sake, Mr. Keane?" I demanded.

"That's them fancy buzzards of Miz' Winthrop," he said in his slow drawl. "They make a heap of racket, about this time."

He lapsed into silence, and we stood there, I rather uneasily, because he kept looking so anxiously at the door. Finally I asked him how his tobacco was, and if he thought the storm had hurt it; but before he could answer Irene Winthrop's voice came, high-pitched and clear as a bell, from the drawing room. A window must have blown open in the wind, and the heavy gold damask curtains had been drawn, so they wouldn't, I supposed, know it was open. And for the first time a sharp torn edge was audible under the gentle imperviousness of that lovely lilting voice.

"Tell Mr. Keane I don't care to see him. The matter's settled, and very liberally, I do think."

Dan's voice was charged with incredulity, and anger.

"You mean you're kicking Mr. Keane off the place, after he's been here half of his life?"

"The matter's *quite* settled, Dan. Mr. Keane has been taken *very* good care of . . ."

Irene's voice was suave, and final. Then I could hear Major Tillyard.

"You're making a big mistake, Irene. Keane's the best farmer in Southern Maryland. He's made Romney pay when every other farm in the county is in the red, and the land's better today than it was ten years ago. You'll never get another tenant that touches him."

"Money, money!" Irene moaned plaintively. "That's all any of you think of! What about Mara! Oh, Rick's perfectly right —if I'd sent Mr. Keane off the place four years ago, Alan would never have come back here, and we'd never have had any of this nonsense of Mara's marrying a . . . a criminal!"

I stared helplessly at the farmer standing there by me, his heavy boots clogged with sand from the tobacco fields, his gnarled hands making futile helpless gestures, his face under his dripping tattered hat numb and stupid with pain.

And we just stood there for an instant, until he said, very simply, "I reckon she don't want to see me," and turned back the way he'd come.

The sound of his feet on the brick path had disappeared when Dan came out. He was angrier than I'd ever seen him, with a deep and sustained and choking anger.

"It's a rotten damn system that lets a bounder like Rick turn a man like Mr. Keane off the land he's had for twenty-five years. I'd like to know what the hell's behind it. You needn't tell me he gives a damn what happens to Mara. I'd like to . . . Oh well, what the hell."

He kicked at the corn husk mat on the flagged porch, and took a deep breath. "I guess I'll go and try to say something to Mr. Keane. I'll be seeing you, Grace."

I didn't have the courage to point to the open window . . . and I don't think it would have made any difference in the long run if I had. The things that were happening at Romney were the noxious flowerings of seeds that had been planted and were full grown before Dan and I barged in on them out of the storm-wracked night. Nothing anyone could have done at that point could have averted the doom about to break over Romney . . . any more than we could have stopped the inky black and murky yellow lightning-torn clouds from crashing down their pent-up fury of wind and water.

As Dan disappeared around the wing that shrill cry came again out of the night, and I saw the dark form of a huge bird soar across the box. I went inside, thinking that all in all I wished I'd not come to Romney.

5

Irene and Major Tillyard were standing in front of the bright wood fire burning behind the great old polished brass and-irons, in what had been the dining room of the original house but was now a sort of family sitting room, with soft chintz-covered chairs and sofas instead of the formal period pieces of the drawing room across the hall—lovely but not particularly comfortable with its delicate Sheraton sofas and straight-backed fireside chairs. They were still talking about the farm, and they stopped abruptly as I came in.

Irene held out her hands to me.

"Oh, darling, it's really so nice to have you here—like old times!" she said, smiling. All trace of annoyance and petulance was gone, like a cloud in April. "And I do hope this dreadful weather clears up, because in the morning we're going to shoot a full Columbia round!"

I'm afraid I blinked, because Major Tillyard smiled.

"Archery, Mrs. Latham," he said.

"Then that lets me out," I said—adding to myself, in the expressive jargon of my younger son, "I hope I hope I hope!" Archery is not one of my favorite sports.

"Why Grace, aren't you awful!" Irene cried. "We really need you! And besides, my dear, it's awfully good for the figure!"

"I'll stick to a horse, if you don't mind."

Irene shrugged her slim bare shoulders. She certainly, I thought, didn't look like fifty-five . . . or act it, I added to myself as she said, "Oh, of course, Grace, if you want to spoil—"

Major Tillyard poked the fire a little abruptly, and she broke off.

"Of course you'll come in, Grace—don't be silly," she laughed.

Major Tillyard put down the fire iron. "I think I'll be getting along, Irene." He took her hand. "I'm sorry about tonight. Don't let it upset you, will you, my dear."

He shook hands with me, and he and Irene moved toward the door. I looked at his broad straight back and thick iron-gray hair, thinking that Irene showed remarkably good judgment at times, and sat down by the fire. As I did I felt a sudden draft on my cheek, and glanced around at the window. And I started, not sure I wasn't definitely seeing things.

A perfectly mammoth creature had pushed aside the curtains and walked in, blinking two light blue eyes through a ridiculous fringe of long dirty gray hair. I don't know what, at first sight, I could have thought it was, because quite obviously under the three bags of curly wool it was a dog. He grinned very amiably and wagged his tail. Irene and Major Tillyard in the door both turned, and Irene said, "Oh, there's Dr. Birdsong," which seemed a little confusing to me until almost immediately the curtains parted again and a very tall man came in.

He was even bigger than the dog, and looked rather like him, in a slightly different way. He didn't have as much hair, and it wasn't gray, except a very little near the temples. His country tweed jacket was rough and baggy, with chamois patches at the elbows, and was definitely for use and not beauty, and his high laced boots and riding breeches were streaked with mud. His hands were enormous, and yet gave an impression of being extraordinarily mobile and sensitive. His eyes, like the dog's, were a light pale bluish-gray, his face was burned almost black and looked more like corrugated iron than skin. And somewhere about him there was an astonishing quality of detachment, in his eyes probably—as if they seldom looked at the things close by.

He didn't smile as he strode in through the window, and the dog looking up at him, and apparently realizing that he had been a little previous, took the grin off his face, walked over to the fire and lay down with a solid comfortable grunt, divorcing himself from whatever unpleasantness was about to ensue.

"There's a tree down in the road, Sidney. You can't get your car out. I thought if you were ready I'd pick you up."

The smile died on Irene Winthrop's face. Whatever she'd started to say went with it. Her lips tightened.

"Why doesn't Mr. Keane move the tree?" she said sharply. She reached for the needlepoint bell pull hanging from the carved overmantel. "I'll send—"

"Mr. Keane has been fired, Irene," the tall man said curtly.

Irene's delicate face flushed. "That's silly! There's no reason for his letting things go just because—"

Dr. Birdsong—I took it that he, not the dog, was the doctor—jammed his ancient felt hat on his head and interrupted her brusquely.

"Some day you'll find you can't have your cake and eat it too, Irene.—If you're ready, Sidney. We can take your car to the tree—mine's on the other side."

He strode out. The dog, who apparently had been quite sound asleep, got up and ambled after him.

Irene held out her hand. "Good night, Sidney." She closed the door sharply, came back to the fireplace and stood looking down into the yellow flames. She was very angry.

"If they think they can bully me into letting that man stay on, they're wrong," she said quietly, after a long time. "I must say I can't understand Sidney Tillyard. He acts as if Alan Keane was completely in the right, stealing from the bank. He wanted to take him back, at the time—goodness knows what would have happened if his Board had let him have his way. Just because I've taken his advice from time to time is no reason for him to think he can dictate my affairs."

"Is he trying to?" I asked. He had seemed to me amazingly patient, that night.

She drew a deep breath and shook her head. "He thinks I ought to give each of the children an allowance, and let them live wherever they please . . . including Mara, for heaven's sake, who obviously isn't capable of taking care of herself. He thinks it's a mistake to divide the estate, and that if I give Rick his share now I'd have him back on my hands in two years."

"I thought you were going to give Rick an allowance when he married," I said.

"I certainly had every intention of doing so, until he flew in the face of all my . . . my prayers, and married a total stranger, that he picked up heaven knows where!"

"She seems to me like an extremely nice girl," I said.

She looked at me with a slow astonished expression on her lovely face.

"My dear Grace, how can you say such a stupid thing? Anyone can look at her and see she's nothing but an adventuress. And this business tonight certainly proves it. You didn't see the look on Dan's face when he saw her! At the table in his own home, his own brother's wife, was certainly the last place in the world he expected to run across her again."

I smiled. That part of it was certainly true.

"And I'm glad Rick's eyes are finally opened," Irene went on. "I've made it—I think—perfectly clear to him that as long as he's married to her, he needn't expect anything from me. I think he sees now what a fool he was not to be the one to marry Natalie."

"Do you think Dan is going to marry her?" I inquired.

"Of course. He's got to."

"Why?"

She came over and sat down in the deep love seat beside me.

"Grace . . . the reason I sent for you this week end is this.—My husband was your husband's own first cousin."

I nodded.

"When he died, Grace, he left his estate entirely to me, except that at my death, or before if I chose, and if the need arose, three-fourths of one quarter of it was to go to his sister's child. The other one-fourth of that quarter was to go to your two children."

I looked at her in complete surprise. It was the last thing in the world I should have expected.

"And . . . Natalie is that sister's child."

"You mean she's Dan's cousin?"

She made a quick impatient gesture.

"That doesn't make the least difference—she takes after her father and Dan takes after me, so it's exactly as if they weren't at all related."

It seemed very convenient, and definitely, as Dr. Birdsong had said, of the eat-your-cake school.

"Does she know about this—the will, I mean?"

Irene shook her head. "The point is, however, that she's an orphan, and a very nice girl, and a really quite beautiful girl . . . and if one of the boys marries her, I won't have to divide the estate now . . ."

She got up abruptly.

"At least that was my idea this morning!"

Her slim white hands moved in a limp, weary gesture.

"I don't know, now. I don't suppose you realize how awful that scene at the table was, with Rick and Dan and Mara at each other's throat, hating each other . . . and me. Of course, nobody understood but Sidney and myself that Rick is bitterly opposed to my marrying. He's always hated Sidney. I think if Sidney hadn't been in the bank Rick would have stayed on and perhaps amounted to something. Perhaps if I gave him his money now he'll still do something. Sidney's opposed to it, but it's because he doesn't understand Rick."

She leaned her head on the mantel and stared down into the fire, the flames lighting her filmy crimson gown, making the shadow of her body seem too light and fragile to hold up against her strident warring family.

"I wonder if any other mother ever felt the way I do, or if I'm nothing but an unnatural beast," she said quietly, after another long pause. "But Grace . . . sometimes I almost hate Rick, and . . . Mara. And I know they hate me."

Her voice had sunk almost to a whisper. Outside a gust of wind buffeted the windows, a shutter banged. Above it came that dreadful shrill shriek. I got up abruptly.

"You're being stupid, Irene," I said, rather brutally, I'm afraid. "You'd better go to bed and forget tonight."

I went to the window to close it, and for some reason that I wasn't quite aware of I drew the curtains aside and looked out. Someone slipped quickly behind one of the white fluted columns, but not quickly enough to escape the shaft of light falling on her auburn hair. I let the curtains fall . . . wondering what difference it might make that Natalie Lane had heard all this too.

I drew the window down and came back to the fire.

"Who was the man with the dog?" I asked.

"That's Tom Birdsong," she said dully.

"Is he a doctor?"

"Among other things. He doesn't practice—nobody knows why. He's the local man of mystery."

I started out.

"Please go to bed, Irene."

She kissed me lightly on the cheek.

"You probably think I'm a very wicked woman," she said softly. "Good night."

It wasn't, I thought as I went up stairs, the old pine banister satin-smooth under my hand, as much a matter of thinking that Irene was wicked as of thinking that since I'd seen her last she had really changed incredibly . . . or that perhaps I'd never really known her, never had seen her before in a situation that was anything but rather charmingly casual—certainly not one as fundamentally emotional as this night's.

I went to bed and turned out the light, but I didn't go to sleep. Even if it hadn't been for the wind moaning in the old chimneys and tearing like dead hands at the wooden shutters, and the eerie screaming of those birds, like souls lost in hell, Romney was still too full of ghosts for me, ghosts of my own dead past. I must have dropped off at last, however, for I'm sure I woke up hearing hushed frantic voices outside my door in the hall.

"You can't leave now, you can't! Don't you see it's just what they want you to do?"

It was Mara's voice, urgent and passionate.

"Cheryl—you *can't* go!"

"But I've got to go, to-night! You don't understand, Mara! A horrible thing has happened . . . please let me go, I tell you I've *got* to!"

"But you *can't!* The tree's down over the road—you can't walk, you can't stay in the village all night!"

"But you can phone Alan—he can take me to Washington. I've got to go, Mara."

There was a long silence. I heard steps on the polished pine floors then, and in a few minutes the tinkle of the country phone. I looked at my clock. The hands pointed to twenty minutes past one. I lay there as long as I could without going quietly out of my mind, and got up. However bad the situation was, it seemed utter folly for Cheryl Winthrop to go barging off into the night in Alan Keane's open car . . . it would only give Irene and Rick another stick to thwack her with, and it wouldn't help Dan.

I put on my dressing gown and slippers, opened the door into the hall, and went along the hyphen corridor to the main upstairs hall where the phone was. The receiver was hanging down, but neither of the girls was there. Then as I stood there, wondering what to do, I heard low and bitterly intense voices below. I looked over the pine rail. Down in the lower hall, cowering in a corner, was Mara Winthrop, in front of her, a riding crop in his raised hand, was Rick. His voice was like a hissing madman's: "Where is she, damn you! Tell me where she is, or I'll—"

Mara's answer was a strangled terrified sob. "She's gone, out there!"

For a moment I stood there, not knowing what to do. Then I saw, quite suddenly, a figure standing in the shadow of the landing just below me, watching this as I was watching it, and my blood froze with horror. It was Irene Winthrop . . . just standing there, not raising a hand or saying a word to save her youngest child in that moment of abject mortal terror. My hands on the dark wood rail were cold and shaking like a leaf. Below me then I saw Mara sink down on the sofa and sit perfectly rigid, staring white-faced at the door that had slammed on her brother's back.

Irene hadn't moved. I stood there for a moment, frightened and angry—angrier, I think, than I ever remembered being in all my life. Yet I knew that if I made a scene it wouldn't help —anybody: Mara, or Cheryl, or Dan. I could, however, keep something pretty terrible from happening to Cheryl. I thought of that riding crop and of Rick Winthrop's face, convulsed with rage.

I turned as silently as I could and crept along to the other wing, the dining room wing where Dan's room had always been, and opened his door. In the dim light I could make out the great fourposter bed and its blue resist print curtains. I could see Dan's bags still unpacked on the rack. I ran across to the bed and put my hand out to wake him, and touched the soft cool linen sheet still folded neatly back.

My heart stopped dead at a sudden wild shriek outside, and beat again as I realized that it was only one of Irene's fancy buzzards. My knees were shaking and my hands were icy, and

36

I don't know how long I stayed there, just standing by the bed, afraid to go back for fear of meeting Irene. I had a profound conviction in my heart that she would make Mara, and Cheryl, suffer for that night . . . so charmingly and delicately that no one but they would know what was happening.

Just as I was gradually realizing that I had to go back, I couldn't stay here, I heard slow cautious footsteps coming down the hall, something in them so secret and stealthy that without fully realizing what I was doing I slipped behind the tall painted screen in the corner. I heard the door close and the latch uncatch, and a match strike. Looking out between the sections of the screen I saw Dan Winthrop go very quietly to the window and pull down the blinds. Then he took off his shoes and went into the bathroom and turned on the light. I saw him look in the mirror. A long streak of blood trickled down from a cut above his right cheek bone. He mopped it off with a cleansing tissue and painted it with iodine, and examined another cut on the side of his mouth. Then he came back into the room, took the pajamas off his bed, went back into the bathroom and closed the door.

I got back to my own room . . . with a feeling of considerable satisfaction at the idea that if Dan had been marked up a bit, Rick Winthrop was probably unrecognizable.

It was half-past eight when I went downstairs the next morning. Breakfast at Romney is served English fashion, in the summer, on the terrace of the dining room hyphen, overlooking the lawns stretching down to the Potomac. As I came down the wide staircase it seemed incredible that it was less than eight hours since I had seen Mara cowering there in the corner, her brother's upraised crop, her mother watching, detached and impassive, from the landing by the grandfather clock. The hall was quiet, a fresh breeze from the river came through the front door and out the garden door where Dan and I had come in. It was the cool airy silence of a summer morning in the country, before the day's life begins and the sun becomes hot and drowsy. A humming bird hung motionless like a jewel in the white wisteria on the garden porch, a wasp nosed at the copper screening on the door.

The old rubbed pine made the hall dim and shadowy inside. I pushed the screen open and stepped out onto the pillared portico, and stood looking down at the green lawns sloping to the glistening waters of the river, almost blue under the clear cobalt sky, and the white urns full of brilliant flowers, and the Italian marble balustrade and benches, drenched with sunshine, that marked off the formal gardens on each side of the long dark alleys of box; and I caught my breath at the loveliness of it. The night, and the storm, and that passionate scene

37

at dinner, were a nightmare—the wind whipping the cedars and the box, the buzzards in the oak, were as unreal as remembered pain. My heart rose inside of me with a sensation of almost physical release . . . and dropped again as suddenly, out of all this loveliness and light and sunshine came that horrible scream again.

I turned my head, hardly knowing what I must see. There parading majestically out of a tiny domed and pillared temple of love set in a crimson sea of roses, came a long troupe of peacocks, strutting the living beauty of their coverts, spread like great jeweled fans above their soft iridescent breasts. I watched them move sedately across the garden, their trains spread, glittering magnificently, a shimmering glory in the sun, to where an odd-looking woman in a wide straw sombrero was sprinkling corn on a marble rose-colored balustrade and calling them in a strange high-pitched voice.

I turned quickly toward the terrace, a quite sheepish flush rising to my cheeks. The glamorous entourage parading through the sunlit flower-decked lawns of Romney made the fantasy of the night an even madder child of my disordered brain. I wondered with some amusement even if the rest of the night was also a horrible imagining: Cheryl's flight, Mara cowering under the upraised crop, those tell-tale cuts on Dan's face.

I stepped out on the terrace, and stopped dead. Cheryl Winthrop was sitting at the table, in a blue backless tennis frock, her warm gold skin unbelievably lovely under her thick wheat-gold sleekly waving hair, her eyes as blue as hyacinths, her brown legs bare except for short white socks, her feet in stubby woven grass slippers. And beside her in a Lincoln green archery costume with a peacock feather in her hat, and looking very gay and lovely, was Irene.

"Darling—good morning!" she cried. "I'm so glad *somebody* can get up in the morning! Do hurry and have a bite of food, and then come along to the range. Cheryl's not going to shoot, so you really must."

I steadied myself against the walnut hunting table and poured myself a large cup of coffee from the fluted Sheffield urn. I must, I told myself, be quietly losing my mind. I was convinced of it a minute later when Irene said, "There comes Mara!" and in Mara came, dressed in tan mud-spattered jodhpurs, her jodhpur boots wet and muddy too, her yellow shirt open at the neck, her dark eyes shining, her pale cheeks flushed. She tossed her hat and crop and a yellow glove on one end of the table and sank down in her chair. Then she sprang up again.

"Let me get something for you, Grace. Kidney stew—ham

38

and eggs? Did the peacocks keep you awake all night? I think they're ghastly, but you get used to it. They're only vocal once a year—mating season."

I shall never know how I got through that breakfast, though it didn't take long, Irene was waiting with such marked impatience for me to finish. She chattered gaily along like a bird among the apple blossoms while Mara and Cheryl ate in silence. When I got up she took my arm, and we went through to the hall and out on the back porch. I glanced up at the spot where she had stood silently looking on at that scene between Rick and Mara. It seemed utterly incredible.

We went out onto the porch.

"Dear, dear, look at that!" Irene cried suddenly. "One of my best bows!"

Lying at the edge of the porch was the bow Dan had fallen over. It's shaft was broken, the string tangled and snapped at the servicing.

Irene picked it up. "You wouldn't think these things cost money, the way they're treated," she said irritably. "Young people simply haven't any sense about things."

She tossed it back on the stone flagging and held up her arms suddenly to the morning, her annoyance over the broken bow completely vanished. "My dear—isn't it *divine!* Do come along!"

We crossed the oyster-shell drive, toward the big target that my lights had picked out in the driving rain the night before. It was glistening in the sun now, and a peacock was perched on it, exhibiting the glory of his outspread train to a crowd of gray little peahens.

Irene waved her arms. "Isn't he lovely!" she cried.

The cock sailed slowly down, alarmed but dignified, as Irene hastened down the green stretch. The sun glistened on the raindrops caught in the tiny cups of the box leaves. I saw it glistening also on some little glass pebbles lying in the close cropped grass not far from the target. I bent down to look at them, they looked so like diamonds fallen there; and as I did so I saw Irene stop suddenly, ahead of me, and heard her give a strange strangled cry, so frightening that I stopped myself, bent halfway to the round. She ran quickly past the target then, toward the box hedge that formed a back drop for the range, stopped again and stood perfectly rigid, staring down at something on the ground.

I straightened up and stood for an instant staring at this odd pantomime. Then, still rigidly poised there, one hand out in front of her as if to ward off some terrible sight, she moved her other hand in an almost mechanical but so imperative a summons that I ran toward her.

Lying huddled at the base of the box hedge was Rick Winthrop, and a slender, feather-tipped shaft was buried in his throat. A stream of blood had trickled down, dyeing his white coat an ugly brown, and dried along the white folds of his collar.

I stood there for an instant, as petrified with horror as Irene Winthrop. Then I felt my eyes moving back, almost automatically, to the golden ball of the target. The arrow that had been there last night, that Dan and I had seen in the beam from my headlights as we rounded the white oyster-shell drive, was gone.

It seemed to me a thousand years that my eyes had to journey from the empty gold back to the inert figure huddled under the box, and at the feathered shaft stained with blood, to realize that it was an arrow, to understand that Rick Winthrop was dead. It seemed a long time too that we stood, his mother, all the jauntiness gone from her archer's suit of Lincoln green, and I, staring down at him. I didn't see as much as simply know that her hand was moving out to touch that arrow. As it closed on the green and yellow crest I felt something cold and wet and alive touch my own trembling fingers.

I couldn't move my hand, or could hardly look down, without forcing myself to do it. When I did, I was looking into a pair of pale, almost white eyes, very alive and strange, behind a fringe of long curly gray hair.

"It's Dr. Birdsong, Irene . . ." I managed to say.

"Oh, my God, no! No!" she whispered frantically. Her sharp red nails were buried in my arm.

6

It sounds absurd, I suppose, to call Irene's hand clutching at my arm, and her frantic broken whisper, a jarring note, because obviously the whole business was jarring in the extreme . . . our coming so abruptly on Rick Winthrop's rigid ghastly body in its sodden white dinner coat, lying there in the sun-drenched grass, the arrow buried in his throat, the oozing dried blood on his jacket and collar . . . and then the cold wet muzzle of that extraordinary dog thrust so silently—and significantly, it seemed to me—into my hand.

Probably if I'd known more about Dr. Birdsong then, and less—or perhaps more—about Irene Winthrop, I shouldn't have been so disturbed as I was. Disturbed isn't, of course, quite the word. And shocked is too strong, although it was literally a kind of shock; not the sort that would floor one, but the kind one gets touching a door knob after crossing a heavily carpeted room. It sank like a tiny sliver of ice into a remote unhappy corner of my mind, and crept out to plague me again and again.

If I'd known more about Dr. Birdsong—if, for example, besides telling me he was the local man of mystery, Irene had told me that if you mentioned his name at a dinner in Washington somebody would always look up and say, "Oh, do you mean Tom Birdsong? Do you know him—really?" and then lapse into abrupt and quite inexplicable silence . . . just that might have made my part in it all quite different. Sometimes so many people were apt to lapse into silence that the hostess was grateful to some western senator's wife who'd look up brightly and say, "Oh, it *must* be twenty minutes past the hour!" And I suppose sometimes it must have been. It could happen in London too, and in remote spots on the globe where many other names would pass quite unnoticed.

But I didn't know that then, nor did I know that Irene Winthrop carried beneath the sunny gay surface of her life, with its vanities and affectations, anything that fear could touch, and touching, wither like hoar frost a garden of autumn roses. I didn't, for example, know that she disliked Dr. Birdsong, nor why. I only guessed, from what he'd said the night before, and the glance he gave her as he stopped beside us now, and looked down before he stooped quickly and touched the

41

rigid heap that had been Rick Winthrop, that he hadn't any too great admiration, or even tolerance, for her.

She stood now, her face ashen, her lips quite blue where they showed under the bright outline of geranium-red, her thin nostrils pinched and quivering. I think if she hadn't been steadied by her convulsive grip on my arm she would have swayed like a drunken person.

Dr. Birdsong stood up as abruptly as he'd stooped, and turned to me. I had a sudden sinking feeling in the pit of my stomach. It wasn't the first time that I'd been where a person had been killed; but it was the first time anyone had looked at me with cold and inexorable eyes that had so definitely the effect of putting me instantly in my place. Before, I'd been, if not an official, at least a tacitly accepted member of the hounds. I was now painfully one of the hares, if persons suspected of such a thing as this could conceivably be called hares; and I was to learn before the week was out that nobody, no matter how innocent he is, can be normal under the cold and jaundiced eye of suspicion.

And there was suspicion, definitely, in the remote gaze that Dr. Birdsong fixed on me.

"Go and phone the sheriff," he said curtly. "Tell him what's happened, and tell him I said I'd wait here till he comes. His name's Dorsey."

It may have been because I'm not used to being ordered about, or perhaps it was some of Irene's emotion communicating itself to me. Anyway, I felt the color rise in my cheeks and the adrenalin content of my viscera increase perceptibly.

His steely eyes sharpened, but he added instantly, though I'm afraid with a barely perceptible irony, "—if you don't mind?"

"I'll be glad to," I said shortly.

"And also will you tell everybody in the house to stay there.—And Irene, will you move out of the way? It's important to keep this place from being messed up."

I didn't hear Irene Winthrop's reply. I don't imagine in fact that she made one. It didn't occur to me, however, as I hurried down the hundred yard range to the house that this was probably part and parcel of what Dan had so aptly referred to as the hell's broth for somebody to stew in, and whether it was Irene Winthrop who had stirred it up didn't seem to matter very much. All of us, apparently, were going to stew, and stew properly, under the frosty objective eye of the gentle man in the rough baggy Harris tweeds and riding boots caked with dirt from the tobacco fields.

And when I'd realized that, in a vague way, I hadn't yet

42

realized that it was also to be done under the personal supervision of that odd dog of his. It wasn't until I'd stepped out of the glaring sun into the cool hall that I noticed he'd come along with me and that I'd rudely closed the screen door in his face. For a second I thought I'd do nothing about it. Then I saw those gray white-rimmed eyes looking at me through their chignon of dirty wool. It sounds silly, of course, but I opened the door with a sudden feeling that if I didn't he might very well go back and tell his master, and probably put a very bad face on the entire incident. As it was, he grinned at me and gave his ridiculous tail a perfunctory wag, and waited for me to proceed.

I hesitated. Through the great open door leading to the pillared verandah I could see two heads, one dark, one shining gold in the sun, close together, as Mara and Cheryl sat side by side on the top step, so deep in conversation that they must not have heard me come in. For a moment I thought I'd go immediately and tell them. Then I changed my mind, and to keep from having to use the living room phone, where they'd hear me if the window was open, I went upstairs to the one on the landing.

The house was perfectly silent with that drowsy summer silence that a bumble bee buzzing at the clusters of white wisteria outside the palladian window on the upper landing seemed only to intensify and make more profound. I found myself thinking, as I wound the little crank at the side of the phone and picked up the receiver, "But it's a live silence, it's got nothing to do with the silence that hangs over Rick out there."

A voice said, "Number, please," and I said, "The sheriff's office, please." After a minute a tired voice at the other end said "Sam Dorsey speakin'," and I said, "There's been an accident at the Winthrops', at Romney, Mr. Dorsey. Dr. Birdsong said to tell you he'd be here till you come."

I put down the phone. The dog was sitting there beside me, grinning. He looked at me, and then down the hall, and back at me . . . for all the world as if he were saying, "Don't look now, but there's somebody listening to us." It may not have been what he meant at all, but I did look . . . and as I did I saw, in the old gilt mirror over a Pembroke table against the wall, a door closing softly, very quietly, and in its dark cloudy surface I saw the bright glint of auburn hair.

I glanced back at the dog and nodded. He grinned, pricked up his ears and looked down the other wing, just as Dan Winthrop, barefooted, in his bathing suit, a towel around his neck, came whistling cheerfully from the opposite wing.

"Did I hear you say there'd been an accident?" he asked.

When I saw the alarmed look come into his eyes I knew I must be paler than I'd thought.

"It's not . . ."

I shook my head. "No. It's her husband," I said. And then, because the look of relief on his face was so complete, I added, pretty callously, I'm afraid, "He's dead, Dan."

He looked at me, his eyes blank and perfectly uncomprehending, his big mouth opened stupidly.

"Rick's dead, Dan," I repeated, more gently. "With an arrow in his throat. Your mother and I found him—she's out there now, with Dr. Birdsong. You'd better get some clothes on and go out to her."

I glanced at the cut on his cheek. He'd plastered it with some adhesive tape. The skin around his eye was swollen a little and rather discolored, and his mouth was swollen a little too. It didn't look serious—not in itself. I could easily see the cold look that Dr. Birdsong was going to give it.

He stood there dumbly, staring at me. "Does . . . she know?" he got out at last.

It never entered my mind to think who "she" was, knowing that so far as Dan was concerned the feminine creation existed solely in one exemplar. I shook my head, aware curiously that while I was saying I didn't know, he was of course understanding that she didn't. He stood there silently a moment, then turned and hurried back to his room.

I looked down at the dog, trusting he'd remember in his report to say that Dan's face was certainly bewildered to the point of stupefaction when the news was broken to him, and started out to the porch. The quicker the two girls out there were prepared for the descent on Romney of what sounded over the phone like a Keystone comedy sheriff, and for all I knew a khaki-colored car bearing brown-jacketed State Police, the better. That they might conceivably have a deeper concern with Rick's death seemed irrelevant at the moment. And while normally I'm really not a completely callous person, Rick's performance of the night before had raised the threshold of my mind gainst him so definitely that I couldn't actually think of his death as anything but a fact. Not even a tragic fact . . . only an ugly one. And ugly, I thought, in its effect on Dan and Mara and Cheryl and Romney, more than its effect on himself.

I went down the wide pine staircase, the dog at my side. I'd begun to think of him as definitely detailed to keep an eye on me, and I was surprised, therefore, when we got to the landing and I started to go through to the porticoed verandah overlooking the Potomac, to see him go to the screen door and push it with his immense wooly paw. I was more surprised to see that it didn't open; someone had hooked it. I glanced out on the porch. The two girls were still sitting there, their heads close together. I wondered, idly at first and then with more interest, who had come that way, why had they moved so silently, why had they locked that door? If one of the servants had heard what I said, either to the police or to Dan, he would have showed more interest. They'd all been born on Romney or close by—in fact had practically raised the three young Winthrops.

I started over to unfasten the door, but as I did the dog raised up on his hind legs, balancing with one paw against the frame, and calmly nosed the hook loose. He then pushed the door open and padded down the stone steps toward the range . . . the death range, as the papers were to be calling it in so terribly short a time.

As the door slammed back, Yarborough, the gaunt white-wooled old colored man who had come with the house when Mr. Winthrop bought Romney, came out of the dining room, muttering darkly. He had on a fresh white linen coat and the thickest-lensed pair of gold rimmed spectacles I've ever seen. He padded to the door, saw me and said, "This yere do' got to be kept shet. They's flies, and they's waspes, and Missy she make out it's case we don' keep the pantry do' shet. It's this yere hard-name ol' do' that makes th' trouble. It's got to be kept shet."

With that he locked it firmly and turned back to me. He hesitated. Then he took off his spectacles, and beamed suddenly, like an ancient ebony cherub.

" 'Deed, Mis' Grace, Ah didn't reco'nize you in that costume. La, chil', you's pretty as a picture, 'deed you is."

I thought it was odd he hadn't recognized me. I looked at his glasses.

"You must be having trouble with your eyes, Yarborough?"

He gave his old head a mournful shake. "Mus' is, Ah reckon Ah gettin' ol' Mis' Grace. An' eye strain is health strain, as the sayin' is."

He put his spectacles back on. I didn't know then they were an extra pair left behind by an exceedingly myopic member of the German Legation after a weekend at Romney and that Yarborough had just adopted them . . . or that when he had them on he was practically as blind as a bat. He only made his way around the house safely because he knew the shape of every room and stair and the position of each piece of furniture by heart. Nor did I know that that was why the Romney murderer was able to pass so close to the old man—blinded quite literally by his pride and his vanity—as almost to touch him. But no state policeman would ever believe that, and I

45

suppose it is incredible unless one has lived with colored people, or children, or known—for instance—an otherwise quite intelligent man of fifty who thought the small patch of brown on the top of his head remotely resembled hair, as did the rector of the church we went to as children. And I'm not sure, now, that the strangest thing about the whole affair of Rick Winthrop—and what followed—wasn't that when life and death hung so delicately in the balance at Romney, the two-fold vanity of an old darky should have weighed death's side down: the personal pride that made him wear the gold-rimmed spectacles that almost blinded him, the pride in his career that made him labor stubbornly to keep that screen door locked to keep out flies and waspes. But that night when life and death swung in the balance, and death was the throw because a screen door was locked, was still mercifully in the future.

I looked at his brown old eyes, lost fathoms deep in the concentric rings of those spectacles. He took them off again, and said gently, "Mis' Grace, you lookin' mighty worried. Is they sumthin' wrong?"

"It's Mr. Rick, Yarborough."

"He did'n had no accident?" he asked quickly. His eyes bulged a little—almost hopefully, I realized with a definite shock.

I nodded. "He's dead."

His face faded slowly into the color of old putty. He put on his spectacles again, turned and went blindly off without a word; and I really had no doubt that the reason he staggered against the door was that he was overcome with emotion. I heard the pantry door swing shut, with the sort of suction sound it has, and I heard a door slam shut upstairs, and Dan Winthrop's quick heavy tread on the narrow back stairway.

I crossed through the hall, opened one side of the front screen, and stepped out on the wide sun-bathed verandah. The two girls sitting there stopped their low-voiced talk abruptly, and sat motionless for a moment. Then Cheryl glanced around, said "Oh!" and got up quickly. Mara looked back and got up too. It didn't take much to see that it hadn't been I they had expected, or to see that they were both living in a state of mute anxiety that was straining their nerves to the breaking point. Mara's eyes were like two blurred dark wells, the yellow handkerchief in her hand was a tiny tight wad of linen that fell when she got up quickly and rolled like a ball down the stone steps and lay unnoticed in the grass. Cheryl Winthrop's blue eyes had the look that I've seen in women's faces standing in hospital corridors, waiting.

I looked from one to the other of them, and for the first

46

time, I think, the necessary corollary of murder struck me full in the face: if there is murder, there must be a murderer. I don't mean that that's something I hadn't known before, but only that it came with startling newness as I looked at the two girls there, one the dead man's sister, the other his wife . . . the sister who hated him, the wife whom his brother loved.

All that went through my mind quite instantaneously, for Cheryl said almost as soon as she rose, "Is Irene waiting for us?"

I shook my head. "There's some pretty awful news for you, Cheryl," I said, as gently as I could.

Pale gold as she was, she grew paler, until her blue eyes were dark lakes in the waxen pallor of her face. She stood quite motionless, and Mara's slim little figure, still in tan jodhpurs and yellow shirt open at the throat, grew as still also as a candle flame when a window beside it is suddenly closed.

"Is it . . . Rick?"

Cheryl's voice was almost soundless.

I nodded.

"He's dead."

For a moment neither she nor Mara moved a muscle or quivered an eyelid. And yet something about them had changed so completely that it was hardly believable. It was almost like seeing them turn almost imperceptibly to marble. They didn't look at each other; they simply stood, silent and immobile. For a moment I thought Cheryl was too dazed to speak . . . and then I knew, in some way, that she was not, that she had known, and Mara had known, and that this had been what they had sat there together on the porch waiting for.

7

Cheryl turned around suddenly and leaned her slim young body against the white fluted columns at her side, and bent her bright head with its gay little red ribbon bow. Mara's dark eyes rested on her for an instant. Then she went to her, and touched her arm in some mute appeal I could not fathom. Cheryl's brown hand closed on Mara's browner one, as if she understood and assented. Mara turned back to me.

"Where . . . where did they find him, Grace?"

"Your mother and I found him on the archery range, behind the butt," I said.

Her eyes widened slowly. "Behind the . . . oh, how awful!"

"I should think both of you might change into something else, and be ready when the police come," I said, a little brusquely, I'm afraid, trying to cover up my own sharp bewilderment.

Cheryl looked down at her smart short blue linen frock and brown bare legs as if she had suddenly seen them for the first time.

"Yes . . . of course," she whispered.

Then I saw that Mara's calm control had suddenly snapped. She was staring at me, her eyes wide with terror. "The police! Oh, Grace, they shan't come, you mustn't let them!"

Cheryl caught her arm.

"Oh, don't, darling, don't! You just make it so much harder! Come on, please, and change your things!"

"But you don't know what they're like, Cheryl!"

I heard her voice, almost hysterical, as Cheryl took her into the house. As I stood there, more bewildered than ever, not knowing now at all what to think, Irene's voice came from the living room. She was obviously at the telephone, and trying, it was equally obvious, to sound as casual as she could.

"Sid, this is Irene. Rick's had an accident. Could you come over—*just* as quickly as you can?—But this is *dreadfully* important . . . can't your meeting wait? I *do* want you here when the . . . the rest of them come."

Then there was a silence, and in a moment Irene came out through the open window and stood beside me. "Let's go down here," she said softly. We went down the three shallow bevelled stone steps and across the lawn. A peacock perched on the marble bench, his glorious tail spread to the morning sun, and a drab little peahen pecking aphids off the rose bushes, moved grudgingly out of our way. Irene drew me down beside her and glanced uneasily at the house.

"My dear, you can't ever tell, at a time like this, *who's* listening," she said, her grip on my arm tightening nervously. "I'm literally terrified. Do you know what that horrible man has done?"

I shook my head.

"He's had Mr. Keane put a barrier up around the range, and he won't let anyone go up on the porch. He thinks . . . somebody shot Rick from there. Oh my dear Grace, it's too, too horrible! Two policemen have come, and they're ordering everybody about as if they owned the place."

She clasped and unclasped her hands convulsively.

"If only Mr. Purcell would come, Grace! He's the State's Attorney, and an old friend . . . I *know* he'll put a stop to this terrible mockery."

I looked at her, wondering in spite of myself about a lot of things. Her lips were pinched and her face drawn and gray. For the first time since I'd known her she looked her fifty-five years . . . and more, I thought, just then, in the bright glare of the morning sun. She looked away quickly as her eyes met mine. There was something in them that I couldn't fathom.

"Grace, you must help me," she said suddenly. "We've got to stop this thing!"

"I'm afraid it's rather late, Irene," I said gently. "And anyway, don't you want them to . . . to find out what . . . happened?"

Her eyes were wide with surprise and dismay, question and horror, and under them stark living fear.

"And have it all in the papers? His quarrel with Sidney Tillyard, and . . ."

"Did he and Major Tillyard quarrel?"

I thought, just off-hand, that there were other more important quarrels that seemed infinitely more likely to make the public prints.

"Oh, yes. Rick didn't want me to marry Sidney—he threatened to kill him . . . and me too. Rick was insanely jealous. He always was, even when he was a baby. He was jealous of Dan—and even of his own father."

"Irene," I said, as calmly as I could. "Do you mean you think Major Tillyard killed Rick?"

She turned full on me. "Why, Grace—what a *horrible* thing to say!"

"Then I'd be awfully careful about about saying anything

that seems to imply it," I said. "Especially if there are any policemen about."

She seemed shaken, and paler, all of a sudden.

"Of course I didn't mean that. It's ridiculous and wrong of you to pretend I did. After all, he's my own son."

I managed to follow that.

"And you're going to marry Major Tillyard . . . and Rick's been going around, I suppose, shouting that he's a fortune hunter."

"But he's not, Grace." She was very indignant. "I mean, he's got much more money than I have. I've explained that to the children, thoroughly."

It seemed to me so strange, then, that Irene should be talking this way with her first-born son lying dead so close by . . . and not only dead, but—as eleven men in all probability now being gathered from the neighboring fields would be saying so soon—dead by the hand of a person or persons unknown. Looking at her, I wondered again . . . pretty sick, I'm afraid, at her shallow heartlessness. After all, whatever Rick Winthrop had done or not done, he was her child; it was she who had set his feet in the path they were to go.

"All I mean is," she said plaintively, "is that everybody will think of that the first thing as a motive, and no telling what might come of it, with a man in Sid's position."

I looked at her with a new awareness.

"You mean, Irene, that you're *really* in love with Major Tillyard . . . you really *very much* want to marry him?"

A little cloud settled on her smooth forehead.

"It doesn't seem quite right to be talking about my marriage—at this time, I mean. But I do want to marry him. I suppose I'm in love with him. I'm certainly very fond of him. He's been asking me to marry him ever since his wife died, three years ago. It seems too bad that now . . ."

She trailed vaguely off.

"You don't need money, do you, Irene?" I asked.

"Oh, no." She laughed lightly. "Although money's the one thing nobody ever gets too much of. You know, I've almost doubled the estate Joe left me—I've been very lucky."

If I had known Irene better at that moment, I would have known a great deal more than I even faintly guessed about what had been going on at Romney . . . but know her as well as ever I might, I could never at that point have guessed why Rick Winthrop lay out there with an arrow in his throat.

"But what I wanted to tell you, Grace, is this: you mustn't let on if the police question you about any of the things I said last night."

"You mean what you said about almost hating Rick."

She looked at me in amazed horror.

"Why Grace Latham, are you mad? How can you sit there and say such a thing!" she cried. Her blue eyes were saucer-wide. "—Hate my own son?"

Maybe she *had* forgotten words that no doubt she hadn't seriously meant.

"I'm sorry," I said. "I must have been thinking about something else. Just what is it you don't want me to let on about?"

"I mean about dividing the estate, and all that. Because I really promised Rick I'd give him his share. I really did. So you see that couldn't possibly have had anything to do with it, could it, Grace?"

I looked away. Her gentle insistence seemed rather odd. Had she promised him his money, I wondered, or was she only trying to make me think so . . . and if so, why, in heaven's name?

"There *is* one thing that disturbs me, though." She'd changed again, suddenly, and was speaking almost as if she were thinking out loud. "I mean, if the police do come, and all that. It's about Cheryl. I wouldn't want it known . . . but she wasn't in her room last night, Grace.—And we certainly ought not to let it get out that she's an astonishingly good shot with a bow. She taught archery when she was a councillor at a summer camp in the Adirondacks."

She was bent forward, her weight on her two hands spread palm down on the marble bench, swinging her tiny handsomely shod green feet, crossed, back and forth over the daisies and buttercups in the grass. She looked as sweet and charming and lovely as the flowers themselves. And my blood froze in my veins.

"Irene!" I gasped. "That's the most horrible thing I ever heard anybody say!"

She looked at me innocently. "My dear, I was just warning you. I wouldn't think of mentioning it. Heaven knows I don't want to cause the girl any trouble."

She shrugged airily. "It *is* unfortunate, of course, that there's been all this talk of divorce."

I'd got past the point of doing anything except just wait, staring stupidly, for the next thing she'd say. I was well beyond surprise or shock any longer. I couldn't, however, help noticing the ever so faintly calculating wrinkle that deepened at the corners of her eyes so guiltless of the crow's feet that plague most women past thirty.

"Because you know Rick had finally made up his mind to get a divorce. It was just a question of how cheap he could get off.—At least he had until Dan barged in last night."

It seemed to me that since sitting down on that marble

51

bench that Irene's husband had picked up for a song in some Italian garden, I had run through my entire emotional gamut. I had now finally got to anger.

"Look," I said. "I know you don't like Cheryl. I don't see why, except that I suspect you wouldn't like any girl one of your sons married. But you can't do this sort of thing, you simply can't! If she were a Polynesian leper you couldn't do it!"

She raised her brows, maddeningly casual.

"Don't get excited, darling. Wait till some penniless nobody marries one of your sons. We'll see whether you'll be so detached about it."

"If one of them is bright enough to marry a girl like Cheryl I'll thank heaven on my bended knees," I retorted . . . knowing all the time how stupid I was to let her get under my skin. I got up.

"There's only one thing I've got to say, Irene," I said, as calmly as I could. "If you start—however disarmingly—the notion that Cheryl killed Rick, I'll feel perfectly free to tell Dr. Birdsong, and everyone else, everything you told me last night.—And everything I saw, as well."

She looked inquiringly at me.

"Where, for instance, were you, when Rick was shot?"

I knew it was stupid to ask that, the minute I did it.

"I? Why, my dear, I didn't leave my room all night," she said quietly.

"Then how did you know Cheryl wasn't in hers?"

A little smile played on her delicate porcelain lips.

"Quite simply, my dear. Her husband came and told me so."

I didn't believe it—naturally—and she knew I didn't. But it left me out on a limb . . . unless I wanted to tell her I'd seen her out on the landing, watching Rick and Mara in the hall below. Which I didn't . . . almost instinctively, I supposed, analyzing it later.

Irene got up suddenly and held out her hands to me.

"Oh come, Grace, we're old friends—let's not quarrel. We're both upset. I'll not even mention Cheryl. She can leave this afternoon, and I'll never see her again."

I looked at her in blank surprise, in spite of myself.

"Are you forgetting," I asked, "that she's your son's widow?"

We'd started to the house. She turned to me, stopping abruptly, a new oddly bewildered look in her eyes.

"You mean . . . you think she'll expect to inherit Rick's share . . ."

I couldn't help that feeling of hopeless anger again.

"Is money all you ever think of?" I inquired. "I was thinking chiefly of the funeral . . . and the police."

She shook her head. "No," she said shortly. "She's got to get away from here—right away. I can't have her here. Not while Dan's here."

"I thought you said last night," I observed pleasantly, "that Dan recognized her as an adventuress."

She didn't answer, and I glanced at her. She had stopped dead in her tracks and was looking across the gardens, her lips parted. Chugging up the wagon road from the farmhouse was a rickety old truck piled high with chairs and tables, a shiny old brass bedstead topping the lot. It looked like an outpost of a train of flood refugees. And Irene, standing there, said, I think, the one genuinely sincere word, instantly recognizable as such in my new view of her, that I remember her saying that week. She said, "Oh!" and there was no doubting the dismay in her voice.

Then she seized my hand, and we hurried across the garden and came out of the box lined path just as the truck rattled around the big pink and white apple tree at the curve in the road. Irene darted out directly in front of it. There'd never been any doubting her nerve, or her complete confidence in herself—not many people, I thought, would have cared to give an injured person such a handmade plea of accidental manslaughter.

Mr. Keane jammed on his brakes and stalled his old machine, which meant—not that Irene would mind, of course—that he'd have to crank it half an hour to get it started again. Its pitifully meager load wobbled dangerously, but finally stuck, and Mr. Keane hesitated a moment, then climbed out of the cramped seat and took off his hat. He had on a blue denim work shirt, unironed but freshly washed, the top button sewed on with red thread. I remembered there'd been no woman on the farm since his daughter had married and gone away four or five years ago. I'd known that because Irene had worried about his marrying again . . . chiefly because the right kind of woman would insist on having a bathtub put in the tenant house, and she didn't, of course, want the wrong kind there, and she couldn't think of going to the expense of plumbing, for after all they had electric lights.

I'd only seen Mr. Keane, this time, in the semi-light from the hall. Now in the full sunlight I saw his face, lined and weather-beaten under his short shock of thick gray hair, a curiously tragic face, lined with toil and with suffering too, I imagined, but certainly with nothing meek or fawning in it. The impression I got was one of a sort of kindly dignity and simplicity that most people, I think, would not have tried to take advantage of.

I glanced at Irene. She was standing there in the road, looking up at him with a hurt, almost tragic expression in her blue eyes.

"Why, Mr. Keane," she cried, "I don't see how you can do this to me! At a time like this, after all the years you've been at Romney . . . and you know how I've always depended on you, ever since Mr. Winthrop died, you're the one person I always thought I could count on!"

Mr. Keane's face reddened uncomfortably.

"I was told last night I wasn't wanted any longer at Romney, ma'am," he said.

"Oh, but Mr. Keane!" Irene cried. "You know the trouble I've had with Rick! I've been simply at my wit's end—I was ready to do anything to keep peace! But poor, poor Rick!"

She turned away. Mr. Keane would have had to have a heart of granite to withstand that. He turned redder still, fumbled in his pocket and brought out that blackened stumpy pipe, and stood uncomfortably poking the dark shreds of his home-cured tobacco into its bowl.

"I'm mighty sorry about Rick, ma'am," he said.

Irene turned back, her eyes bright with tears.

"Oh, Mr. Keane, you won't leave me, will you? I couldn't run the place without you! I've always felt Romney was your place as much as mine—and you know how miserably I feel about the way Mara has acted about Alan, but you know as well as I do neither of them would ever be happy a moment!"

Mr. Keane frowned a little. "Alan's a good boy, ma'am," he said quietly. "But I don't blame you. It wouldn't be the thing. I've told the boy that. He knows the way I feel. He couldn't never do for her like he ought to if he was to marry her. I've told him so many a time."

"Then you will stay, Mr. Keane? And we'll make a new contract, you really deserve more . . ."

"I don't want more'n I've got now, ma'am," Mr. Keane said. "Jus' to have the boy let alone, and nobody interferin' with the farm, is all I want, ma'am."

Irene smiled through her tears and held out her white delicate hand with its scarlet nails. Mr. Keane wiped his hand on the seat of his pants and took hers, his face a dull mahogany.

He was still cranking his truck when Irene and I were almost to the house.

"Thank God!" she said practically. "The whole crop would have been a dead loss if he'd gone. I intended to go see him the first thing this morning. I could never get anyone to do what he does. I can't see what I was thinking about, to let Rick . . ."

"And—Mara and Alan?" I asked, when she didn't go on.

"I'll have to arrange that some other way," she said calmly.

8

As we came up to the house she gripped my arm sharply. "Ssssh—there's Dr. Birdsong."

I glanced up. He wasn't in sight, but his dog was sitting on the porch, looking at us. He grinned as we came up the steps. Dr. Birdsong was standing in the doorway, with a tall completely emaciated figure in an old black alpaca suit and a soiled panama hat, and another man in spruce freshly laundered gray seersuckers and a new clean panama hat. The first man was hot, his scanty gray hair sticking to his moist forehead; he had white mustaches stained with telltale tobacco juice and wore a badge pinned to his white shirt. The other man looked enormously upset. He came toward us and held out his hand to Irene.

"I'm sorry!" he said. It seemed to me he was genuinely moved.

Irene pressed her lips together and looked away, gripping his hand tightly. "Oh, Barney, it's too horrible!" she whispered. She turned to me, her hand still in his. "Grace dear, this is Mr. Purcell the State's Attorney. This is my cousin Mrs. Latham, Barney. She's never liked poor Rick, but now that he's gone . . ."

I'm afraid I must have looked as completely stunned as I really was, for she gave me a pale smile.

"Oh, I know, dear. You couldn't possibly approve of so many things he did. No one could."

The idea that I had established myself as a moral censor to Rick, or anyone else, was definitely new to me. Rick could have lived his allotted three score and ten completely submerge in a tank of alcohol and it wouldn't have bothered me. But it did bother me, rather, to have the State's Attorney give me a swift inquisitorial glance out of his brown ferrety eyes, almost in a sort of "You'd better watch your step, my good woman" way.

I glanced without meaning to at Dr. Birdsong. His light blue eyes were resting steadily on me. I thought I detected the faintest ironical gleam in them. Whether it was a smile or a sort of comment on a confirmation of his own worst fears, I hadn't an idea. I know I was annoyed and looked away quickly.

Mr. Purcell was a man of about sixty, and obviously quite susceptible to beauty in distress. He turned back to Irene.

"You can count on us to make this as easy as we can for you, Irene," he said gently, patting her slim shoulder in its Lincoln green twill jacket.

She smiled gratefully up at him—and I don't for a minute mean that she wasn't genuinely grateful. Indeed I think that now he was there an enormous load had fallen from her shoulders; and as I learned more about Mr. Purcell I understood better why that was so. He had the old Comegys place next to Romney, and having been brought up on fatback and corn bread on a run-down farm in the next county he enjoyed, rather more than most, the frosted mint juleps in silver goblets and the candlelight and all the period elegance at Romney, and the flattering charming deference of a lady like Miz' Winthrop. His own wife stayed at home most of the time, and there were those who said that if anything ever happened to her Mr. Purcell wouldn't look around long. But that was county gossip, and anyway he could have looked longer and further—or so I'd thought until just recently—and done much worse.

The point, however, was not Mr. Purcell and his susceptibility to Irene as much as Irene and her susceptibility to herself. It's useless to say that she hadn't, in each of the guises and moods she'd appeared in so far that morning—and the night before—, been perfectly sincere. Everything she ever did was sincere . . . just as I'm sure Duse and Bernhardt were sincere in each role they ever played. For Irene was born an actress, and her life had developed her talent amazingly—on a stage far from Broadway, but just as much a stage. Every act of her life that I'd seen was motivated, consciously or unconsciously, by the effect it would have on her audience, let it be a group of tattered little colored boys or a dinner of foreign ambassadors. It made no difference to Irene, except in the role she chose, and she had a perfect sense of the fitness of any occasion. She could be a grand lady giving pennies to the little darkies, or a simple and oh, so charmingly ignorant woman to a stuffed and decorated white shirt.

And I think that what she had seemingly developed under her gay chameleon exterior was something that no one, least of all herself, would ever have predicted her being or becoming. Her own beginnings were well on the wrong side of the tracks—but neither Mr. Purcell nor Mr. Keane would ever have dreamed it. They were so lost and shadowy, and Irene so lovely, that no one, not even my husband's two Back Bay aunts, one of whom had been her mother-in-law, remembered them any more. I'd never have thought of them myself, or

57

dreamed that Irene remembered them even, until all her talk about Cheryl being a penniless nobody . . . and I only thought of them then because that's precisely what the Winthrop family had called Irene.

All this is merely by way of explaining that it wasn't, therefore, particularly designing or hypocritical of Irene that she seemed suddenly on the point of collapse after the harrowing experience of the morning. And of course it wasn't odd that Mr. Purcell, as the oldest friend of the family present, should support her fragile drooping figure into the cool house.

The sheriff put his hat on, took it off, scratched his bald head and put his hat on again. He turned to Dr. Birdsong.

"Maybe she can give us the dope." He nodded at me.

I saw that odd gleam again in Dr. Birdsong's eyes.

"Mr. Dorsey wants to know, Mrs. Latham," he said quietly, "how many people here can shoot an arrow in the dark, and hit the mark the first time?"

"I wouldn't have the foggiest notion," I said. "My guess would be none of them. Here, or anywhere else."

He nodded. "That was mine, too."

"It looks mighty like somebody did," Mr. Dorsey drawled. "Rick couldn't 'a done it by himself, now, could he?"

I looked at him with rather more interest. I took it that he plainly had a kind of common-sense point of view that his sallow emaciated face and his threadbare alpaca suit hadn't quite prepared me for.

"Of course, we don't want to make any trouble we ain't obliged to—but facts is facts."

"I know," Dr. Birdsong said. There was an ironic flicker in his eyes again. "That's what makes it hard. I mean, it was an extraordinary hit."

He had started to speak to me again when Mr. Purcell came to the door and beckoned the two of them inside. I stood there, wishing rather that my friend Colonel Primrose were here so I could go along. I didn't, some way, trust Irene Winthrop, not with an audience of three men and herself in the tragic role . . . though I wouldn't have cared, of course, if it hadn't been for Cheryl and Dan and Mara. But Colonel Primrose and his Sergeant Buck were on their way to Alaska, doing something about alien fishing rights in the Bering Sea for the government, and Dr. Birdsong obviously regarded me as alien corn. And so for once I had the privilege of minding my own business and keeping quietly out of the way.

Or so I thought. I could, at any rate, have gone quietly up to my room, at that moment, and that was what I had in mind as I passed the door of the sitting room. Inside I saw Irene seated in the sofa by the fireplace, her head back against the gay flowered chintz curtains, her eyes closed. Mr. Purcell sat beside her, with troubled eyes; Mr. Dorsey the sheriff, obviously ill at ease, was standing by the door. At the other end of the room, visible to me in the Chippendale mirror over the mantel, was Dr. Birdsong. His hands rested lightly in the pockets of his tweed jacket, his head bent a little, watching the other three in a kind of grimly detached fashion that for some reason was rather disturbing. Whether he actually then knew all the things about Rick and the rest of us that came out later, and whether, knowing, he planned then to keep them to himself, I don't know. I knew he was a strange man. But I believe it's true that under different circumstances he would have let Irene's personal influence with Mr. Purcell, and Lieutenant Regan's inexperience in murder outside the colored, Saturday night and bootleg classes, together settle the unpleasant fact of Rick's death in the pleasantest way possible. I even think he would have preferred doing it that way, if it hadn't been for Dan . . . and for Mrs. Jellyby.

I hadn't thought of Mrs. Jellyby then, nor for a long time, and I don't suppose I should have then, except that as I came to the staircase and started up I heard a voice that it took me a full second to recognize as Natalie Lane's at the telephone on the upper landing.

"You're *sure* he was coming to Romney?"

It must have been the urgency in her voice that stopped me from going on up, that and the fact that Natalie Lane seemed to me to be acting, on the whole, in a definitely quaint fashion —this being the third time I'd come upon her hovering about in the background of the curious things that seemed to be going on at Romney. At any rate I promptly went downstairs again, with as much clatter as my sneakers could make, and out the back garden door, the one Dan and I had come in the night before. The broken bow was gone, I noticed. Old Yarborough appeared in the hall and hooked the screen door, and padded away, muttering under his breath. I went down the stone stairs to the white oyster-shell drive, and stopped.

A uniformed state policeman was sitting on the running board of a khaki-colored car, smoking a cigarette. I looked past him down the grassy range to the big target, its golden heart gleaming in the sun. Beyond it, covered with a gray tarpaulin, poor Rick's body lay, profoundly still. The policeman got up as I came down, pushed his helmet back on his boyish head—he couldn't have been more than twenty-two— and came toward me.

"Say, who is that old dame in the straw hat with the bag of seeds?" he said. "I guess they're seeds."

59

And when I looked blank he said, "She's nuttier'n a fruit cake, if you ask me. She gave me these."

He took a little white cloth sack out of his pocket and handed it to me. It had a paper tag, on which was written, in an old-fashioned delicate script, "Columbine from Romney."

The young cop put it back in his pocket.

"I told her she couldn't go over there." He nodded toward the range, where they'd put up a couple of saw horses to keep people from treading on the grass. "She says to me, 'Young man, my work won't wait,' and she went right ahead, picking things off the bushes. Jeez, I hope it's all right."

"Oh, well," I said. "That's Mrs. Jellyby. It's all right."

"Jeez, I hope it's all right," he said dubiously.

And that's when I thought of Mrs. Jellyby again. Mrs. Jellyby is what is called in Maryland "a *real* character." In fact she's more than that. Who she is, what her name really is, where she came from, no one, unless it was Dan's father, has ever known, or ever asked. She appeared out of the blue at Romney in 1918. Irene was doing war work in Washington, Mr. Winthrop was home on sick leave from Fortress Monroe, Dan and Rick were in bed with the flu, and even Mara, a year old, had it. The one old doctor the war had left in Port Tobacco was driving himself in an old buggy from place to place, his own eyes glassy, his own temperature a hundred and two. The morning he collapsed Mrs. Jellyby walked up to the front porch of Romney with a leather satchel in one hand, a stout oak stick in the other, a canvas rucksack on her tweed back and a pair of men's shoes on her feet. She had come, she said, for seeds. She stayed, and nursed the three children and half a dozen darkies back to life; and when she wasn't in the sick room she was gathering little bags of seeds in the garden and stowing them away, neatly labeled, in her rucksack.

No one ever knew exactly how it was that she came to stay on, year after year, in an old slave cabin under the big weeping willow you can see from the house at the head of a tiny inlet at the foot of the kitchen garden, beyond the up-river wing of the house. But stay she did, even after Mr. Winthrop died. Everybody had thought she'd leave then, but she hadn't. Some people said Irene was afraid to put her out, but I doubt that. The darkies thought she was a witch, but a beneficent one, and they planted her little bags of seed with holy care. I have a bleeding heart against my garden wall in Georgetown that I grew from a bag she sent me.

I wondered, thinking about Mrs. Jellyby for the first time in many years as the young policeman returned to his car, what she would be making of all this. I glanced again down the range, where the little glass nodules on the grass were gone, and the arrow in Rick's throat was gone, like the broken bow on the porch. and like Rick himself soon, and I turned back and went along the herring-bone walk past the library wing and through the high walls of arbor vitae into the herb garden. At the end of the long vista I could see Mrs. Jellyby's tiny white cabin with its red chimney overgrown with ivy and trumpet vine, under the feathery streamers of the old willow, the water of the river glistening beyond it in the sun.

I thought then that it was amusing, rather, that I should be going that way, amusing and true to form, as all the troubles of Romney were sooner or later taken down that walk to the little house. Dan in his first year of French had taken to calling Mrs. Jellyby a sage-femme, I remembered suddenly, until he'd learned that that word didn't mean quite what it said. I was just thinking that as I came to the white fence that enclosed Mrs. Jellyby's half acre to keep the sheep and dogs out. I opened the gate and went along the narrow walk, bordered with old-fashioned spice pinks and tiny bright flowers whose names I didn't know, flanked with columbine and bleeding heart and canterbury bells and foxglove.

I stopped as I heard a girl's voice inside that it didn't take an instant to recognize.

"She's terrified, Mrs. Jellyby. If the police find out that Alan quarreled with Rick last night—"

Another familiar voice as harsh as a rusty lock interrupted:

"Don't be a rattle, Cheryl. Rick quarreled with everybody on the place last night, at one time or other."

"I know, but Alan's the only one who . . . who's been in jail."

"Not the only one who ought to be."

"And it was Rick who testified against him—"

"Oh, nonsense," Mrs. Jellyby said.

And because that seemed to settle that, I decided not to go back but to go on in. So I rapped at the white-washed door and stepped into the room. Mrs. Jellyby was perched on a stool at the end of a mahogany dropleaf table completely covered with trays of dried and drying seeds. She looked up, her weather-beaten face that I suppose had never had a grain of powder or rouge on it bright and amazingly alive under a short thatch of crisp snow white hair.

"You're too thin," she said frankly. "All women today look emaciated. I'll send you something. Put Grace's name down, Cheryl."

Cheryl opened a thick gray ledger on an old walnut bureau desk between the little windows and wrote my name down. Mrs. Jellyby pushed back her stool and got up. She was wearing an old blue polo shirt and an ancient gray tweed skirt that came just below her knees. Her thick legs were covered with gray wool stockings, and she had on men's shoes—whether the same pair or not I didn't know. She took her straw sombrero off the hook behind the door and put it on.

"I can't be bothered today," she said, and walked out. But at the door she stopped and looked back. "Try to remember that death isn't the worst thing that can happen to a man, Cheryl."

Cheryl Winthrop nodded slowly. Just looking at those words they don't seem to hold much sympathy or comfort; but hearing them, from that square hard woman whose life was given up to saving flowers at their death for a new awakening, there was, some way, and Cheryl felt it. I watched her go, thinking she seemed no older to me than she did when I ran into her tying short strands of red ribbon around the great blue heads of the morning glories on the paddock fence the first day I came to Romney, the year I was married. It didn't seem to me at all that Mrs. Jellyby, who seemed old then, was eighteen years older now. Her step was still as firm and her eye as steady, and her manner as brusque as it had been rather terrifyingly so then, for I'd picked a morning glory I hadn't known was being saved for seed.

9

Cheryl had changed from the blue linen tennis dress with the bare back. She looked almost like a cloistered nun now, in the simple black sheer frock with narrow white collar close about her firm slender throat. Her hair looked lighter, her skin a paler gold. As she turned to me her eyes under their long gold-flecked lashes were as blue as the great stalks of delphinium in Mrs. Jellyby's little garden.

"I can't find Mara," she said. "I'm so afraid she'll do something she'll . . . regret."

"She doesn't think Alan Keane had anything to do with this?" I asked. "Or does she?"

Cheryl looked away.

"I don't know how long anyone can go on, believing in someone," she said quietly. "She's held out so long, in this other business."

"There's not much doubt about that, is there?"

"Oh, I don't know . . . I wish I did!" she said. "I don't think Mara would be so belligerent if . . . if they'd let him alone. They did have *something* on him, and they've never got the bonds back. He did get a long prison term, and Major Tillyard and Dr. Birdsong got him paroled. Irene was furious. Oh, it's all so stupid. You see, in the summers he and Mara had had a sort of idyllic romance, while he helped Mr. Keane on the farm."

She came back from the window and sat down near me.

"You see, at first it never occurred to Irene that they were both old enough to fall in love, not until Alan got his job in the bank. It was Major Tillyard who said one night at dinner —more to tease Mara than anything else—that after all this was the great universal romance . . . the farm boy working up and marrying the Lord of the Manor's daughter. Irene nearly hit the ceiling, and just after that came the business of the bonds. Rick was working in the bank too, and she made him quit, and Alan went to prison for eighteen months."

She shook her bright head slowly.

"Major Tillyard was grand about it. I think he . . ."

She came to a full stop, and then went on, I thought almost defiantly.

"I think he thinks Alan was . . . innocent. But he doesn't dare say so. Irene threatened to take her account to Washington, and they couldn't afford to lose it."

I supposed they couldn't, actually, but it seemed strange that Irene could dictate to a bank—though not as strange as it would have seemed a couple of days before.

"And Alan," I said. "What has all this done to him?"

"What do you suppose?" Cheryl said. She spoke with a sudden passionate bitterness, without moving her eyes from the charred logs in the fireplace. "How can anyone go on living even, if everything they do is misinterpreted and if they're treated as if they were—"

She stopped abruptly. "I'm sorry! I guess I'm being what Irene calls 'dramatic.' I only mean I know exactly how he feels, and I've never been in prison. If I'd had the courage Alan's got, I'd have run out the first week I was here. But I was sorry for Mara . . . and then it was too late."

"But you're running out now?"

"Not exactly. Irene doesn't want me here, and I'm . . . I'm glad to go."

She got up and stood looking out the door toward the great house, and beyond it at the glistening waters of the Potomac.

"When I came here it was all covered with snow. I'd never seen any place so lovely," she said slowly, after a little while. "I kept thinking how it would look in the spring, when the lilacs and roses would be out, and then the magnolias and the crepe myrtle and jasmine. But . . . I guess things don't work out. I knew the minute Irene looked at me she'd never like me. But I thought she'd see that I . . . well, that I . . ."

She stopped. After a minute I said, "Cheryl—why did you marry Rick?"

She rested her head against the white-washed door frame, gazing out with unseeing eyes.

"I . . . thought I was in love with him. He . . . reminded me of someone I knew I'd never see again, I guess. I . . ."

She hesitated. Then she said quietly, "I just . . . mistook the shadow for the substance."

"And you didn't know they were brothers."

She didn't answer.

"And when you thought of what the place would be like, you forgot the oleanders and the wheat fields at Vezeley . . ."

She didn't look at me, but a faint smile touched the corners of her mouth.

"Then he . . . remembered it, too?" she whispered, more to herself than to me.

After a moment she raised her head. Her eyes were really very like faded hyacinths, blue and gray and soft.

"It's crazy, isn't it," she said.

I didn't have time to answer, because just then a colored girl came running down Mrs. Jellyby's walk.

"Dat man say you all supposed to be in the libin' room directly, an' Miss Mara and Miz' Jelly too."

Cheryl looked at me in alarm. "What'll we do?" she said quickly.

I shook my head.

"We'd better go."

She nodded slowly, her lips trembling and her face the color of old ivory.

I took her arm. We went back together, up the garden path and into the house, every step, I suppose, harder and rockier for the girl whose sin had been mankind's commonest sin . . . taking the shadow for the substance.

In the hall we heard the murmur of voices, and Irene's voice above them. "I'm afraid my daughter-in-law has left the place . . ."

Cheryl's eyes widened. I think she sensed as clearly as I did the danger that lurked in that pleasant, almost anxious tone, and in Mr. Purcell's "Tch, tch, that *is* unfortunate."

I looked at her. She nodded, and we walked in together.

Seated on a sofa at one side of the room was the grotesque figure of Mrs. Jellyby, in her men's shoes and straw sombrero. Beside her sat Mara Winthrop, like a wild orchid beside an oak. She looked at Cheryl. I don't know what the message was that passed between them, but Cheryl went over and sat beside her, and I went down by the window where Dan was standing. And I stopped dead as I saw him, staring at him open-mouthed. He looked as if he had been through the nine circles of hell. It was utterly inconceivable that such a change could have come over any human countenance in so brief a time, that this was the man I'd seen grinning and tousle-headed in his bathing suit, a bath towel round his shoulders, whistling debonairly on his way to the river, only that very morning. He couldn't possibly have cared so much for Rick, I thought desperately—not possibly!

His mother was there in the room, and Mr. Purcell, and Major Tillyard, and Natalie Lane, sitting quietly behind a bridge table in the corner. Not far from her, looking too awfully like an ad for What the Smart Young Man Will Wear in the Country, was a man I'd seen at a night club once, and only once, and for some reason had never forgotten. I even remembered his name, which is something I seldom do. It was Fellowes Dunthorne. I remembered it largely because I remembered thinking, when the two very decorative if rather intoxicated young women he and Rick Winthrop were with went out to the powder room and Rick brought him over to our table, that he had been born neither with that name nor his accent, which was as English as he obviously now thought his clothes were. But what Mr. Fellowes Dunthorne was doing here, in his yellow vest and new plus fours, except looking hot and uncomfortable, and very much as if he'd rather be digging a nice deep ditch somewhere above the Mason-Dixon Line than sitting in that handsome straight-backed wing chair in Romney's living room, I hadn't a notion. Mr. Dunthorne was large and fortyish, with a not too high forehead and a rather heavy jaw, and his hair was black and sleek and carefully tended. Neither he nor Natalie Lane, for some reason I couldn't quite analyze, appeared to belong, exactly. Nor did Mr. Sam Dorsey, the sheriff, though he was sitting there as firmly entrenched behind a maple butterfly table as if he had produced it from his own chrysalis.

As Dan's eyes met mine I saw they were sick with pain, and I looked away again and sat down quickly to keep my knees from shaking.

Mr. Purcell cleared his throat.

"This isn't the way we ordinarily do things," he said slowly. "But under the circumstances—and I want to say Sam here is with me one hundred per cent—and to avoid as much trouble and anxiety for the family as we can, I want to say I appreciate the frankness and honesty of certain people here."

I couldn't make that sentence make any possible logical sense, but I realized that it made, in some way, another extraordinary kind of sense, and that everybody else in the room was breathless before it.

Mr. Purcell bent down and picked something up from the hearth. I didn't recognize it at once, and then I saw that it was the bow Dan had tripped over, that Irene had found broken on the porch that morning, before we came on Rick's body with the arrow through its throat.

I looked for some reason at Dr. Birdsong. He was looking, oddly enough, not at the broken bow but at Irene.

"I won't go into it except to say that we all realize a very terrible accident happened," the State's Attorney went on. "—One of those queer cases where the truth is stranger than fiction. But there's no doubt it is the truth. And nobody here is going to be fool enough to think for a minute that when Dan picked up this bow and fitted an arrow to it, and shot it out in the dark at that target, he had any idea that his brother was at the end of the range."

The silence in that room was so profound that his voice, perfectly normal, sounded in my ears at least like a clap of thunder.

"Dr. Birdsong has pointed out that nobody could possibly

66

shoot a single arrow, in the dark, and hit such a mark. And that goes along with what is undoubtedly the fact of the case. —Dan says that last night, as he came past the target he pulled out an arrow that was stuck in it, to put it in the quiver on the porch. But instead he picked up the bow he'd tripped over earlier in the evening, just on the merest impulse, to try a shot with it. It was dark, he could only guess where the target was. The bow was a woman's bow and too light for his draw. As he let fly it snapped in his hands, cutting his cheek, as you see."

I sat perfectly motionless in my chair, not looking at Dan, not daring to look at him. If it was true, and he had killed his brother . . .

"We all know the deep bond that existed between Dan and his brother," the State's Attorney went on. "We can all sympathize with Dan's horror when he got up this morning, and found that this awful thing had happened.

I look at Cheryl. Her face was as white as death.

"It was the kind of thing that wouldn't happen once in a million times. I am confident that the coroner's jury will bring in a verdict of accidental death, and that time will heal the tragedy for both Dan and his mother."

I couldn't help looking over at Dan. There was no doubt of the truth of part of what Mr. Purcell had been saying. Dan's face was drawn with agony . . . the deeper, I knew now, because he knew in his heart how much he would have given to have the girl who was his brother's wife. But what would the Freudians, for instance, who won't allow accident to account for a broken tea cup, or the most trivial slip of the tongue, say about such an accident? What would Dan himself, in his own heart, be saying?

I looked back at Cheryl Winthrop. Mara was gripping her hand with all her might to keep her from fainting dead away. Mrs. Jellyby near them was sitting bolt upright, looking fixedly at Irene. Natalie Lane was laying out cards for a game of patience. Her cigarette, lying on the edge of a silver tray, had burned its full length of undisturbed ash; the smoking tip had fallen off the tray and lay, quietly burning a hole in the top of the table. Major Tillyard had moved over beside Irene, and had taken her hand. There was a subtle air of relief in the room that was suddenly almost unbearable to me.

I got up abruptly and went over to Dan, and as I did I saw Dr. Birdsong's crazy dog lift his head from the floor and grin through his crimped bangs.

There was a sudden rasping sound in the room as Mrs. Jellyby cleared her throat, and a sudden suspension of everyone's activity.

"Now is the time for you to say something, Tom Birdsong," she said.

Dr. Birdsong nodded.

"Yes, I think it is," he said. He leaned forward, his great hands resting lightly on the back of the chair in front of him.

"Dan," he said, very quietly. "What kind of an arrow was it you shot from that bow?"

He pointed to the broken wood lying on the table where Mr. Purcell had put it.

Dan raised his head. His voice was rough with pain as he spoke.

"What do you mean?"

"I mean, what kind of an arrow was it? Was it a target arrow, or—"

"It was a target arrow, of course," Dan said.

"You're quite sure?"

"Of course.—So what?"

Dr. Birdsong crossed the room to the fireplace. He lifted a feathered shaft from behind the Lowestoft garniture on the mantel, and held it carefully between his thumb and forefinger.

"Only that this is probably it," he said. "Mrs. Jellyby found this in her nasturtium bed, behind the box hedge, this morning. She says it was not there when she looked at the bed last night."

I think every eye in the room was fixed on that slender wooden shaft with the green and white casting and white cock feather swinging delicately in that huge hand. I heard no motion, no breath even. Irene's cheeks flushed, and Dan looked suddenly like a man hoping against hope for a last moment's reprieve from the gallows.

"And in any case," Dr. Birdsong said steadily, "if you shot a target arrow, you didn't kill Rick." His eyes rested for a moment quite impersonally, on Irene, and turned to Dan, by his side. "It wasn't a target arrow that killed Rick. It was a broadhead—the kind that's used for hunting game."

He turned round then to the rest of us, his gaze directed very steadily at the State's Attorney.

"A target arrow has a short steel pile. A broadhead has a sharp steel shaped like an Indian arrowhead. A target arrow could conceivably kill a man . . . but if a man wanted to kill with an arrow, he would use a broadhead. It was a broadhead arrow that was found in Rick's throat."

I saw the color seep slowly back into Cheryl's waxen face, and ebb slowly from Mara's until she was paler than death. I glanced at Irene. She was looking at Cheryl. The room was alive with embattled hatred.

68

10

If I live to be a hundred, I shall never forget the rest of that day. I kept thinking Rick Winthrop's epitaph should be "No One Wanted to Know Who Put Me Here" . . . and found myself wondering grotesquely what some passerby fifty years from now would think, coming upon it carved on a lichen-covered stone in the little Romney cemetery under the weeping willow beyond the pear orchard. Whether it actually was what, in part at least, it seemed to be—a conspiracy of silence —I wouldn't know. I do know that if the villain had to be picked out by virtue of being the most stubborn objector, then Irene and Major Tillyard and Mr. Purcell the State's Attorney would have been quietly taken out and hanged forthwith on the highest branch of Romney Oak.

And it wasn't what they said, so much, because after all, all Major Tillyard said was that he thought Dr. Birdsong ought to be very sure indeed before he implied that whoever shot Rick had done it purposely. Irene said that Dr. Birdsong didn't seem to understand that what he was saying meant murder, and that no one she could think of could possibly want to murder poor Rick. And Mr. Purcell said nothing at all, but only looked as if he was ready to burst with choler.

Or if, conversely, as is always done in fiction, the person who had so calmly upset the applecart turned out to be Rick's murderer, then that, beyond a doubt, would have been the stocky tweed figure of Mrs. Jellyby, planted four-square and solid on the sofa beside Mara. As that preposterous idea came to me, I thought instantly that even Mrs. Jellyby wasn't so anxious to hang the person who killed Rick as she was to take the brand of Cain off Dan's forehead. But I couldn't know about that, really. I only know that a little later, after she'd gone and taken with her, in some way, her kind of dependable open air sanity, a sort of hysterical fear seemed to settle on the room.

Dan had already gone—almost immediately, in fact, after Dr. Birdsong had stepped in—and when old Yarborough came in to tell Mr. Purcell and the sheriff that some men were waiting for them outside, I escaped with an almost unbearable sense of liberation, and went to find him. I saw him, eventually, from the top of the shallow brick steps that go down from the lawn to the river. He was sitting on a bench at the end of the narrow float, just looking out ahead of him. He reached over, as I sat down beside him, and gave my hand a hard squeeze without turning his head.

"What if I had killed him, Grace?" he said, after a long time. "God knows I could have, last night. In fact, I damn near did."

He spread his two great brown hands out in front of him, looking at them as if he'd never properly seen them. The knuckles of his left hand were cracked, and had broken and bled again as he'd clenched his fist tight during that ordeal in the house. My heart sank a little as I saw that, and glanced at his forehead.

"Or what if it hadn't been for Birdsong, and I'd gone on *thinking* I'd killed him."

I lighted a cigarette.

"I trust you're not planning to brood much about either possibility," I said, more casually than I felt.

"No, but what if I had?" he said doggedly. "I'd always have thought I did it so he couldn't have . . . her."

A flush darkened his face.

"The old unconscious, if you know what I mean."

"Yes, I know," I said. "I'd thought of that too."

We sat there, watching the slender white sail of a catboat bobbing up and down in the yellow river.

"You know, it's funny," he said at last. "I never knew till last night that finding her was the only thing that's really mattered to me for a long time. I mean, that's why I've stuck in Paris grubbing away—so when I did find her I could take care of her. I guess I figured I couldn't count on Mother."

He ground his cigarette slowly to brown powder under his heel.

"It sounds crazy, but I've waked up at night in a cold sweat, thinking what if something happened to her, like an auto accident, or a plane crash. But the idea that when I did find her she'd be married to somebody else just never entered my head."

He laughed, very mirthlessly. "I got to thinking of her like a kind of destiny. Not that I took the veil or anything, but other girls just didn't mean anything.—And now, it's all shot."

"Well," I said, "—now that you *have* found her . . . and Rick's . . ."

I suppose it just goes to show that women are more callous —about some things—than men. Or maybe only more egocentric and practical. Dan frowned and got up.

"It isn't the same," he said briefly.

"Just more adult—and realistic," I said.

"I didn't mean that. Its just—"

At that moment that ridiculous dog with the pale uncanny eyes behind their fringe of dirty gray hair materialized on the top step between the urns of dubonnet petunias, stood there for a moment wagging his tail, and glanced back to tell his chief he'd found us.

Dr. Birdsong's large figure came into sight. He looked rather grim, it seemed to me. In fact I saw now that I hadn't realized before just how grimly hard-boiled, in a perfectly impersonal way, that face of his was, or how cold those light blue eyes of his were.

He came down the stairs to the float.

"Purcell and Dorsey have rounded up a coroner's jury. The verdict's death by shooting with a bow and arrow, accidentally or on purpose, by a person unknown."

"I ought to have thanked you—" Dan started. Dr. Birdsong shook his head.

"For what?" he said curtly. There was a sort of arctic gleam in his eyes. "You'd better wait and see. At the moment Purcell's hunting for you. I'd stick around up there if I were you."

Dan nodded and strode up the steps. Dr. Birdsong watched his long rangy figure disappear in the box alley, and turned back to me. He looked down at me for a moment. I could almost see him tabulating me on a Bertillon chart, or something: hair light, eyes dark brown, height five feet seven, weight one-thirty-five, age thirty-eight (I hope). Then he said, his voice as impersonal as his gaze, "Can you shoot a bow and arrow?"

"Not without taking all the skin off my arm, fingers and nose," I replied. "And if I made a hit, it would be entirely by accident. I suppose, however, that's just what qualifies me for the present round."

He smiled—I was surprised to see that he could—and just sat there for a moment, his curiously sensitive fingers scratching absently at the shaggy head of the huge dog sitting between his knees.

"You know, I can't make this damned business out," he said, after a time. "Nobody could possibly have shot Rick, in the position he must have been in, and been sure of a hit. It isn't possible. But nobody would shoot a hunting arrow at a target, at night, just for fun."

I got the impression, somehow, that his remarks were not really addressed more to his dog than to me—as they'd have appeared to be—though I dare say the dog looked the more intelligent of us. He was certainly the happier, for Dr. Birdsong's cornering me down there was not, I was fairly certain, as unpremeditated as it seemed on the surface.

"Another puzzling thing," he went on, with a kind of grim abstraction, "is that when they moved Rick's body, they found his cigarette lighter under him. It was open, and there's a scorched spot on his shirt front. He apparently fell on it when it was still lighted."

"So that the flame of the lighter might have made a target for . . . someone to aim at?"

He looked at me with an oddly interested flicker in his cold blue eyes.

"Did you . . . deduce that, or—"

"Or did I already know it?" I asked sweetly. "The answer to that, Dr. Birdsong, is no."

He shrugged his heavy tweed shoulders. "You'll have to forgive me, Mrs. Latham. I'm rather confused by the apparent lack of interest everybody has in Rick's demise."

"You wouldn't be if—"

I stopped abruptly and bit my lips. I'd stepped full into his trap. And oddly enough, the only way I knew it—for his own expression hadn't changed, or the tone of his voice—was that I was suddenly aware that the milk-blue eyes of his dog had opened and were fixed intelligently on me. I supposed he must have sensed a quickened interest through those fingers moving in his matted hair. I felt exactly as I imagine a laboratory rat must feel when he's escaped the door in the maze that leads not to the carrot but to the charged plate.

Dr. Birdsong glanced at me then with the look of rather ironical amusement that I suppose the experimenter would give the rat.

"Look," I said. "It'll be a lot simpler if you'll just ask me what you want to know. I don't like devious people. And while it doesn't make a lot of difference to me—frankly—that Rick's dead, I do, I'm afraid, have a certain amount of just natural curiosity about who did it—if anybody. On the other hand, if it's going to cause a lot of unhappiness to Dan, or Mara, I'm willing to let my curiosity go unsatisfied. I happen to like Dan, and I'm finding myself rather moved by Mara."

He took a bright new corncob pipe out of his pocket and filled it slowly from an ancient rolled oil-skin pouch patched with adhesive tape.

"Mara could do with a friend," he said.

When he didn't go on for quite a while I said, "You're sure Rick was killed—deliberately, I mean? It really couldn't have been an accident?"

He shook his head.

"If it had been a target arrow, in the first place . . . or anybody else in the second. But Rick's been asking for something like this, as far as I can make out, for just about twenty-eight years."

I looked a little surprised, I suppose.

"No," he said, as if I'd asked a question. "I've only known him five. But I've heard a lot since I've been around. He was a bully, in the first place. Take the case of the Keanes, for instance."

"Isn't it rather . . . dangerous, to be taking the Keanes?"

He looked at me.

"I mean, when your State's Attorney starts gathering motive, and opportunity, and all the rest of it, aren't the Keanes going to be right out in front?"

"I don't think either of the Keanes goes in for the aristocratic sport of archery," he said. "Now if it had been a pruning hook, or a tobacco knife . . ."

"I should think it's not unlikely Alan knows how to shoot —with everybody else in the place going in for it."

He nodded slowly. "He may. He's an interesting boy, by the way. Sensitive and ambitious, and he's worked like a dog."

"You don't think he's as black as Irene paints him, then?— or what I'd rather know, really is . . . why do you dislike Irene?"

He gave me a quick glance, amused and a little surprised, I thought.

"I don't dislike Irene."

"You certainly don't like her."

"I don't like bullies, male or female. Irene's just as much of a bully as Rick was. More, actually—she's smoother. She uses her charm and her money so they amount to actual brute force, in the end, to get her own way . . . and she glosses it over so well that it generally looks as if she's doing it for somebody else's good. Like Rick and Cheryl, for instance, or Mara and Alan Keane."

"You don't think it's for their good?"

"Cheryl was the best thing that could have happened to Rick, or any other man," Dr. Birdsong said shortly. "And if she really wanted to break up Mara and Alan Keane she could have sent Mara to New York, or Paris—anywhere to get her away from here, where she sees Alan every day and never sees anybody else. No, Mrs. Latham, the point about Irene is . . ."

He hesitated.

". . . is something else again."

He gave me a cheerfully irresponsible grin. The dog grinned too, and glanced up the terrace steps. A peacock had perched himself on one of the urns and was posing his magnificent iridescent fan to the midday sun.

Dr. Birdsong turned back to me. "That's what Irene's like. Only her vanity's not as harmless."

There was something in it, I supposed. Romney and the wealth and old glamour that it represented were to Irene what his glittering plumage was to the peacock, and she displayed them with a charming apparent naiveté quite as effective. I glanced back at the bird. His head went up with sudden interest as he strutted there, and he scrambled down from the urn and scuttled across the lawn to where the short square figure of Mrs. Jellyby, with her peaked straw sombrero and seed bag—like the Pied Piper—led a procession of strutting cocks and scurrying hens toward their feeding ground.

An affectionate light kindled for a moment in Dr. Birdsong's strange face.

"There's a woman," he remarked. There was a sudden warmth in his voice. "It's she that's been the Winthrops' mother—not Irene. Mother and father-confessor."

It seemed to me I detected a note of bitterness in his voice too, that didn't match that apparent detachment of his.

"You don't, by any chance," I inquired with what pretended to sound like casual indifference, "happen to be in love with Mrs. Winthrop yourself?"

A wintery gleam flickered in his eyes.

"Not consciously, Mrs. Latham," he answered. "But I see what you mean. I suppose I do sound like it. And the fact that she's fifteen years older than I am doesn't prove it isn't so."

He shook his head.

"No, it's just that in a community of this sort you tend to get involved in other people's lives, and when you see the wanton damage that a person like Irene can do to half a dozen people, it gets under your skin. At least it does mine."

He shrugged, trying, I thought, to keep his tone completely casual.

"I just happen to be one of those people who're more moved by individual injustice than by collective injustice. The sight of four hundred and eighty-nine starved coolies doesn't make me as sore—for example—as seeing Irene let Purcell make a decent chap like Dan go through the rest of his life thinking he'd killed his own brother."

It seemed to me this was being pretty rough on Irene. I was a little sore myself.

"You don't really think Irene *knew*, do you?" I asked. "I mean, give the devil his due."

"You're like all the rest," he said evenly. "Irene's never held accountable for what she does. Everybody assumes she couldn't possibly know what she's doing. Look here: Irene

74

knows more about archery and bows and arrows than anybody else at Romney. She knows a green and white crested broadhead from a green and yellow crested target arrow. They don't look alike at all, if you know anything about nocking and fletching and woods. And Irene does."

He knocked his pipe out on the edge of the bench.

"I've been around here several years, and I've seen a broadhead hunting arrow in just two places. One's over the taproom mantel at the Fountain in Port Tobacco. The other's down in the game room in the cellar here at Romney."

He didn't go on for a long time. There was something so definitely odd about the way he'd said that, or it seemed to me there was, that a terrible idea leaped for the first time, clear and sharp, into my mind, and I felt my heart freezing inside me. I knew at the same moment, automatically, that it was an idea that had been persistently trying to get into my mind, and that I'd refused to let in because it was too horrible a thing to dream, much less to say.

"Dr. Birdsong," I managed to get out, "—you *can't* think that Irene . . ."

I didn't finish it; and I was shocked again to hear how hushed and how deadly in earnest my voice had become.

11

He nodded, to show he knew what I meant without my finishing that sentence.

"If I could only figure it out," he said slowly. "How could anybody have shot him in the dark, even with his lighter burning? It couldn't be done, not surely. It just couldn't be done—and perhaps it wasn't."

I steadied my voice.

"I thought, if you were a really good shot," I said, "you could hit pretty consistently in the fifties."

He looked at me very oddly.

"Look, Mrs. Latham," he said. "Everybody who shoots around here uses what they call the point-of-aim method. Nobody shoots point-blank—which is what shooting at Rick with his lighter for a target would have meant. Nobody could have been sure of a hit that way. When you're hunting with a bow and arrow it doesn't matter if you miss the first time; the arrow's silent, it doesn't frighten an animal. I've hunted game with a bow and arrow in Zambesi, which is how I happen to know. If you're hunting a man it's different.—And nobody hunts game here, and everybody uses a point-of-aim."

I had then even less knowledge of archery than I ended my week at Romney with, so I hadn't a very clear idea of what he was getting at.

"I suppose a point-of-aim is something you aim at so you can hit your target?"

"An arrow describes an arc when it's projected from a bow, Mrs. Latham," he said patiently. "If you aimed at your target you'd go a long way over it. They put something on the ground in front of the target to aim at."

"And . . . if they could have had a point-of-aim?" I inquired.

"Several people qualified," he said, with an ironic glance. "Irene's about the best. Mara's almost as good. Cheryl's even better if she's at top form. Tillyard isn't bad, Rick himself was about even with Irene. But there couldn't have been a point-of-aim—not at night."

"Which lets out Irene, Cheryl, Mara and Major Tillyard."

He shook his head.

"Which lets out the point-of-aim."

"Well," I said, "if—in some inconceivable way—there had

been a point-of-aim, are they really the only ones who could have killed Rick? I mean, would it let out Natalie, and Alan Keane and his father, and Mrs. Jellyby? And Mr. Dunthorne is already out, and Dan . . ."

"Dunthorne was at the Fountain in Port Tobacco," he said quietly. "And all I've said about Dan is that if it was a target arrow he shot, he didn't kill Rick with it. It isn't going to be easy for him to explain the cuts on his knuckles and the bruises on Rick's face."

I said nothing.

"You see, no matter how bizarre a method anyone uses to murder a person, the fact still remains, Mrs. Latham, that the two important points to consider—in any murder—are first, motive, and second, opportunity. The business of detection begins there. They are the points-of-aim, Mrs. Latham. They may seem pretty pedestrian, but there they are."

"So if it turned out that Irene was the one person in all Charles County who could have let fly an arrow that could have killed her son, she still didn't do it, because she's also the one person who'd have no motive for killing him."

He looked at me oddly again.

"If you'd been around here for the last six months, Mrs. Latham, you'd think Irene had about as much reason to kill Rick as . . . anybody."

That quarrel of the night before—and no doubt many other quarrels too—was public property then, I thought.

"Rick's opposed his mother's marriage to Sidney Tillyard as bitterly, and violently, and publicly as could be done. There was a scene at the Fountain bar the other night that hit a local all-time high. I doubt if the Colonial clergyman who was convicted of bigamy made a worse noise."

"What happened?" I asked.

"Oh, Rick had had too much, and Tillyard dropped in on his way home for a nightcap."

"Which gives Major Tillyard—not Irene—a motive for killing Rick, doesn't it?"

He nodded.

"And he can shoot a bow and arrow?"

"Yes. On the other hand, he was with me, on the other side of Port Tobacco, eight miles away."

"Well," I remarked, "if you've ever read a detective story, you know eight miles is nothing if there's an obstacle between a man and the woman whose money he wants to marry."

"Tillyard has as much money as Irene, if not more. And has rheumatism in his knee, furthermore. I mean, he couldn't possibly have got back here. He'd left his car. Even if he could have borrowed or hired one in Port Tobacco at that time of night—which he didn't, so far as I can find out—he couldn't have walked to the house from where that tree was down across the road."

"He wouldn't have had to," I observed. "His car was out there."

Dr. Birdsong frowned.

"I'm not insisting," I said. "I just thought that while we were going in for motives, there's no use not seeing the one that's closest under our noses."

He smiled.

"I think you're tilting at windmills to keep from having to see the motive just under your nose."

"What do you mean?" I demanded.

"What about this?—Irene has kicked like a steer at giving Rick his allowance or his share of the estate. She agreed to make him an allowance when he married. He did, and she didn't—on the pretext that she didn't approve of the marriage. That just doesn't make sense. If he'd married a hoofer, or a waitress, it might have. But he didn't. The point is, Mrs. Latham . . ."

He stopped. I had the feeling that he was suddenly aware of being pretty serious, and was also a little surprised at finding himself in the position of discussing his neighbor for all the world like the village barber. He shrugged his shoulders and went on more casually.

"The point it . . . that Irene Winthrop is a miser—just as surely as one of these old women who dies on relief and has ten thousand dollars cached in the mattress. The difference is in the externals of it. If Irene conceivably killed Rick, it wasn't because she was opposed to his marriage or he was opposed to hers: it was because he was demanding his inheritance and she didn't want to let him have it. If Tillyard killed Rick, it would only have been in self-defense, and this obviously wasn't. Rick wasn't a serious obstacle to his mother's marriage. Irene is just as determined to marry as Tillyard is. Perhaps more so. And while each of them sees the advantages in it, they're not starry-eyed lovers, like Alan and Mara, ready to sell their souls as well as risk their necks to have each other."

The idea of Irene being a kind of miser kept going around in my head so that I scarcely heard the last of what he was saying. If true, I thought, it explained many things. But it was hard to reconcile that with the lavishness of Romney or with Irene's own personal extravagance, in clothes and jewelry and furs.

"Of course," Dr. Birdsong went on—and his voice, de-

78

tached and casual, struck like a white-hot poker into my consciousness—"it's Cheryl that's on the spot."

He turned and looked at me with startling abruptness, with that sudden uncanny awareness of unspoken truth that all good doctors seem instinctively to have. And he smiled faintly. "So that's what you're trying to sidestep, is it, Mrs. Latham.—I didn't know you knew her."

"I don't," I said. "I never saw her until last night."

He looked at me steadily for a moment and turned away. After a while he said, very soberly, as if speaking from something pretty deep inside him, "Money has always seemed to me to be the most powerful corrosive in human life. Those old Hebrew johnnies who said the love of it was the root of all evil hit the nail on the head."

As this tack seemed to me to veer directly opposite any path that would lead to Cheryl, and eventually to Dan, I clutched at it.

"I don't see who gains by Rick's death," I said, "except people who already have a good deal of money. Irene, and Major Tillyard, if she really did intend to divide the estate, as she says she did."

"Or any of the others who'll come into it some day, like Dan and Mara."

He apparently didn't know about Natalie, I thought, or my own two sons, who'd some day get one-fourth of one-fourth of the estate. I tried vaguely to think how much that would be. More, of course, now that Rick was dead.

"And chiefly Cheryl, as Rick's widow."

"But Irene has the apportioning of the estate," I said. "She doesn't have to include Cheryl—just as she didn't even have to include Rick."

Dr. Birdsong gave me an ironic smile. "Thanks," he said. "I've been wondering about that."

"I shouldn't imagine it was a secret," I said. "Mr. Winthrop's will is probably registered at Port Tobacco. If the county registrar is anything like the one in the town I was brought up in, everybody knows what's what without even having to bother to go to the court house."

He nodded.

"I forgot Mr. Winthrop died here.—That ought to absolve Cheryl . . . knowing as she does that her mother-in-law regards her as complete poison."

I don't know how long this conversation would have gone on if the big bell outside the kitchen that once called in the hands from the tobacco fields and now calls in the family and guests hadn't broken it up. In one way I was very glad . . . for I don't know how long I could have gone on being

79

immune from something in him that made me—quite against my better judgment—want to open up and tell him everything I knew, and a lot, probably, that I didn't.

Because there was something about Dr. Birdsong that was curiously . . . fascinating is too much of a word, intriguing too little. Perhaps fascinating is nearer to what I mean, because it does imply a certain sense of danger, and at the same time indicates that one is free to take it or leave it alone. I suppose it also implies that one hasn't sense enough to do the latter. And I gathered, abundantly I may say, in the next few days, that I wasn't the first woman who had found Dr. Birdsong pretty irresistible with practically no encouragement of any kind . . . except a willing ear and a detached smile. But let any attractive man reach the age of forty unmarried, and he's bound to become legendary in the countryside. If he's also a doctor, the fact that every woman adores a good bedside manner and an understanding professional ear that won't send her a bill oughtn't to be entirely ignored. Not, I hasten to say, that I didn't stoutly demolish every impulse I had to talk about my sinuses, or that my surprising visit to him wasn't wholly inadvertent. But that was still to come. Now we went up the stairs together, each with his own thoughts, and not—if the truth were told—very flattering ones at that.

The peacock strutted before us up the broad alley of box like something out of the Lord Mayor's show. Half-way up to the pillared portico I said, "Would you mind, by the way, telling me why you've been asking me so many questions? Or why I answered them?"

"You asked me just as many," he said, with an amused sudden grin. "And I answered them—or evaded them just as you did. Except rather more reasonably. You see Mrs. Latham, I'm trying to find out who murdered Rick Winthrop. I'm a special officer." He held open his jacket and I blinked at the silver badge with "Special Officer—Charles Co." on it.

"Then you're . . . you're *official?*"

He nodded. If it's true that drowning people re-live their whole lives in one swift moment, they're certainly cleverer than I am. I couldn't even re-live the last half hour of mine, try desperately as I did to remember what I'd said—or implied—and what its consequences would be.

"The only thing you told me that I didn't know already, Mrs. Latham," he remarked casually, with that exasperating intuition of his, "was that Cheryl had some strong motive for wishing Rick out of the way that has nothing to do with money."

80

"Did I tell you that, or are you guessing it, Dr. Birdsong?" I asked quietly.

"It's true, isn't it?"

"Not that I know of," I said. There must be times when God forgives people for lying.

"I hope you're right," he said.

It was not only a lie, of course, but a very foolish one; and it didn't need the insight of a highly trained observer of human behavior—which Dr. Birdsong definitely was—to spot it instantly. Dan and Cheryl could no more be in the same room without establishing a magnetic field than two parts of hydrogen could come in contact with one part of oxygen and not form water—if that *is* what they do. They didn't seem to look at each other, and hadn't, so far as I knew, said two words, beyond "Good morning," but each was so intensely aware of the other that anyone not as blind as a bat couldn't help seeing it. And when, after the simple buffet lunch in the dining room, Irene excused Cheryl and Mara, Dan's eyes unconsciously following her were so poignantly revealing, Dr. Birdsong's level gaze so undeceived, that I whispered to him, "Stop it, you're being indecent."

But for the rest of that day I saw Dr. Birdsong's slate-blue eyes resting on him with a new tranquil interest.

12

I don't think, looking back on it, that that in itself was the
reason for the slow sick feeling of apprehension that curdled
the spoon bread and deviled crab in the pit of my stomach. It
was much more the sudden sharp-eyed calculation in Irene
Winthrop's blue unclouded eyes, the almost imperceptible
tightening around her red mouth as she glanced from her
son's face to Cheryl's taut gold-tipped figure going through
the carved rubbed-pine door before she turned her back and
held Mr. Purcel'sl cup to the silver coffee urn.

I should have liked to see her face just then. I have the
feeling that that moment crystallized her antagonism to her
elder son's young widow . . . and I'm not sure, as a matter
of fact, that it wasn't the most justifiable moment of that
otherwise totally unjustifiable week. I doubt if any mother,
even one with as rudimentary a maternal feeling as Irene had,
could have been completely composed just then. She couldn't
have helped realizing, just at that moment, that whatever hold
she had on her son was powerless.—Or most mothers
couldn't. Ordinary norms didn't seem to apply to Irene.

I glanced back at Dr. Birdsong. He was looking at Natalie
Lane, auburn-haired and handsome, with Fellowes Dunthorne
by the Chinese Chippendale serving table. She looked at me
exactly as I imagine a very well-bred and stream-lined tigress
would look, waiting in a jungle bower for a chattering well-
fed monkey to drop into her paws. And somehow I had the
feeling that if any of the Winthrops was to be the monkey, it
was not Dan but Irene.

Mr. Fellowes Dunthrone I couldn't, I'm afraid, entirely
make out. He had turned, for some reason—or maybe it was
his natural color, intensified by the very horsey jacket, cravat
and pin he had on, though I must say without any olfactory
tinge of the stable—a curious mustard color. His eyes roamed
the room, avoiding the people in it but resting with something
more than interest on the Sheraton banquet table, the Aubus-
son carpet, the Chippendale chairs, the oil painting of General
Washington over the carved pearwood mantel. It may have
been accidental, or I may have been imagining things, but I
certainly thought I saw his thick very practical fingers move
caressingly over the leg of the Hepplewhite sideboard and
along its satinwood inlay. I know I saw him turn the heavy

three-pronged fork over, and frown as if slightly confused by the 999/1000 on the back of it. I know that, because Major Tillyard, standing near Irene at the other sideboard opposite the fireplace, saw him too, and smiled as our eyes met.

I wasn't particularly surprised, therefore, later that afternoon as I started out of my room, to hear Dan's voice saying, very offensively, "Is there something in my brother's room you particularly want, Dunthorne?" and Mr. Dunthorne's hasty denial: "No, no—I was just looking at that table with the spade feet."

And I heard Dan, who on occasion could be quite necessarily rude, answer, "Guests at Romney usually stay downstairs when they aren't in their rooms, Dunthorne."

He closed his door. I saw Mr. Dunthorne beat a rather hasty retreat down the hall. I didn't hear him going down the stairs, but when I looked out the window I saw him down on the oyster-shell drive, by his car, an elaborate silver-gray European number with yellow leather upholstery and so much chromium trimming that it was too dazzling to look at comfortably. It occurred to me that I hadn't heard him go along the hall to Rick's room either, though I'd been listening because I wanted to speak to Cheryl when she came along. I looked down at the thick composition soles of Mr. Dunthorne's shoes. It seemed very odd.

Then I wondered if it was so very odd after all, and I found myself suddenly very much interested in Mr. Fellowes Dunthorne. And for some inexplicable reason it dawned on me then that it must have been he that Natalie Lane was talking about over the phone that morning.

Her words and her urgent tone came back to me: "You're *sure* he's coming to Romney?"

I sat down on the love seat between the open windows. For the first time the problem of who had killed Rick Winthrop, and why, seemed to me to be extremely important . . . and extremely bewildering.

I looked down on Mr. Dunthorne's dazzling vehicle again, and on the bald-spotted top of Mr. Dunthorne's head. Just then he glanced up with sudden alert interest. Old Yarborough had come out on the porch and was peering down at him through his thick lenses. Behind him, some way back, was Mara. Yarborough drew himself up in all his very considerable dignity, and said, in the deep voice he reserves for rather special occasions, "The public ain't admitted to Romney at this time, suh . . . so we wish yo' good day, suh."

The expression on Mr. Dunthorne's thick face was definitely indescribable. It turned from mustard to deep red.

And Mara giggled, and then controlled herself, and stepped forward with a dignity almost matching Yarborough's.

"This gentleman is a guest, Yarborough," she said.

The old darky pulled off his spectacles.

"Mr. Rick's guest."

" 'Deed an' Ah'm sorry," Yarborough said. He turned to Mr. Dunthorne. " 'Deed an' Ah is, suh. But yo' sho' don' look lak no guest to me."

He scuttled back into the house. Mara came down the steps.

"I'm terribly sorry, Mr. Dunthorne," she said sweetly. "But you do look awfully public, you know. We never see people as grand as you except Garden Week. And by the way, didn't I hear you telling Mr. Purcell you didn't try to come out to Romney last night? Because if you really didn't, you ought to speak very firmly to somebody at the Fountain. Your tire marks are all over the mud just beyond where the tree fell. You ought to look into it, Mr. Dunthorne."

She crossed the drive with that, went down the brick path and disappeared behind the tall green screen of arbor vitae.

For a moment Mr. Dunthorne stood stock still, watching her. Then he bent down and examined the thick distinctive tread of his handsome white tires. He straightened up and wiped his forehead with his handkerchief, still looking at them.

That jettisoning of Mr. Dunthorne by Dan, Yarborough and Mara was not the only reason for my leaving my room to go back downstairs with a definite sense of relief. It was, I think, chiefly because Mara, giggling behind old Yarborough's impressive posterior, and then coming down the stone stairs like a young chatelaine to put Mr. Dunthorne neatly and permanently in his place, seemed, all of a sudden, like a girl again—not like some dark tragic little wraith moving in mortal fear. And that was why the next shock I was to get was worse than it would have been before.

Downstairs the house was drowsy and cool, the Venetian blinds drawn against the hot glaring sun. Irene and Dan had gone in to Port Tobacco with Mr. Purcell and Major Tillyard. Natalie Lane was lying, protected with white-rimmed sun glasses, in a chaise longue with white and green cushions under a mimosa tree down by the river, her magazine face down on the grass beside her. Cheryl was nowhere in sight. Mr. Dunthorne, in bathing trunks and also with white-rimmed sun glasses, was sprawled out on the end of the float. Dr. Birdsong, Yarborough said, had gone to Washington to take some things to be analyzed, and Mr. Sam Dorsey the sheriff had returned to his office. I went through the hyphen that leads to the library. Romney is, of course, a typical tidewater five-unit house. The library used to be the plantation office, in the old days, just as the present dining room was the kitchen once; the hyphen that was merely a passage way then was now a card room, as the dining room hyphen was now a breakfast and lounging terrace with its brick sides converted into long French windows.

I opened the pine door with its broken pediment cornice and narrow fluted pilasters, and stepped down into the cool book-lined room, with its eighteenth century prints and the Lazlo Orpen portrait of Mr. Winthrop set in the elaborate baroque overmantel. I stood for a moment looking up at his strong, not handsome but very human face, wondering what he'd think of the mess things were in at Romney. Mara had been his favorite . . . and what would he think, I wondered, if he could know how his will had managed to exclude and thwart her?

Then I thought how much he would have liked Cheryl, and then I pulled a deep leather chair with its linen slip cover over between a couple of bookcases jutting out at right angles to make a nook in a corner overlooking the river, and sank down in it, watching Natalie under the mimosa tree and Mr. Fellowes Dunthorne sun-bathing on the float, not bothering to open the book I'd picked up from the old taproom table with the pewter trough on it full of scarlet roses. I don't know how long I sat there, except that Mr. Dunthorne had turned over five times and anointed himself with sun tan oil twice, when I realized that somebody had come stealthily into the room, not from the house but from one of the doors that balances the fireplace.

I glanced around. Through the angle of the bookcases I saw a man in a crumpled white linen suit, his eyes haggard, his hands holding a match to his cigarette trembling as he kept watching the opposite door.

Suddenly I saw him start, and stiffen his shoulders, waiting. Then his face was so instantly transformed that I hardly recognized it. I heard the door close softly, and a little cry; and Mara flew across the room and into his arms.

They clung together there like two lost creatures, for hours, it seemed to me as I sat there. I thought I'd saunter out, as soon as they'd released each other, and say "Don't mind me," and retire as gracefully as I could under the circumstances. But that's only what I *thought* I'd do . . . for almost instantly I saw it was the one thing in the world I couldn't do, really—not and ever look at the spring, or the sickle moon, or anything young again. For I realized in one startled intuitive flash, and even before Alan Keane had loosed his passionate hold around her slim body and stood, her dark radiant little face cupped in his hands, gazing down into it rapt and hungry, kissing her lips and eyes so gently it was almost heartbreaking, that this wasn't any longer just an idyllic summer romance.

I realized that instantly, and somehow without nearly as much surprise or shock—shocking as that may sound—as when Mara drew away from him at last and whispered: "I'm so scared, Alan! What if Rick told Mother we were married? He said he would, last night—that's why Cheryl came back. Oh, if he did, what can we do?"

She buried her face in his arms.

While I have the sketchiest notion of what a jailbird's voice sounds like, I'm very sure it doesn't sound like Alan Keane's then.

"You'll come with me the way I want you to now, sweet— and we'll get away, somewhere, anywhere away from here . . . Oh, why don't we now, Mara? I love you so much! Let your mother keep her money—we don't need it."

She raised her head and stood looking up at him, straight as a young fern, her arms clasped loosely about his neck.

"You promised you wouldn't say that again . . . don't you see it would just be telling all of them we can't take it? And you couldn't go anyway, the parole board wouldn't let you, and anyway, it's not . . . it's not right! Oh, Alan, tell me again you didn't . . . No—don't! I know you didn't . . . only they're so—"

"I know it, dearest. Sometimes I even wonder about it myself."

"No!" Mara cried. "You mustn't say that, ever, ever!"

They sat down on the deep sofa in front of the fireplace.

"Listen," she said, her voice urgent and frightened suddenly. "Alan—you didn't see Rick, last night, did you? I mean, they *mustn't* be able to say you . . ."

"Killed your brother?"

Alan's voice was bitter and disillusioned.

"Is that what you mean? Go on, say it. God knows there's enough without brooding over something you're afraid to say."

"Then—where were you last night? I tried to phone you a little after one—Cheryl wanted you to take her to Washington. I . . . I couldn't get you. Oh, Alan, forgive me —but where were you?"

"I was helping my father get his stuff together," he said steadily. "And I did see Rick. Dad made me promise I wouldn't tell anybody. Rick came down to the house. I'm telling you, because I've never told you anything but the truth. You've got to know that, Mara, no matter what happens."

"I do know it!"

"But I'm not telling anybody else, because of . . . my father. Rick's the only thing he ever hated in his life."

They sat there silently for a moment, Alan bent forward, his hands clasped between his knees, staring into the empty hearth, and Mara a little away from him, her body taut and rigid. Something—doubt, or resentment, or just accumulated strain—had crept between them, separating them as wide as the poles. Suddenly Mara looked quickly around, and sat there poised and intent, listening, her eyes wide with alarm. I heard a chair in the hyphen move as if something had bumped into it, and shuffling steps near the door. My heart sank as I heard the door open, and stopped dead for an instant, until I heard Yarborough's voice, low and smooth.

"Miss Mara, yo' mother's cah comin'. Yo' bettah hurry, honey."

"Thanks, Yarborough."

Alan got up as the door closed softly.

"We can't go on like this, Mara."

His voice was almost unrecognizable with torment.

"Wouldn't it be better—"

"You don't know Mother. No—please go, quickly! It isn't only us! No, don't touch me—please! Just go!"

I heard a car outside. Alan must have heard it too. He went over to the door, hesitated, and slipped out. For a moment the room was as still as death, and then I heard Mara throw herself on the sofa, in a storm of sobbing too infinitely bitter and lost for anyone as young as she.

13

Out of the window I saw Yarborough crossing the lawn with a tray of tall frosted mint juleps and put them down on the white wrought iron table under the huge green and white umbrella. Natalie Lane under the mimosa tree stirred herself, and Mr. Fellowes Dunthorne on the float sat up, touched his red legs and redder shoulders experimentally, as one does a cake to see if it's done, got up, straightened his back tentatively and bent over, and for the next few moments went through a lovely pantomime of a man who'd lain not wisely but much too well in the sun. I realized without shame that I was grinning like an ape. Nothing that I know of makes a guest—male or female—quite as unpopular in any country house as a severe case of sunburn . . . except possibly getting, and giving everybody else, the whooping cough.

As I turned back from the window it flashed through my mind with the most startling clarity that neither Mara nor Alan had once asked, actually, what would seem under the circumstances a natural and even obligatory question. Was it, I thought, because they already—by some awful chance— knew who had killed Rick Winthrop? Was it that knowledge that had come between them there, or was it that each of them was afraid to ask it?—Or Mara, anyway: was she afraid to ask it of Alan?

I felt a strange coldness settle on my heart, like going from a warm hall into an unused room where there'd been no heat all winter. I heard Mara get up, and saw her cross the bare old pine floor quickly and take a large red book from a shelf in the open corner cupboard. I don't know what I expected her to take from behind it, but I had a definite sense of relief when I saw it was only a vanity and a comb. She dabbed quickly at her nose and her reddened eyes and ran the amber teeth through her short dusky hair. I saw her bend down and pick something from the floor near the door Alan had gone out of, raise her head, listening, and slip quietly out that door and into the garden path, just as the hyphen door opened and I heard her mother's voice. It was even sharper than it had been that morning.

"Are you *sure* Alan Keane hasn't been here this afternoon?'

" 'Deed an' Ah ain' seen him aroun', Miss Irene, an' that's gospel, an' Ah was talkin' to Miss Mara right in this room."

No one could have failed to hear the ring of truth in the old darky's voice.

"No, *ma'am*. Ah ain' seen him *no* where. You said he ain' to come in this house, an Ah ain' *lettin'* him in."

And, of course, he wasn't. Alan had let himself in, and out. I thought of Dr. Birdsong, saying Mara could do with a friend, and wondered what he would think of this one. I was still thinking of it a few moments later, when I'd escaped out of my corner and slipped upstairs. As I reached the top landing I saw Dan stop at my door and rap softly. When I came up to him he turned with a grin.

"You're under arrest," he said.

"What for?" I asked. "Eavesdropping?"

It popped out of my mouth before I could stop it.

His blue eyes sharpened. Then he grinned again. "No—I just wanted to try my hand."

He held his white linen jacket open. I blinked. A nickle-plated badge was pinned to his inside pocket.

"I persuaded Dorsey to appoint me a deputy sheriff. So next time I run into somebody prowling around the house, I shoot him—in my official capacity."

"Oh," I said.

"Dorsey didn't think it was a very good idea. Birdsong's his deputy already."

"Yes, I know," I said.

"Dorsey said it would be awkward if he had to arrest me. You know, it's not a bad idea, Grace. I mean, if you've got something you want to cover up."

"You, or Dr. Birdsong?" I asked.

"I was speaking generally. Look—come in here. See what you make of this."

I followed him along the corridor to Rick's room.

"You know, it's my idea this bird Dunthorne's a phoney," he said, closing the door.

"Why?"

"Just look at him, the big heel."

"You're not implying he's not a friend of Rick's, are you?" I asked. "Because I've seen them together, at Twenty-One. They seemed pretty intimate.

"Rick's finances were always so rotten he couldn't pick his friends."

He crossed the big room with its handsome Empire day bed and green leather upholstered chairs. It was the kind of room a very smart decorator would do for a very smart bachelor about town—one with no place for a woman in it . . . except casually. He picked up the tooled leather desk pad on the open Sheraton secretary and pointed to a sheet of buff paper lying on the polished wood. It had Romney's crest at the top and was dated two days before, and in Rick's heavy undisciplined scrawl was written:

"Dear Dunthorne,—You'd better put off your visit. I don't think it'll sit very well at the moment. If I can keep Mother from marrying Tillyard, you won't have a ghost of a chance. If I can't, I can probably raise enough stink to pry loose sufficient cash to take up those damned notes. It isn't that I personally wouldn't be tickled to put you up here, but as—"

The writing broke off there. I read it again, and looked at Dan, rather more bewildered than ever.

"Dunthorne was going through the pigeon holes when I happened along. Maybe he's responsible for this too."

He nodded toward the fireplace. All I could see was a couple of logs lying across the polished andirons. Dan bent down and pointed behind them, and I bent down too and saw a charred sheet of paper, one tiny corner of it untouched by the flames. It was the buff paper that had meant Romney on my breakfast tray as long as I could remember.

"You mean you think Mr. Fellowes Dunthorne was doing a little light housecleaning before the sheriff got around to it?" I asked. "—But what could possibly be the point?"

"That's what I wouldn't know," Dan said—rather grimly. "But I'm going to find out."

"It would also be interesting to know," I advanced tentatively, "what was behind Rick's opposition to your mother's marriage."

He was about to speak when we heard a car come in the drive. I looked out. The door of the light roadster out there opened, and that huge absurd dog got out, like one of Cinderella's sisters, and stood grinning up at the house.

"It's Dr. Birdsong," I said. "Are you going to show this to him?"

He shook his head.

"Why not?"

"I might not want him to know it."

He picked up a snapshot lying on the mantel and put it down again as if it burned his fingers. It was Cheryl in shorts with a bow drawn just ready to shoot. She was laughing, the sun on her golden hair.

I went to the door. He started after me, then went back. I saw him pick up the snapshot again and put it in his pocket.

"Another clue you don't want Dr. Birdsong to have?" I asked.

He grinned very cheerfully.

"One I don't want anybody to have," he said.

A couple of straw hats were lying on the horsehair sofa in

the hall. I recognized one of them as Mr. Purcell's. The other, apparently, was Major Tillyard's. The two of them were in the living room, with Irene and Dr. Birdsong, when Dan and I came in. They were standing around the center table. On it was lying a large manila envelope, and beside it an odd assortment of things: a sodden cigarette, a blood-stained arrow with a long shaped steel head, its edges, I noted with a little thrill of revulsion, freshly sharpened, so that where the blood hadn't dried on it I could see the bright marks of the file. Also lying there, a little apart from the other members of this grisly exhibit, all neatly labeled, was a very handsome gold cigarette lighter.

Dr. Birdsong turned as we came in, his blue eyes resting on us momentarily with a slightly amused glint in them, and went on talking.

"I had these at the Department of Justice this afternoon. There's no doubt Rick was killed by that arrow; and the arrow was filed to a sharper point than hunting arrows normally are even when they're new—which this isn't. It's at least ten years old. We can find out if necessary. I'm not sure that's important. The important point is, there's no doubt that the intention behind it was to kill. Furthermore, it was no spur of the moment business: it was premeditated, planned and arranged. And after it was done, the arrow was wiped off very carefully, so that it shows no fingerprints whatsoever."

He looked around at us, and went on slowly.

"It was wiped off with a yellow string glove—if you happen to be interested."

He didn't actually look at Dan, but he might as well have, I thought.

"And there's something more important than the arrow and the bit of yellow string caught on it. Namely, this."

He pointed down to the gold cigarette lighter on the polished surface of the old mahogany table.

"We found this, you remember, under Rick's body. There was a scorched smudge on his shirt front. That cigarette had been lighted, and dropped on the grass. The assumption was that Rick was lighting it as the arrow struck him, the flame of the lighter acting as a target for the archer."

He glanced from Irene and Major Tillyard, who was standing beside her, his arm steadying and protective about her slim shoulders, to Dan, and then to Mr. Purcell the State's Attorney.

"The curious thing about the lighter, however, is that—like the arrow—it has no trace of fingerprints on it. Not anybody else's . . . and above all, not Rick's. Which would seem to indicate, very clearly, that Rick was not holding that lighter

91

in his hand when he was shot. He was not holding a target for his own destruction."

We couldn't, the lot of us, have looked more stupid or bewildered if Houdini himself had been lecturing us. The look of bewilderment on the State's Attorney's face particularly was too good not to be true.

"What do you mean, Tom?"

A cold gleam crackled like fire in Dr. Birdsong's frostbitten eyes.

"I mean that since Rick didn't hold this lighter to that cigarette, he couldn't have dropped it as he fell. It was put under him *after* he fell—to create an illusion. Moreover, it was put there by someone who took it from Rick's pocket after he was dead . . . or of course, conceivably, who already had it in his possession."

He stopped as Cheryl and Mara, passing the door, saw us inside, hesitated a moment and came in. Cheryl's hyacinth eyes, moving past his tall figure to the exhibits on the table, widened. She seemed slimmer, and more vulnerable, just then than she had seemed before. I saw Irene's eyes resting on her harden as she came forward quickly, her lips parted, her long gold-flecked lashes suddenly moist. It was the first time any memory of her short life with Rick that I'd seen called up had seemed to move her, or bring back anything that didn't put her still further on the defensive.

She came up to the table and stood looking down at it, her face a little pale.

"He . . . he was asking for it, last night," she said.

In the silence that fell in the room Dr. Birdsong's voice was oddly quiet, though alive like his dog's eyes.

"For what, Cheryl?"

I glanced quickly at Dan Winthrop. He had one eye on Cheryl and one on Dr. Birdsong, and the muscles under his sun-bronzed jaw were thin white ridges.

"The lighter," Cheryl said. "It was the only thing he had that he really liked very much . . . that he'd never sell when he needed money. He won it from Mr. Dunthorne. It always brought him luck, he said."

She turned toward Irene.

"He told me to be sure to remind you . . ."

Her voice caught for a moment.

". . . to remind you to give it back to him. But so . . . so many things happened I forgot about it."

We all stood there, totally breathless. Only Irene's blank horrified face as she turned slowly and looked up at the man beside her showed that it was not herself but Major Tillyard —the man she was about to marry—who was, in light of

92

what Dr. Birdsong had just been saying, being quietly and with complete unconsciousness of the act, accused of the murder of her son.

We all stood, utterly aghast. And Major Tillyard, I may say, was as aghast as the rest of us.

14

The fact that Cheryl—and no matter if with the utmost innocence and naïveté—was virtually accusing her mother-in-law's prospective husband of murder was of course absolutely incredible. It was also a very awkward thing to cope with according to the established rules of etiquette. I don't know who turned the whitest there, Major Tillyard himself or Irene . . . or Cheryl as she realized, without understanding, that she must have done something pretty awful. She looked from one blank face to another—at Irene's, at Mr. Purcell's, at mine.

"Have I . . . I'm terribly sorry . . ." she stammered.

Major Tillyard took a very deep breath and ran his finger around under his collar.

"It's . . . it's the timing that makes it . . . well, rather overwhelming, Cheryl," he said.

The color came gradually back to his face.

"Now, Irene!" he added quickly—for Irene Winthrop had also recovered herself, and was, I saw, on the point of becoming exceedingly vocal.

He turned to the State's Attorney.

"I did have Rick's lighter. He handed it over for me to hold yesterday afternoon when you and he and Natalie were in swimming. I forgot to give it back to him until I started home with Birdsong. When I remembered it then, I came back."

He glanced at Dr. Birdsong, who nodded.

"I put it on Rick's desk, and on my way out I met him, and told him I'd put it there. He asked me to wait a minute and get a letter to post for him as I went through Port Tobacco— Jim had already taken the mail pouch down to the barn. Which I did."

He glanced again at Dr. Birdsong, who nodded again. I remembered that letters at Romney had to be in the leather pouch in the hall by ten o'clock so that the colored stable boy could take it down to the barn, where the first milk truck picked it up in the morning without disturbing the household.

"It was to Mr. Fellowes Dunthorne in New York. If I'd known Mr. Dunthorne was spending the night at the Fountain Inn, I could have delivered it in person, but I didn't, so I posted it."

Major Tillyard's arm tightened around Irene's slim black-clad shoulders. "Now, now," he said. "She hadn't any idea of what she was saying. How could she have known I returned the thing?"

"Oh, of course she didn't mean anything, Mother!" Mara cried. "What—"

Irene's voice breaking in was icy calm, but her face was still pale with anger.

"Then perhaps one of you can tell Mr. Purcell who took Rick's lighter off his desk?"

"When did Rick tell you to remind him of it, Cheryl?" Dr. Birdsong asked.

"When he was dressing for dinner.—Oh, I'm so terribly sorry!"

Major Tillyard turned to the State's Attorney.

"I'm afraid I don't have much in the way of proof, Purcell."

Irene's face brightened.

"But you have!" she cried. "Rick had his lighter when he came in my room to ask me where Cheryl was! He showed me a letter he'd got and burned it in my fireplace. The reason I remember he used his lighter is that I don't smoke, and so I never have any matches in my room. I wanted to light a candle earlier in the evening, because the light in the attic closet is burned out, and I had to ring for Yarborough to light it for me."

Major Tillyard took another deep breath. "Thank you, my dear. I hope you aren't just making that up to help me out of a tight spot."

"Or if you are you'll stick to it," Mara said, with perfectly inexcusable flippancy.

Irene looked at her and reached for the petit point bell pull. When Yarborough appeared in the door she said, "Did I call you upstairs just before dinner, last night?"

"Yas ma'am, yo' sho' did—when Ah was tryin' to get th' table set," the old darky said. He shook his white kinky head. "Yo' couldn' fin' no matches, to light a candle with."

"Did you leave a box of matches in my room?"

"No ma'am, Ah forgot, but Ah'll go do direc'ly."

"Don't bother," Irene said curtly. "That's all."

She looked at Mara.

"I'm sorry!" Mara mumbled. "I was just being funny—I didn't mean what you said wasn't true."

Irene was so angry that she had quite forgotten to be charming. She turned to the State's Attorney. And I suppose her distress was quite genuine.

"This is all terribly . . . unfortunate, Barney. It makes it just that much more imperative to find out who did . . ."

She turned away and put her handkerchief to her mouth, trembling uncontrollably.

And poor Cheryl! The color had seeped gradually back into her face, and burned now in two intense spots under her steadfast hyacinth eyes. Mara, standing a little behind her, tugged gently at her belt. Immediate retreat, I saw, was clearly her solution for the situation. It struck me abruptly that retreat had always been Mara's solution of her mother . . . and that it was strange, and rather fine, that in spite of that she wasn't letting Alan Keane retreat when it would have been so much the easier way.

Cheryl was different. I don't think retreat was in her nature. It certainly didn't show now, in her lovely head as proud as a race horse's, or her level unflinching gaze. It seemed to me that her chin had come up, defensively; and then I realized why when I looked away from her and saw Mr. Purcell the State's Attorney, his rather viscid gray eyes resting on her with about as much enthusiasm as you could see in the eyes of a buck shad on the end of a trolling line. He had furthermore the air of a pretty shrewd observer to whom this was no surprise of any kind—this was, in fact, precisely what he had been waiting for.

"It seems to me, Miss Cheryl, that this would be a good time for you just to tell us what happened between yourself and your husband here last night."

Irene raised her head sharply.

"Barney—you promised me you wouldn't drag out all Cheryl and Rick's difficulties! What can the point be, except to distress and mortify everybody!"

"That was before anybody had been practically accused of murder, Irene," Mr. Purcell said.

Major Tillyard managed a smile.

"I don't think it was Cheryl who accused me of murder," he said dryly. "It was all the rest of you. Cheryl merely stated a fact that was true as far as she knew.—Just because you're coming up for election again, Barney, is no reason for chucking your weight about unnecessarily."

Mr. Purcell's eyes and mouth hardened. He was, I thought, a man who could be flattered and enticed, but he couldn't be pushed. He still looked at Cheryl. And she couldn't have been more adequate to the situation.

"I'm perfectly willing to tell you what I know about last night, Mr. Purcell," she said quietly. "It's quite simple, really. You probably know Rick and I weren't particularly . . . compatible. I don't think it was all Rick's fault."

Irene's hand winding in her pearls stopped still.

"—Or all mine. It . . . just didn't work. Rick wanted a

96

divorce. I was brought up to believe that divorce, if it's ever justified, is only a last resort—not a first. But I didn't realize that Rick felt very . . . very differently about a lot of things. Before dinner he offered me a certain sum to divorce him. He'd been drinking, and I knew he didn't have that much money."

She flushed as Irene drew a sharp breath.

"It wasn't that I wanted the money—it was that since I knew he didn't have it, I didn't think he seriously meant what he was saying. I said we'd decide it in the morning, when he was . . . more himself. But after dinner I realized he had meant it. And I realized also that I'd never been anything but a means to an end, and that the end hadn't panned out, and the sooner I got out the better, for everybody."

She raised her wide tranquil eyes to Mr. Purcell's shrewd face. I didn't know whether either Dr. Birdsong or Mr. Purcell realized how much she was leaving out of this story that would have made her so much more sympathetic and appealing to any unbiased judge. Certainly the rest of us did. I thought even Irene must have had a twinge of conscience.

"Anyway, I left," Cheryl said quietly. "But Rick had changed his mind. He said . . . a lot of things I can't seem to remember."

"But you came back?"

"Yes. The tree was down over the road, and I couldn't get a car out, and I . . . I didn't have courage enough to walk as far as Port Tobacco by myself, so late."

"I see," Mr. Purcell said slowly. "What time would it be that you came back?"

"About half-past one."

"Then how do you account for the fact that one of the men on his way to milk saw you come in with your hat and furs in your hand?"

I could see Dan's arm tense, resting on the mantel, and his eyes change, never moving from Cheryl's face.

"I didn't say I came back to the house. I didn't. I went to Mrs. Jellyby's and stayed till morning."

"Why did you do that?"

"Because I didn't want to come back here."

"Then why did you sneak back this morning?"

Her lithe body stiffened, the blue of her eyes deepened. I didn't dare look at Dan.

"I didn't sneak back. I came back because Mrs. Jellyby . . . persuaded me it was the sensible thing to do."

"Because you knew Rick was dead?"

"Because I thought he was very much alive," Cheryl retorted coolly.

There was an amused gleam in Dr. Birdsong's eyes that seemed to be focused on everybody in the room simultaneously.

Mr. Purcell took a cigar out of his pocket and bit the end off with considerable deliberation. "I take it you were alone when Rick persuaded you to stay?"

"He didn't persuade me to stay."

"Did he threaten you?"

She hesitated a fraction of an instant—trying, like old Yarborough, I thought, to avoid, as skilfully as possible, the lie direct. I found myself wondering whether, if she'd known that Irene had stood on the landing watching Rick with his raised riding crop, and realized that Irene must know now that she was not telling the whole truth, she would have played so directly into Irene's hands. I doubt actually if it would ever have occurred to her that Irene, no matter how deeply she resented her, would have gone to the lengths she did. Because it was Mara, of course, that Cheryl was trying to save, and it was Mara that Irene was perfectly willing to sacrifice in order to hurt Cheryl. At that, I don't think Irene knew—not really —what she was doing to Mara. If she had, I think sheer vanity would have dictated another course. I'm not sure even now that it would have made any difference in the long run, however, or that the deluge set in motion could have been averted. Too much water had run under too many bridges, and backed into too many stagnant pools and stopped there.

When Mr. Purcell stood there asking Cheryl if Rick had threatened her, her quiet "No" seemed very game and true, with perhaps a higher quality of truth than the literal statement of evasive fact that Yarborough went in for. Rick hadn't threatened Cheryl. It was Mara he had threatened. He probably knew quite well, I thought, that for herself she was fearless. I suppose it was that about him that made Dr. Birdsong say he was a bully. At any rate, it seemed pretty nauseating to me that that denial of Cheryl's should have been twisted around so that Mr. Purcell had practically no alternative, later, but to assume that Cheryl had just deliberately lied to save herself.

But that was all in the future. What surprised me a little at the moment was that nobody seemed to be conscious of the fact that Mara Winthrop's face was the color of old newspaper, or that as she and Cheryl went out it was her step that was unsteady, not Cheryl's.

15

I'd followed them out chiefly because ever since I'd read that unfinished note under Rick's desk pad, and heard that he did finish some kind of a letter to Mr. Fellowes Dunthorne, I'd found myself more and more interested in that gentleman. If Natalie Lane had felt the necessity of calling him up in Port Tobacco, she must have known he was there. If she'd known that, why hadn't Rick known? Why had he written to him in New York the night before? How well did Natalie know Mr. Dunthorne, and why, if she knew him well enough to phone him, had the two of them spent the afternoon within fifty yards of each other without speaking?

It seemed very strange to me, and it seemed stranger when I wandered into the library to see Mr. Dunthorne there, all elegantly got up in a white dinner coat like the one Rick had worn the night before, down on his knees going through the bottom shelves of a corner cupboard that I'd never seen opened before in my life.

"Looking for something, Mr. Dunthorne?" I inquired.

I must say he was remarkably cool about it.

"No, no. Just having a look at the dowelling on this door," he said airily. "Extraordinary how those old chaps got things together, what?"

"The old chap that got that cupboard together," I said, "has a shop in Queen Street in Port Tobacco. The old one's in the other corner."

He had the grace to blush. I don't know whether we'd have got along any better after that or not, for the problem didn't come up. I heard Dan calling me, and I went back through the hyphen to the hall.

"What about driving me in to Port Tobacco?" he said. "I had the boy bring your car around, on an off chance."

"Look, darling," I said. "You're not taking yourself too seriously, are you?"

I was rather startled by the expression on his normally quite irresponsible face.

"Because that's practically fatal, even to a deputy sheriff."

"No," he said. "I just want to check up on a couple of things."

He stopped, looking out at the square figure of Mrs. Jellyby, in her peaked straw sombrero, moving methodically along the wire backstop of the tennis courts, tying bits of red string around the sweet peas she'd planted there and wanted saved for seed.

"Fiddling while Rome burns," Dan said, with something like his old familiar grin. "Mother says it's got so every flower she wants for the house has a claim staked on it."

He shrugged.

"At that, she's probably the only happy person at Romney."

We turned out of the circle and started down the long white oyster-shell drive between the rows of cedars.

"What are you checking up on, and in which of your capacities?" I asked. "Official or unofficial?"

"This—and both."

He pointed toward the roadside, and I put my foot on the brake and stopped the car at a hole in the black cedar line as gaping as a missing front tooth. It was a good half mile from the house. The old tree lay out in the tobacco field. I don't know why it reminded me of a big dog lying dead at the side of the highway, except that it's a grave defect in my psyche that I can't bear to see a dog or tree torn ruthlessly down. That the wind had done this, and that it was all quite impersonal, didn't help much.

Dan opened the door and got out, and I followed him. The stump of the tree was quite rotten inside a thin circle of clean splintered wood. Dan examined it carefully, then clambered over the drainage ditch, full of wild roses and honeysuckle, and examined the tree. I started to follow him, snagged a new pair of stockings in the briar and thought better of it. After a few minutes he came back. He looked even grimmer than when we'd started out.

"What *is* the matter?" I demanded.

He shook his head.

"Just dirty work at the crossroads," he said, and went back to the stump of the old cedar. He began rooting around in the grass. Mysteries, I've usually found, defeat themselves, so I gave up and went along the road a little ways, looking for the print of Mr. Fellowes Dunthorne's tires that Mara had so pointedly mentioned to him. I found it, without much trouble. He'd tried to turn around, apparently, but his car was much too long, and he'd obviously given up, after three or four tries, and backed out.

I called to Dan, and when he came I told him about Mara and Yarborough and showed him the tire tracks. His face brightened for a moment, and then he stood gnawing at his lower lip, looking back at the stump and down at the tracks.

"Look, Mr. Winthrop," I protested, after an interminable

time. "Are you rehearsing for a Christmas pantomime, or what?"

"I'm just trying to figure out what the hell the connection is," he said.

"Between what?"

"Between anything," he groaned. "Just come back here."

We went back to the stump.

"See that?"

"No," I said. "What is it?"

"Well, can you see what this is?"

"I can," I said patiently. "It's a chip—probably off the old block."

"Precisely. And the point is this. Mr. Keane says he saw Rick out here with an axe, yesterday afternoon, chopping at this."

We both looked down at it.

"What for?" I said.

"I don't know. What would you think?"

"Well," I said, "it seems a rather circumlocutious method of forestalling a visit from Mr. Dunthorne. It would have been simpler to burn down the house, or wire a stick of dynamite to his battery. I could think of lots of better ways to keep Mr. Dunthorne at home. It just doesn't make sense."

Dan nodded. "I know. But the tree has been chopped."

I looked at it again.

"Are you sure Rick did it? You know Mr. Keane hasn't any particular reason to love Rick."

"And a lot of very good reasons to hate his guts.—Look here, Grace," he added suddenly. "What if he did it himself, to give Alan an alibi?"

He whistled softly.

"That's what it did. I mean, Mr. Keane pointed out to Sam Dorsey that Alan couldn't have got in unless he walked through the mud."

"Except that he—" I started to say that he was in, and stopped, remembering I'd got that information by eavesdropping. I'd got information by eavesdropping many times before, but this was different, someway.

"Except that weren't you out there," I said, as casually as I could manage, "and didn't you see a lot of things that must have interested you in your capacity of deputy sheriff?"

He brought the French lighter—one of those things with a dozen yards of rope on it—to a dead stop half-way to his cigarette.

"Just how much of this are you in on, Grace?"

"You'd be surprised," I said sweetly. "For instance: Dr. Birdsong, who's hunted game with a bow and arrow in Zambesi incidentally, tells me nobody could have shot Rick, even with the flame of his lighter as a target—because everybody around here shoots in the approved target method of ladies' archery classes, with a point-of-aim. None of them, except possibly your mother—whom he can't abide—could possibly hit a target without it. Or so he says. And your mother, on the other hand, says Cheryl is the best shot on the place."

"And she can't abide Cheryl."

"Precisely. But the point is that that's what Dr. Birdsong says, and it's Dr. Birdsong who found the lighter, and it's Dr. Birdsong who says the lighter hasn't got Rick's fingerprints on it."

"That was the Department of—"

"I know. But it was Dr. Birdsong who took it up there, . . . and who could have wiped all the fingerprints in China off it between here and Pennsylvania Avenue. And it was Dr. Birdsong who shot game point-blank in Zambesi."

He looked at me very oddly.

"Look here, Mrs. Latham—I've always thought you had a nice mind."

We'd got in the car again and had come almost to the end of the long white lane. The sun, down in the western sky, slanted a few last rays across Romney's tobacco fields, and glistened in the tiny discs in the Stop Boulevard sign at the gate. I slowed down in semi-obedience to it. And then I jammed my foot on the brake and stopped dead, stalling my engine, staring at that sign.

Dan looked at me patiently, the way men look at women who kill their engines.

"What is it?" he asked.

I sat there in a complete daze for a moment . . . and then what had been tugging at the shuttered windows of my mind all during the conversation Dr. Birdsong and I had had about shooting bows and arrows down at the float that morning came sharp and clear into my consciousness. And I knew now why he'd come down there, and why he'd stayed there at what must have been a dreary session for him.

"I suppose *you're* in the Mid-summer pantomime," Dan said.

I shook my head, opened the door of the car, and got out, the memory of a thing I'd seen there the night before, when Dan and I had come in in the storm, very clear in my mind. I crossed the oyster-shell road to the double right-angle sign to the left, on the highway, that indicates a road coming in on one side only, and stopped again. Three of the small glass buttons were gone out of it, and I could see the marks of a sharp instrument that had pried them out.

Dan peered over my shoulder, looking perfectly blank.

"This morning, when your mother and I went out and found Rick," I said slowly, "there were three little glass discs in the grass, about the middle of the range. I bent over to look at them, because with the sun on them they looked like Aladdin's jewels in the grass. I didn't think of them until I went back and noticed they were gone. But don't you see?"

He didn't, or didn't seem to, anyway. And maybe it was too fantastic.

"Dr. Birdsong," I said, "who seems to be the village expert, says Rick couldn't possibly have been shot with that arrow that he was obviously shot with unless William Tell was here in person. Even if Rick's lighter was lighted and made a first-rate target. No one here could have been sure of such a hit; no one would dare to take such a chance, because in such a case you couldn't afford a miss—Rick would know, and all that. The only way anybody here could have been fairly sure of hitting that mark—assuming he was a very good shot—would be by using the scientific point-of-aim method. And he couldn't possibly have used the point-of-aim method at night."

A light dawned slowly in Dan's big face.

"I get you," he said. "They did have a point-of-aim, even in the dark. Those glass buttons were it?"

I nodded.

He shook his head. "You don't think they'd catch the light from a cigarette lighter, darling?"

"No," I said. "I don't. But they'd catch light from the hall, or the upstairs windows, or a flashlight, or the parking lights of a car, or the long lights if the car was parked even as far down the drive as that fallen tree."

He took out a pack of cigarettes and stood, apparently absorbed in the business of opening it.

"I don't know what Dr. Birdsong was trying to prove," I said. "But there's one thing that interests me very much."

He glanced over at me.

"What's that?"

"Why didn't he see these glass things in the grass himself? He was there with Irene after I left. If he didn't see them then, somebody else who knew what they meant picked them up."

He looked down at his cigarette for a moment.

"You think it was Mother?" he asked, quietly.

103

16

"Look, Dan," I said. "I wouldn't put it beyond your mother, if it was anybody but Rick. I can't bring myself to believe that she'd . . . Oh, well, the point is that she wasn't the only person on the range."

His eyes sharpened.

"You don't mean Birdsong?"

"Why not?" I demanded. "I mean, is there any reason, just because a man barges in and takes charge of a thing like this, that he's automatically excluded from suspicion himself?"

"But he hasn't any reason—"

"You mean so far as you know, darling. And he *has*. He told me himself he's got a sense of justice . . . and the fact that Mara and Cheryl and Mr. Keane are getting a tough break at Romney apparently burns him up. That's aside from any personal quarrel he might have had with Rick. And I certainly couldn't prove that when he came down to the river to tell me nobody could have shot that arrow without a point-of-aim, he had the point-of-aim neatly tucked away in his own vest pocket; and I couldn't say the pebbles he kept shying out into the water were it. I'm just saying he had as much chance to get them as Irene did. And it seems to me now that he was trying to find out if I'd noticed them."

Dan shook his head. "He wasn't on the place—he went home with Tillyard."

"Yes," I said. "I know. But—unlike Major Tillyard—he had a car."

"You think he drove back and walked in from the tree?"

"He could have, easily enough. But he didn't have to. He had very neatly arranged with Major Tillyard to take his car as far as the tree, and get into his own on the other side. So all he had to do was get Major Tillyard home, come back to the tree, change to Major Tillyard's car, drive in, and out again. I should think a first-rate deputy sheriff would arrange to find out if any of all that happened."

We'd gone back to the car and were just going over the brow of the hill. Spread out below us, Port Tobacco lay nestled in the twilight, in the narrow valley of Potobac Creek. The lighted clock face in the tiny steeple watched like Cyclops over it. Lights flickered among the fishing craft and sailboats and yachts moored in the basin, like chicks swarming over the feeding pan. Up the hill at our left the chimneys of Rose Hill stood dark and somber against the sapphire sky.

Neither of us had spoken for a couple of miles. I was thinking—myself rather somber, I suppose—that in effect Cheryl had accused Major Tillyard of murder, I had accused Dr. Birdsong of murder, and it sounded, at least, as if Dan had accused his mother of murder. I started, eventually, to suggest as much to Dan, and glanced at him. He was gazing through the windshield with what, in a younger man, I would call a moon-calf glow in his eyes. Or maybe it was just the odd light from the slate roofs of the village. Anyway, I didn't interrupt him.

After a minute he said, "How soon could I decently marry Cheryl?—I mean, if she'd have me?"

"I thought that was all off," I said.

He shook his head.

"I didn't know what a tough break she'd had here, or that she and Rick were on the point of splitting up. I guess that wouldn't have mattered, anyway."

"Your mother will cut you off with a shilling, if you do marry her—any time," I said.

"That's okay."

"With Cheryl?"

"You don't think she married Rick because she thought he had money, do you?"

"No, I don't," I said. "I think she married Rick because of just one reason—he reminded her of you. And she never thought she'd see you again. You do have a definite resemblance, you know . . . especially when Rick was being decent, and when he wasn't being hounded to death by his creditors."

We crossed the bridge over Potobac Creek.

"Where do you want to go?"

"To the Fountain."

I pulled up at the curb behind a small roadster that had been reduced to its lowest terms. The top was gone, and the spare tire was gone, and the left rear tire was practically devoid of rubber, and the right rear tire was just as bad.

Dan looked at it. "Isn't that Alan Keane's?" he asked.

"I wouldn't know," I said. "If it is he'll have to start hitch hiking shortly."

17

We went up the verandah stairs of the old inn. It had been the center of the more abundant life when Port Tobacco was a center of trade in early days. A bronze plaque by the door had most of the names that colonial history remembers on it. Washington had dined there, Jefferson, Madison. John Wilkes Booth had dined there, I remembered, but his name wasn't on the plaque. Now a half dozen farmers from the country were sitting in the old green rocking chairs strewed along the verandah, talking about the price of tobacco. The light in the ceiling was virtually obliterated by mosquitoes and gnats and millers.

Inside a radio bawled swing music, and an old Chesapeake Bay dog was biting the fleas out of his webbed front foot. Two little boys about eleven were mending fishing tackle under a reading lamp on the table littered with old magazines and newspapers. Through the door at the side I could see a couple of fishermen from the city playing a slot machine. The big fireplace at the end of the main room was the only recognizable sign of the Fountain Inn's past glory, or its antiquity. It had an old crane with an iron pot hanging from it, and above it on the mantel three fine if rather battered pewter tankards. Over them a couple of oyster rakes and an old-fashioned long barreled flintlock rested, as they had always done, on wood brackets in the pine overmantel. And hanging from one of the brackets was a leather bag that looked like a child's golf bag, except that it wasn't. It was a quiver, smoked and dust-covered, and sticking out of it were three smoked and dust-covered feathered arrows.

And more disturbing to my mind than the quiver and arrows was the tall lank figure in the rusty alpaca suit standing in front of the empty fireplace, talking to Mr. Chew the proprietor and his plump red-headed daughter Betty.

Mr. Chew was scratching the back of his scrawny neck.

"I can't rightly say, Sam, just when them arrows was missing," he drawled. "There was five, at one time, wasn't there, Betty?"

The red-headed girl nodded vigorously.

"Yes, dad. Because old Mr. Winthrop shot a sea-gull that got tangled up in the church clock hands, is how we happened to have them," she said positively. "He shot four, and they got all of them back, out of the ivy, but one, and that was lost. I was in the eighth grade and we were reading the Ancient Mariner, and I kept thinking they'd killed an albatross and used to dream about it."

She looked up at the dust-covered quiver—Dan and I standing there fascinated.

"I don't know when the other two went. I never pay 'em much mind. Anybody could take one and nobody'd notice it."

She giggled. "It doesn't look like anybody's been disturbing 'em lately. I'll get a rag and do a little dusting."

"I wouldn't do that if I was you, Betty," the sheriff drawled. "Dr. Birdsong he's a great one for fingerprintin' every thing he lays his hands on. Maybe there's fingerprints on that."

The girl turned and saw us, and came across the room, her brown eyes sparkling.

"Hello, Mrs. Latham! Hello, Dan! I heard you were back! Pa, here's Dan! I was just talking about the day your father shot the seagull. Remember?—You and me and Rick were out in the kitchen . . ."

"Eating gingerbread," Dan said. "I remember. Dad bet old Colonel Masson he could bring down the gull, and Dr. Comegys said he could shoot at the steeple if he'd put up for the damage, because there wasn't anybody could climb the stairs, they were so rotten."

I don't know how long these childhood reminiscences would have gone on if Mr. Chew hadn't offered us a drink, which we refused and Mr. Sam Dorsey the sheriff accepted on our behalf. But as soon as the two of them had gone into the bar the plump red-headed girl, her face sobered, drew us away from the bar door.

"Listen," she said. "They're trying to make out Alan Keane swiped one of those arrows to kill Rick with."

She looked around at the dining room door where her mother was talking to one of the colored waiters.

"Can't you do something, Dan? Alan never killed anybody —not even Rick. But he's going to do *something,* unless they let him alone. He came in here tonight looking awful. Pa's been giving him a room when we aren't full. Ma feeds him when he'll take anything but Pa can't give him a job because your mother holds the mortgage on the Inn, and she'd be sore on account of Alan and Mara. And now she's found out he's staying here, and she told Pa she didn't think he was co-operating with her. So poor Pa had to tell Alan. He won't go on relief like other people.—You've got to do something, Dan! Can't you talk to your mother? She don't realize what she's doing to the kid. Honest, Dan, Alan's okay."

107

I don't think I've ever seen Dan Winthrop's jaw in quite as ugly a stance.

"Where is he?" he said quietly.

"He is 321, third floor. It's the only one empty."

She giggled suddenly, her brown eyes sparkling again.

"I hope Pa don't find out I sent two men in a swell car over to Miz' Foster's Ye Touriste Home. But I don't guess he'd be very mad with me."

We went up the dark worn stairs of the old tavern. How it had escaped fire all these years I couldn't imagine. The wood in it was so old that it must have been like a tinder box. The red light bulb up there with the painted hand pointing to the fire escape seemed hopelessly inadequate.

"Your mother is thorough if nothing," I said, as we went up the third floor stairs.

"She can't see anybody's side but her own," Dan said. He added, with a grin that had as little mirth in it as I've ever seen, "Me, I'm noted as a master of understatement."

"What are you planning to do, by the way?"

"Take the kid out to Romney, to his father's house, where he belongs."

"And what about your mother, darling?"

I don't think I'd better repeat his reply to that. He couldn't have said it unless we'd been old friends of very long standing.

We turned at the top of the stairs and went along to the room with "321" painted on it in white figures, at the end of the dark narrow hall. Dan, ahead of me, raised his fist to knock on that door, and stopped it in mid-air. I saw then that the old pine panelling between the crossboards had split— with the coming of steam, I supposed—and warped, so that the whole room was visible. I felt Dan's body stiffen, and came up close behind him, and saw, through the wide crack in the old door, in the split second before his hand shot forward and threw the door open, the figure of Alan Keane sitting at the table, his right hand raised with a pistol in it, in the very act of putting a bullet in his brain.

18

It still seems incredible to me that Dan could have moved as trigger-quick as he did. A shot barked out, a bullet hissed past Alan Keane's head and buried itself in the pink plaster by the window. With one great hand on the boy's wrist, Dan wrenched the gun from his hand with the other.

"You God-damned fool," he said.

Alan Keane, his face white as a sheet, his dark eyes burning with tragedy, faced him squarely for just a moment, and sank down on the table, sweeping the envelopes that were lying in front of him under his arms, burying his head in them. Not before I'd seen the names on three of them: one to his father, one to Mr. and Mrs. Chew, one to Mara Winthrop.

The other things on the table were mute but so terribly eloquent. His car key in a worn leather holder, a dime and three pennies, a soiled paper of matches, an empty picture frame. On the brick hearth of the closed-up fireplace were the charred remains of what, I suppose, was Mara's picture that he'd burned to keep the reporters from getting and spreading the length and breadth of the country.

I stood there stupidly in the hot stuffy room. There's something very devastating about suicide . . . especially of a young person, and more here, I suppose, because it wasn't spineless cowardice that moved Alan Keane. It was just utter and total despair. I don't suppose I should have recognized that as clearly as I did if I hadn't seen him and Mara that afternoon, and seen her paroxysm of tears. I could imagine Alan living over that scene, the hopelessness of it, the fear, and then coming here where the Chews had been so kind to him, and learning that he was only bringing trouble to them.

This all crystallized in my mind as my eyes went from the pitiful store on the table to the burned picture on the hearth and moved about the meager unlovely room with its iron double bed and marble-topped wash stand where a pair of socks were drying. They fell on the cheap worsted jacket hanging on the back of the door, a large tear near the pocket, and came back to Alan. He had raised his head. His thick chestnut hair needed trimming, his collar was clean and frayed. A sharp barb of pity went into my heart as I wondered if one of my own kids would do this if he was put to it in this way.

109

Alan pushed his chair back, slid the letters into his pocket and got unsteadily to his feet. He mumbled something that Dan interrupted gruffly.

"You're coming home, kid," he said.

I felt the tears start in my eyes as Alan winced and caught hold of himself.

"I'm afraid I haven't got any home, Dan," he said.

"Look," Dan said. "Romney's just as much your home as mine. I'm sorry, Alan . . . and I'm ashamed. I hope you'll forgive us."

"There's nothing to forgive, Dan. It's my own fault. I just can't take it. I always thought I could, but I guess—"

"Skip it," Dan said. "Get your coat."

The boy shook his head.

"You don't understand—"

"I understand plenty," Dan said, very quietly. "Are you coming?"

Alan shook his head again. Dan pulled the gun out of his pocket and swung it lightly in his hand.

"Get that coat," he said. His big face broke into an irresistible grin.

For an instant Alan Keane's body stiffened and his face flushed. Then he grinned too.

"All right—you big bully," he said.

I think all three of us were on the point of tears. I know I looked out of the window down onto the kitchen roof, and sniffled at the smell of fried chicken and hot biscuits for a moment. When I turned back Alan had taken his coat down. I saw him look at the tear in it. "I guess it isn't cold," he said, and folded it over his arm.

The old stairs creaked under our feet as we went down. When we were children my brothers and I used to pretend stairs had voices, because those at the farm sounded different from the ones in town, and the narrow back stairs had a lowlier note than the wide polished ones in the hall. They'd warn us to slip Dead-Eye Dick under the pillow and put out the light. I wished I'd remembered that then, as we went down. Heaven knows those stairs did their part. We were just too deaf to hear. It wasn't till we'd got to the turn at the landing, just about the parlor, that we were suddenly aware of the voices below.

"There's no earthly way of tellin' how long them arrows have been missin', Barney "

It was Mr. Chew's kindly familiar drawl, and the voice that answered him was Mr. Purcell's.

"That doesn't matter, John. There's plenty of people know he was on hand last night. He's been hanging around out there, trying to see Mara. Rick was dead set on putting an end to it. Sam here knows as well as I do that if he'd made Rick a deputy, like I told him to, he'd have shot him for trespassing a month ago. Stand aside now, John—we don't want any trouble."

Mr. Chew's meager form blocked the stairway.

"He's not up there, Barney. He's gone out, I tell you," he drawled.

But it was too late. Mr. Purcell had already seen us as we stopped at the turn. My own impulse, oddly enough, was to go back and take it, as my younger son says, on the lam, and I imagine Alan's must have been instinctively the same only more so. I could hear his sharp intake of breath as he hesitated an instant. Then he went steadily on down till he'd reached the foot of the stairs.

Mr. Chew moved reluctantly aside.

"I did the best I could, son," he mumbled.

Mr. Purcell turned to the lean form of the sheriff. And Mr. Sam Dorsey, who obviously hated the whole business, cleared his throat with some embarrassment.

"I guess we got to arrest you, my boy."

But Alan Keane was not looking at him. His eyes were fixed beyond all of them—the three Chews, the State's Attorney and the sheriff—on the door. Frozen in it, her face as white as death, stood Mara Winthrop. Behind her, also frozen in the act of holding the screen door open for them to enter, was Cheryl. For one completely humiliating moment that must have seemed a century Mara stood there, watching Sam Dorsey's clumsy reluctant hands fix the handcuffs on Alan Keane's wrist. Then with a passionate cry she burst across the room and threw her arms about the boy's neck.

"Oh, Alan, Alan!"

He closed his eyes, his face white, let his head fall against hers for an instant, raised it abruptly and with his free hand tried gently to unlock her arms.

"Come along now, Alan," Mr. Purcell said. His voice was curt, and uncomfortable.

"Oh no, you can't, Mr. Purcell, you can't!"

Mara threw her dark head back, her eyes wild.

"Oh, you can't, you can't!"

"Now look here, Mara—your mother wouldn't like—"

The child's body froze.

"So it's Mother!"

She drew back from him like a person coming slowly from under some stupefying drug, her dazed wide stare fixed, painfully groping, on each of our faces in turn. Mr. Purcell, who certainly knew all about Mara and Alan's passion for each other, equally certainly, I saw, had never thought of it in any such terms as these. He took a lavender handkerchief out of his pocket and mopped his forehead. He glanced very uneasily at Dan . . . and if I had not seen his eyes light on the shiny deputy sheriff's badge visible where Dan's coat had fallen back, I could never in this world have believed the incredible thing that happened next. A glint lighted in Mr. Purcell's eye. I realized that he was trying desperately to see his way out of any possible recrimination from Irene Winthrop . . . and realized then that it wasn't for nothing that Mr. Purcell had the reputation of being the smartest politician in the county.

"Dan's arrest, I guess, sheriff," he said shortly.

Dan Winthrop, never glib at his best, stood there openmouthed. Alan moved a step away from him as if he'd been struck, an angry flush burning in his pale cheeks. Mara's eyes were fixed on that badge, too stupefied to move. Cheryl, who'd come up behind her, stared at him, perfectly appalled, and so did the plump red-headed girl standing by her side. And Dan, more stunned than any of them—and more by their ready acceptance of it than by Mr. Purcell's finesse—clamped his jaws together in what instantly occurred to me was the true Winthrop fashion, and said not a word.

"Now come along, Alan," Mr. Dorsey said. His voice was kindly and almost pleading. Alan Keane took one step, and held back then, his face suddenly white again.

I saw the terror in his eyes . . . and while I don't as a rule have the least luck with my intuitions, I realized with the most instant and extraordinary clarity just what had happened.

I went quickly up to him and held out my hand.

"I'm afraid you won't be going by the post office, Alan," I said. "Give me back my letters, and I'll mail them myself."

The wave of relief and gratitude in the boy's haggard eyes was almost too poignant to bear . . . and I was afraid almost too obvious to deceive.

"Oh, sure," he said. "I forgot all about them."

He pulled out the four letters he'd written with the shadow of death heavy over him—letters that, if I knew anything about country jails, would have been in the hands of some smart well-heeled newspaper man before midnight, and God knows how far by morning—and handed them to me.

I said "Thanks," and put them in my bag. In the old Victorian pier glass between the side windows I caught Mr. Purcell's eye fixed on me. There was a shade of skepticism in it—or so I thought—and I turned to Mr. Chew and inquired, as innocently as I could without overdoing it, when the next mail went out.

112

Alan said, "I'm ready, Sam," and the two of them walked that sickening distance to the door, while Cheryl's brown young hands tightened protectively on Mara's shoulders, forcing her to control herself. The boys mending their fishing gear under the reading lamp looked on, saucer-eyed, too fascinated, too frightened, to move. The screen door slammed shut. I saw Cheryl raise her eyes, blue resentful coals of fire, burning with reproach and incredulity.

For Mara, numb and motionless, the slamming door released a pent-up torrent of despair. She turned on Dan, her dark pointed little face transformed with helpless fury.

"This is how you help me!" she said, with a quiet so desperately controlled that my heart chilled. "This is what you meant last night when you said you wouldn't tell anyone! Rick was right when he said you never cared about anybody but yourself and the only reason you were coming home was to keep him and me from getting a break. You killed him yourself—and you're trying to make Alan suffer for it! You and Mother! I see it all now!"

She turned with a heart-breaking sob and fled across the room and out before any of us, stunned and dismayed, could move to stop her. Dan stood there still, speechless, hurt and angry, his face pale and hard as granite. Cheryl was the first to recover. She ran to the door. We heard her heels click sharply down the verandah steps to be drowned out in the roar of the station wagon engine. She came slowly back inside as we all stood there, paused a moment at the door, and came quickly across to Dan.

She looked up into his face with those extraordinarily clear and tranquil hyacinth eyes of hers.

"Dan," she said, "—I don't believe you told them?"

His face flushed darkly.

"You can believe anything you like," he said.

I caught my breath.

"Well," I said, as cheerfully as I could, "all the Winthrops act like two-year-olds when they're crossed. It's a family trait."

"That's why people murder them," a voice said behind us. We all turned sharply. Major Tillyard was standing in the door of the bar. How much he'd heard of all this I hadn't a notion—enough, I imagine. He came over to me.

"If you're going back to Romney, Mrs. Latham, may I give you a lift?"

The tiny amused flicker in his eyes made me break off before I'd said what I started to say. I nodded and tossed my keys to Dan.

"Bring Cheryl in my car, will you?" I said.

113

Cheryl looked at me, and at Dan, for just an instant.

"Thanks," she said—and I thought it was only a proper show of spirit; "but I'd rather go with you, if you don't mind."

Dan drew a deep breath, and grinned at me.

"You can either come with me, or walk, my girl," he said amiably.

"If either of you can get the car started," I remarked pointedly.

19

Major Tillyard and I got in his car. "You're really very helpful," I said as we crossed Potobac Creek.

He laughed.

"I have a good deal of sympathy for lovers who'd like to be left alone a moment," he said dryly. "And Cheryl's a pretty fine girl."

"You and Irene don't, I take it, always see eye to eye," I said.

"You take Irene's whims too seriously," he answered. "The trouble with all the Winthrops is that they're too stiff-necked to go around an obstacle. They have to crash right through it. Not one of those youngsters has ever made the slightest attempt to lead Irene. They try to bully her, and she balks. She'd never have objected to Cheryl if Rick hadn't been as insulting as possible to Natalie, and then married Cheryl without a word to Irene. If he'd even brought her down on a visit! You know, Irene's consuming ambition has always been to stage an elaborate wedding at Romney. Rick might have given her a chance. But no indeed—he plunks a wife down on the back steps and says, 'Now where's the income, and make it snappy, the plane's waiting in the alfalfa field to get me back to Broadway in time for the floor show.' You can't blame Irene entirely."

"No," I said. "But it's rather unfair to Cheryl."

"Since when have mothers started being fair to their sons' wives, Mrs. Latham?" he inquired pleasntly. "If Dan would just use his head, everything will work out beautifully."

"And Mara? Will that work out too?"

"That's a horse of another color," he said. "I think Irene has some justice on her side. Even so, the· thing's grown out of all rational bounds. But there again, if Mara'd use a little tact . . ."

"Like Natalie?"

He laughed.

"Exactly."

"It doesn't seem to have got Natalie very far?"

"I doubt if she'd agree with you. It's got her out of a dress shop to Romney. And who knows whither?"

He smiled, rather wryly, I thought.

"It didn't get her Rick," I said.

"Perhaps she didn't want Rick—have you thought of that?"

He didn't speak again until we were going down the cedar lane.

"Who, by the way, is this Fellowes Dunthorne person?" I asked.

He didn't answer immediately.

"I'm interested in that myself," he said, after a while. "He's solvent enough, if that's what you mean. Rick met him about five years ago, on shipboard, or so he told the Chews at the Inn last night. I happen to know he's gone on Rick's notes for a lot of money, at one time and another. Rick's taken him around a bit. I met them once at the Maryland Hunt Cup. Oddly enough, he never brought him here. However, I hope to know more about all that tomorrow."

He smiled suddenly. "I'm wondering if Irene's going to let him spend the night here."

I didn't have a chance to inquire into that any further, or do more than wonder curiously about Major Tillyard's very practical interest in him—which in view of that unfinished note on Rick's desk seemed peculiarly significant. We rounded the Romney Oak and came to a stop at the back porch. Old Yarborough in his white coat, the hall light shining down on his kinky white head, was hooking the screen door behind the solid four-square figure of Mrs. Jellyby. She stalked heavily down the stairs, nodded to us and set off down the brick path to her cottage. Yarborough grudgingly unhooked the door for us, and hooked it again.

"Ah wouldn' go in th' liberry jus' now," he said. "Miss Natalie, she been there, and Miss Jelly, she been there, an' ain' nothin' come out 'ceptin' hard words. An' dinner's been gettin' col' since half-past seben."

He started for the door, muttering darkly. Major Tillyard put his hat on the sofa. His face in the mirror over it was distinctly troubled. He caught my reflection behind his own and turned.

"Mrs. Jellyby's the one person Irene never uses hard words to," he said with a smile. "It must be Mara again."

Yarborough, still muttering, finally closed the door. Mr. Fellowes Dunthorne looked out of the sitting room door, looked at the platinum watch on his wrist, shook it and held it significantly to his ear. Mr. Dunthorne, I took it, was hungry, and with some reason—it was almost nine o'clock.

Major Tillyard glanced at me and went forward genially.

"What about a drink, Dunthorne?" I heard him say.

I slipped up the stairs, and stopped abruptly on the landing. Natalie Lane was standing by the Palladian window looking down into the drive, her burnished head resting on her bare arm. For a moment I thought she was crying—incredible as it seemed. It seemed to me also a very odd place to be crying. It flashed through my head that Dan would probably have pointed out to her that female guests at Romney were expected to do their crying in their own rooms. But she wasn't crying. She was looking pretty grim, however, and her really extraordinarily handsome face had a nacré quality.

"Something wrong?" I inquired cheerfully.

"Does Irene ever stick to the same idea fifteen minutes together?" she asked—too bitterly for a guest, I thought.

"On the contrary, I should say Irene has a singlemindedness one seldom meets in a woman," I answered casually.

"You don't like me either, do you, Mrs. Latham?" she said.

It was so abrupt that I was definitely taken aback.

"Who, me?" I said. "Don't be silly!"

"Then will you do something for me?"

She came over to me quickly, her face and voice suddenly full of the most extraordinary entreaty.

"Please, Mrs. Latham—it's terribly important! You've got to help me!"

I'm afraid I drew back instinctively under the intensity of her emotion.

"Everything in my life depends on it! Won't you please make her let Mr. Dunthorne stay tonight, and get them to be . . . decent to him? It's really . . ."

She stopped. Her hand on my arm was trembling.

"Oh, I'm crazy—but it's . . ."

"Don't be silly," I said. "If you really want him to stay I'll speak to Irene."

Not, I thought, that it would do much good. I closed my door and put my bag with Alan's letters in it on the desk. Natalie had come along with me. She sat down on the window seat and stared out the window. I changed my dress and powdered my nose. She just sat there, and when I was ready to go she got up and came with me. It made me rather uncomfortable, having her tag along after me, as if she couldn't bear to be alone. But we only got as far as the first landing. And there we stopped, both of us, and witnessed what still seems to me the most extraordinary scene I've ever witnessed outside of an old-fashioned melodrama. Not that there was anything in the least melodramatic about it. There wasn't. It was all too horribly real, and at the same time so refined and civilized and unerring in its cruelty that it was almost unbelievable.

I was just ahead of Natalie, a little below the turn in the carved pine stairway. In the hall below, coming from the library hyphen, so white and at the same time so dark that she looked more like a sleepwalker bound by some terrible dream, was Mara Winthrop. Behind her, graceful and casual as a summer breeze, a little smile on her red lips and in her flower-like eyes, was her mother. She held out her hand to Major Tillyard, and drew it back as the sound outside of a car stopping and quick feet, one pair light as thistledown, one heavy as a percheron's, came up the stairs.

Mara, one hand on the newel post, her foot on the bottom step, stopped and looked dully at the door as her mother looked brightly at it, her perfectly arched brows raised ever so slightly. The screen rattled alarmingly, Yarborough appeared from somewhere and unhooked it. And in came Dan and Cheryl.

It seems silly to say that the whole hall was suddenly lighted up, but it's quite true. Or that they came hand in hand through fields of black-eyed susans, because they weren't hand in hand, and there weren't any black-eyed susans nearer than the cow pasture. But that was the illusion I got—and unfortunately I wasn't the only one. Irene's delicate hand completed its downward arc to her side. The smile on her lips never faltered, nothing about her changed. But Cheryl stopped as if she had been struck, and Dan stopped too, a slow dark flush rising in his cheeks. Mara's eyes closed as her hand tightened on the newel post. The silence, broken by the long unearthly scream of a peacock, that I'd got so used to now I never heard it any more, fell on us like a clap of thunder. In it, very clearly, and as smooth and—I couldn't help but think—treacherous as quicksand, moved Irene's voice.

"If you were brought up to regard divorce as undesirable, Cheryl, I'm surprised you weren't taught that death has its conventions too—and that a lady doesn't go dancing about the countryside with an old lover before her husband is even in his grave. But if you have no feeling, I have; and Dan has too, if you will leave him alone. I'll ask you not to come a step further into this house, if you please. You may wait outside—Anna will bring your things, Jim will drive you wherever you wish to go. I'll send the few items you brought with you.—Ring for Anna, Dan."

For a moment that seemed an eternity Cheryl stood there, too stunned to move, her lips parted, ivory pale. And Dan stood there too. And then he turned, without a single glance at any one of us.

"Let's go," he said. He took her by the hand. "We're taking your car, Grace."

I felt myself nodding my head quite mechanically, just as the idea came hurtling into my mind that this would never have happened if it hadn't been for that terrible business of the cigarette lighter.

118

Dan took a step toward the door. His mother's voice was like a bell, and yet I know she never raised it, or changed a note of it.

"Dan," she said. "If you go out of his house with Cheryl, you will not come back . . . nor will you get one dollar of your father's estate."

"That's okay with me, Mother, and okay with Cheryl."

His voice was as quiet, as even, and as rock-ribbed as her own. He took another step toward the door, pulling Cheryl with him.

"Dan!" Irene said. "You're perfectly free to choose your life. I've never interfered with that. I only wish to say, before you make your choice, that if you make this one, not only will you get none of your father's estate . . . Mara will get none of it. It will go—all of it—to Natalie. You're free to choose, my dear, for both your sister and yourself."

Dan's hand gripping Cheryl's tightened; but his eyes, after one incredulous glance at his mother, moved to Mara, still clinging there to the carved newel post.

She raised her head, her eyes widening, lips opening, as the meaning of what Irene had said seeped slowly into her mind. Then her eyes moved, bewildered and stricken, from her brother to Cheryl.

And Cheryl drew her hand away from Dan's. "Good-bye," she said.

119

20

I've tried since to think which was the worst of the individual cataclysms focused just then in Romney's mellowed carved pine hall. Cheryl's, for instance, as the door closed softly but with such dead finality behind her; or Dan's, standing there helplessly, torn between his own heart's desire and his unselfish loyalty to the dark child clinging to the newel post, the memory of that scene at the Fountain Inn still between them. Or Mara's own, as she realized what her brother and Cheryl were giving up for her . . . or Irene's as she saw her own ego triumph once more over the lives of her children.

Or perhaps, I thought, as I became aware of him, the toilworn farmer's standing there like a dim ghost outside the screen, his hat gripped in his knotted hands. How long Mr. Keane had been there, or when he was there no longer, I haven't an idea. I only know that when I looked where Cheryl had been it was his shadowy earth-colored figure I saw, and when Mara turned and crept up the stairs, and Dan without so much as a sideways glance at his mother went grimly up after her, leaving the doorway clear, Mr. Keane wasn't there any more.

I'm sure Irene hadn't seen him at all. She stood perfectly motionless, her face as pale as alabaster, like a medicine man who had willed the sky to fall and finds that it has, and stands stunned, appalled at his own power. Then suddenly it was all over. Her breath exhaled slowly. She moistened her lips with her pointed delicate tongue and glanced quickly around at her guests. They stood, each in his own spot, like a collection of Lot's wives changed to stone instead of salt.

She turned easily to the old darky blocking the hyphen door, putty-colored, his eyes all whites behind their thick lenses.

"It must be time for dinner, Yarborough," she said, as if nothing of this had really happened.

"Mus' is," Yarborough said mechanically. He opened the door, and we went in, Natalie, Mr. Dunthorne, Major Tillyard, Irene and I, to a meal that would have made a Trappist monastery sound like a nest of holiday magpies.

I've tried to remember too whether a little later I was really surprised, or whether by then nothing Irene did could any longer surprise me. We were having coffee in the library. Mr.

Dunthorne—his face the color of a scalded beet, except where his sunglasses had left long whitish rings, so that he looked rather like a dreadfully debauched owl—had excused himself, and had been followed almost at once by Natalie Lane. And Irene suddenly got up, sending her spode coffee cup crashing to the floor, shattering into forty pieces, and stood in front of the fireplace, her fragile body as rigid as a glass rod.

Major Tillyard and I watched her, too startled to make the slightest movement toward the broken cup and saucer. Her lovely Dresden-china head raised slowly, as if it was suddenly aware of the weight of folly upon it, until her eyes rested on the painted face of her husband's portrait in the overmantel. She looked at it a long, long time, her delicate hands clasping the mantel until her scarlet fingernails stood out livid against the old wood. Then she dropped her head against them, her shoulders quivering convulsively. Both Major Tillyard and I stared at her. I don't think either of us believed our eyes. Then he put down his coffee and got up.

"Please, dearest!" he said gently. He put his arm around her trembling shoulders. She turned and buried her face against him a moment, clutching convulsively at his dinner coat lapels. Then she pushed him gently away and turned, facing us, the tears streaming down her cheeks.

"Oh, I'm a beast! A beast!" she said passionately. "I don't know why I do these horrible things!"

She raised her eyes to her husband's portrait.

"Forgive me—oh, forgive me!" she whispered.

She stood silent a moment, then brushed the tears from her eyes and turned to the other man, the living one.

"Oh Sidney, don't think I'm too horrible! You've been right from the beginning! Go get Dan and Mara—bring them both to me! Please, my dear!"

Major Tillyard raised her hand and pressed his lips to it. "I knew you'd come to yourself, Irene," he said quietly. "I'll get them, now."

She watched him go with an expression nearer tenderness than I'd yet seen on her perfect face. When he closed the door she sat down beside me on the sofa. She didn't speak for a long time. Then she said, "I'm going to let them have their money. Sidney thinks it's the only thing, and . . . I guess it is. Dan can . . .'"

Her voice caught, but she went on with it.

". . . can do as he likes. And Mara can go abroad and get away from the Keane boy. And . . . my conscience will be clear."

She made a weary final gesture, dropped her head back on the linen slip cover and closed her eyes.

121

"What if Mara won't go, Irene?" I asked. "What if she's *really* in love with Alan Keane?"

She didn't even open her eyes. "Mara's a child emotionally. She'll forget him in two weeks."

"And . . . if she doesn't?"

She took a deep, vaguely exasperated breath and raised her head. "If she doesn't . . . well, I expect Sidney Tillyard knows enough about him to send him back to the penitentiary until she does."

I looked up at the strong kindly face in the overmantel. There was no change in the painted eyes. The days when pictures fell off the walls and statues off their pedestals to avenge themselves or their loved ones were gone, I thought to myself . . . and I could almost hear old Yarborough answering, 'mus'is.'

I put my coffee cup on the silver balcony tray and got up. There was a great deal I should have liked to say, just then. But I knew if I said anything I'd probably say too much, and make things worse, possibly, than they already were. So I only said, "By the way, Irene, Natalie seems terribly anxious to have Mr. Dunthorne around. I said I thought you wouldn't mind. You don't, do you?"

"Not at all," she said—almost cordially, to my amazement. "At least not until he starts peeling. I should think he'd be awfully unattractive with all the skin off his nose. Still, he has quite a lot of money, I believe. He can have the Green Room. Tell Yarborough, will you, dear?"

I don't know why I should have been so upset by that. I ought to have been delighted that some things at Romney were simple. But I wasn't. I was even angrier than I was upset, and for a moment I stood there struggling against an almost overpowering temptation to speak my mind . . . knowing all the time that it would be a barren momentary luxury that somebody would have to pay for. Irene bent forward, dipped a coffee spoon daintily into the gorgeous cream jug and raised it to her lips. The mood of remorse that had so devastated her seemed to me to be definitely slipping. Perhaps—I thought—if I left her under the clear eyes of the man over the mantel it would last until Dan and Mara came. I moved toward the door, the one that Alan had gone through, and Mara, that opened into the gardens toward Mrs. Jellyby's white vine-covered cottage.

Irene put her spoon down on the tray.

"Grace," she said, a tiny cloud between her arched brows. "Is it just my imagination, or does it seem to you that Natalie's attitude has . . . well, changed, some way?"

"Why?" I asked. "Isn't she . . . co-operating?"

"It isn't that, exactly," Irene said, thoughtfully. "It's just that since this . . . awful business she's been . . . well, I don't mean *ungrateful,* but a little as if being here wasn't a privilege, say, as much as a . . . a right, if you see what I mean."

I thought suddenly of the auburn-tipped figure that I'd seen disappearing behind the fluted columns when I'd looked out the open window the night before, after Dr. Birdsong and Major Tillyard had gone.

"It sounds insane, but it's sort of as if she thought—to put it in the most vulgar possible way—she had something on me," Irene said.

"You wouldn't think she knows you're supposed to let her have any part of her uncle's estate, if she needs it?" I inquired, tentatively. "I take it she doesn't need it."

She shook her head.

"She couldn't know, possibly. You see, the will that was probated left everything to me. Joe's instructions about Natalie, and your children, are in a letter to me. I don't actually have to follow them—I mean you're the only person I've ever told. Of course, I wouldn't not follow them for the world— my will does—but as for letting her have the money now, I don't think that's necessary. I mean, I've been very liberal with her. I don't think it hurts a girl to make her own living, it teaches her self-reliance, and of course Natalie's father should have left her comfortably off. He had more money than we had to begin with, but he lost it all in 1929 and jumped off the roof of his club in Detroit. Natalie used his insurance to pay back people he'd borrowed from, which I do think was too quixotic of her—she wasn't obliged to, legally."

I stood there, silently revising my opinion of Natalie Lane.

"Of course, if one of the boys had married her . . . But she acted almost as foolishly as they did. She could have had Rick perfectly easily, if she'd taken the trouble."

I realized she was talking to justify herself in her own mind, not in mine.

"As a matter of fact I can't really say how much there'll be for her. I've spent quite a lot on her. For instance, I got a fur coat for her last year that cost $795.00."

"You mean, you're keeping an account of everything you . . ."

She looked astonished at my stupidity.

"Of course! My dear Grace, I couldn't afford to *give* her an eight hundred dollar coat. Don't be absurd."

"She'd probably rather have worn her old one, or had a cloth coat for a hundred dollars," I said.

"Well, that's being silly. A girl ought to dress well."

123

It occurred to me again that above all odds Irene Winthrop was the most exasperating woman I ever knew.

"I hope you aren't charging her board here," I said, turning to the door. I couldn't tell from the expression on her face whether I'd struck on the truth, suggested a new idea, and I didn't stay to find out. I heard someone coming through the hyphen, and got out. I didn't want to be in on what, in Irene's rapidly changing mood, was bound to be a pretty stormy session.

I closed the door, and stood a moment, the cool fragrant night soothing my exasperated temper. It was very lovely, the stars and the moon on the shimmering river, and on Mrs. Jellyby's little white-washed cabin under the willow tree. The yellow light in its two windows on either side of the open door made it look like a friendly jack-o'-lantern peering up from the river bank. As I watched it the door closed, leaving only the two eyes, and they closed one by one as someone drew down the blinds. Then the door opened again, and two dark figures came out and up the brick walk. They came almost even with me, and stopped. I heard Mrs. Jellyby's harsh voice.

"It's not as easy to do as talk about. Nothing is, if it's worth doing. You go home, and brew some tea from those leaves, and get some rest."

It was Mr. Keane's slow bitter drawl that answered.

"With my boy in jail?"

"If you think it'll help him having you go all to pieces, don't do it," Mrs. Jellyby said. "Alan'll be all right. Jail will keep him out of mischief. We'll get a lawyer for him that'll skin the pants off Barney Purcell."

"I haven't got money to pay any more lawyers," Mrs. Keane said helplessly.

"Stuff," Mrs. Jellyby said. "I'll get the money. You could get it yourself if you'd go to Irene Winthrop and tell her half the money the government paid for ploughing down fifty acres of soy beans, and fifty acres of clover, and all the other practices—sharp practices, I call them—belongs to you, not her."

I could hear the farmer's long-drawn breath as he said, "I've spoken to her about that, more than once."

And I could see Mrs. Jellyby's head nodding grimly.

"The trouble with you is you're a gentleman and you think Irene Winthrop's a lady. She'd skin a flea for its tallow. If you'd go and tell her you'll leave the farm if she doesn't draw in her horns, she'd eat out of your hand."

"I don't aim to have her do that," Mr. Keane said. "All I want is the boy given a chance. If Mr. Winthrop had lived—"

124

"If Mr. Winthrop had lived," Mrs. Jellyby said crisply, "none of this would have happened. Or if he hadn't thought Irene had a man's head. What a woman needs is a woman's head and a woman's heart. Irene's got a man's head and a stone's heart and a woman's vanity.—Good night, Mr. Keane. Don't fret about Alan. If he's in jail he's not hanging around the slot machines in a saloon that calls itself a Bar B Q."

Mr. Keane put on his hat and moved off toward the drive. Mrs. Jellyby stood watching him a moment, and I heard her rusty voice whisper, "Good night—old friend." She cleared her throat violently and turned back the way she'd come.

21

I moved out from the shadow of the boxwood, its eerie rustle and faint nostalgic perfume full of a thousand memories, started toward the back porch, and stopped. Mr. Keane had stopped too, and was standing, looking up at the door. Even in the pale white light I could see the indecision on his face as he took a step up, and backed down again . . . trying, I knew, to get up courage enough to see Miz' Winthrop. I turned back and wandered slowly down the lawn toward the river. At the end, where a stone balustrade covered with starry cypress vine marked the bank, I saw a white figure sitting, looking out over the placid moonlit water, the white smoke of a cigar rising like a spirit picture about his head.

For a moment I thought it might be Dan. Then I realized, from the altogether too expensive aroma wafted to my nose, that it must be Mr. Fellowes Dunthorne, in one of his apparently all-too-frequent solitary moments. I stopped automatically to turn back, and then, remembering that I'd promised Natalie Lane to get people to be decent to him, I decided I might at least have one go at it myself. He turned, rather startled at being approached . . . and from all I'd seen of the people who approached him, he might very well view such an action with misgivings.

"Lovely night, isn't it," I said.

He grunted very noncommittally, and looked at the long ash on the end of his cigar.

"That's a marvelous cigar," I said, sniffing. It really was.

"They're not so bad," he said, modestly. "I get them from a friend in Havana. They're made specially for me—with my name on the band."

"Really?"

"Some ladies don't like cigars," he said.

"I don't like stale cigar smoke," I said. "And by the way, Mrs. Winthrop asked me to tell you she does hope you'll stop on here. Yarborough'll put your things in the Green Room."

Mr. Dunthorne looked critcally at his cigar ash.

"I don't know as I want to," he said, after a moment, and added, "I guess that surprises you, doesn't it?"

"I . . . well, I . . . yes," I mumbled—because it certainly did.

"I had an idea people that lived in places like this"—he

126

waved his cigar out over Romney——"were a cut above the dog eat dog ruckus in there tonight. Of course, I've known a long time Rick didn't get along with his folks. I figured it was because he was an out and out tank, so full of the jitters he couldn't get along with anybody. Don't know as I blame him so much, now I've met his old lady."

Irene, I thought to myself, wouldn't like that, no matter how much money you've got, Mr. Dunthorne.

"You see, I was brought up in Hell's Kitchen, where you don't expect any different. I always figured there was more in environment than there was in heredity. I figured you couldn't do anything about your heredity, but you could do what you wanted about your environment. It looks to me right now that all environment does is teach you how to stage a murder without being sent to the chair."

"We hang them in Maryland," I said.

"Yeh? Well, I'll bet you a thousand dollars you don't hang the guy that bumped off old Rick."

"Oh, dear," I said. "I haven't got a thousand dollars, to bet, but I'll bet we do."

I hoped I didn't sound as little positive as I felt, but I must have, because Mr. Fellowes Dunthorne said promptly, "All right, lady, it'll cost you a hundred if they don't—and I'll pay you one grand if they do."

I felt my hand being shaken and that compact sealed, not with blood probably, because I don't think the skin broke, but very nearly with broken bones.

"You don't, by any chance, *know* who killed Rick, do you?" I inquired dubiously.

"No—but I've got a pretty good hunch," he said. "And I've always been pretty lucky backing my hunches."

I saw the dining room of my house in Georgetown that I'd planned to do over in August staying a spotted Williamsburg blue for another year. Mr. Fellowes Dunthorne had a very convincing air.

He tossed his cigar over the river bank.

"I wish you'd tell me what Mrs. Winthrop's got against Rick's wife," he said, turning to me.

"Just that she married Rick," I answered. "She wanted him to marry Natalie."

I felt Mr. Dunthorne's shrewd eyes indirectly but very intently fixed on my face.

"Why didn't he?"

"I wouldn't know," I said. "Except that Natalie looks to me like the kind of girl that wouldn't marry a man just because he or she would get money by it."

127

I had my hand in the black chiffon folds of my full skirt, so he couldn't possibly see that my fingers were crossed.

Mr. Dunthrone chewed his lower lip a moment.

"You don't think she is?" he asked, not as nonchalantly as he tried to sound.

"Any girl who uses her father's insurance to pay off his debts when she isn't legally required to," I said, hoping suddenly that Irene hadn't just made all that up on the spur of the moment, "and has to get a job and support herself as an immediate consequence of it, certainly isn't. It would seem quixotically honorable, to most people."

"It sure would to the people around here," Mr. Fellowes Dunthorne said. "I'm not sure I don't agree with 'em. She never mentioned that to me."

I covered my tracks as casually as I could.

"Then I wouldn't mention it to her," I said. "Her aunt told me—is the only way I know about it."

"Mrs. Winthrop?"

I nodded. "Her mother was Mr. Winthrop's sister. You probably noticed his portrait over the library mantel. There's quite a resemblance."

I hadn't really noticed much resemblance myself, but if Natalie, I thought, wanted this man impressed, I was delighted to help . . . and I must admit I was a little pleased at my apparent success. It would be funny, I thought quite suddenly then, if it turned out to be Natalie who'd murdered Rick. But I felt safe enough about that. She was the one person at Romney who had no conceivable motive for murdering him, and the only one who wasn't more or less hovering about the scene of the crime somewhere about when it happened.

Mr. Dunthorne took out a thin gold cigarette case and extended it to me. I took one.

"These have your name on them too?" I asked.

"Just the monogram."

He held out a lighter, larger and more golden and more magnificent than the one with which Cheryl had confounded Major Tillyard. I puffed at the cigarette. Whatever his taste in clothes and cars, Mr. Dunthorne had certainly had excellent advice on tobacco.

I was on the point of saying as much, and probably making the usual cliché about the cigarette's having again made Maryland tobacco smokable and Southern Maryland profitable, when I happened to glance back at the house. Under the lantern in the blue ceiling of the portico I saw Natalie Lane's burnished head. She was looking down our way, apparently undecided whether to join us—break in, I expect she thought of it—or not. I imagined she'd had time to think over our little scene in the upstairs hall and was ashamed, perhaps, of having revealed so much of the storm raging inside her.

I turned back to Mr. Dunthorne. "Shall I tell Yarborough to put your bags in the Green Room?" I asked, just enough down my nose to make it impressive.

"Oh, I say, thanks very much," he said, in so much the same tone that we both laughed. And I knew that was what he'd really expected Rick's family to be like—not so simple and unaffected, except for Irene and in spite of the slight touch of murder, as they were. He'd undoubtedly learned his manners from the movies.

I crossed the lawn. Natalie, still standing there, eyed me with a sort of tentative hostility. I went up the steps. "He's staying all night," I said. "I'll have Yarborough bring his things up."

She said nothing. I looked at her, a little surprised, after what I'd just been through in her behalf. Her cold lovely face with its high proud bony structure seemed paler than usual in the silver light, with the filmy brown net of her dinner frock high at the base of the white marble column of her throat. Her yellow-green eyes were like cat's eyes in the dark.

"Did you tell her I asked her to ask him?"

"No," I said—unblushingly.

"Then thanks."

"You're quite welcome."

She went down the stone steps. The fireflies in the grass glided up about the soft folds of her skirt as she moved gracefully across the lawn. I saw her hold out her hand and catch a couple, and watch their light fade out, and light again, between her fingers, like a pale tiny lantern, as she walked toward Mr. Fellowes Dunthorne. If he was at all susceptible to charm and the old South, that ought to finish him, I thought. My grandmother used to put fireflies in a bit of net and tuck them in her hair when she was a girl at a place much like Romney. I shrugged, quite involuntarily, I'm afraid. The conquest—or could it, I wondered, be the propitiation?—of this curious person seemed curiously out of character for Natalie Lane, with that face, and that hair, and with her head too . . . for even Dr. Birdsong agreed with me when we talked about it later that she was a very intelligent person . . . almost too intelligent, I imagine. If it was true that she had deliberately side-stepped Rick, it seemed odd she should be so interested in Mr. Dunthorne, for drunk or sober, Rick, it seemed to me—or would have seemed, up to the night before—was much the more eligible of the two. And as for Dan, so far as I'd seen Natalie hadn't so much as looked at him, much less held out to him a shapely hand full of fireflies.

But whatever it was all about, I said to myself as I took hold of the screen door knob, Natalie Lane was just the girl who could be trusted to take care of her own business, and I would do well to mind mine.

With that definitely commendable resolution I pulled at the screen. Of course, it was locked. I rattled it, expecting Yarborough to sidle out of the shadows muttering about the mosquitoes, but he didn't. After a little I got tired of waiting, and started around the dining room wing to the other door. Yarborough was probably sitting on the kitchen stoop, giving the law to a hand up from the tobacco fields.

I stood for a moment looking down the formal gardens to the broad Potomac. At the right where the white balustrade marked the bank, I could see the outline of Mr. Fellowes Dunthorne's dinner jacket, and the two red tips of his and Natalie's cigarettes. The rest of them was lost in the shadow of the mimosa tree. I could see thin pencils of light through the drawn Venetian blinds of the library, where Irene was by now interviewing her wayward young. At the left, far down the river, I could see the faint light over the door of the tenant house, and beyond it the floodlights in the barnyard. I wondered vaguely why they should be on, knowing they were there largely for protection from prowlers and chicken thieves. The down-river wing of the house itself was oddly dark, it seemed, though why I should have thought then that its darknes wass odd I haven't an idea. It had been dark enough the night before, even with the hyphen lights on and the candles in the dining room, when Dan and I stood where I was now, seeing Mr. Keane emerge out of the shadowy rain-swept path.

I stood there for a moment, letting the silence and peace of the night smooth out the furrows in my heart. Then I went slowly down the shallow old steps and turned into the dark path along the dining room wing. I walked along, aware, now that I'd quit projecting my own consciousness onto the night, of the small lovely sounds and tenuous eerie odors that live after the day is done: the million whispering voices, as remote and inaudible as the stars, in the old box looking dark and gigantic against the silver air, its fragrance that's like nothing else in all the world cool and aromatic above the headier marsh smells from the river; and the fireflies rising up, dying and rising again from its dark bed, too coldly yellow and silent ever to seem very gay to me.

I stopped and looked up at the sky. Among the stars in the trackless paths of that dark infinity poor Rick's soul was wandering, I thought, new and forlorn. A line from somewhere—Shakespeare, I suppose—came into my mind: the evil men do lives after them, the good is oft interred with their bones. I was wondering vaguely why that should have come to me just then when I was aware in the periphery of my consciousness of a new sound, very faint but never for an instant to be confused with the intangible disembodied sounds of the night. I heard the boxwood rustle, but it wasn't only the dark brittle little leaves whispering to each other.

I stopped and waited, my heart quite still. Ahead of me, along the inky path, in a single spot, there were no longer any fireflies. Then one glided into that spot, and sped out, his tiny pendulous lantern still aglow. Someone was standing there, off the path, concealed in the boxwood where I had to pass, unless I turned back now—so close that I could hear a sudden spasmodic breath that could not be held another moment. I started forward. There was nothing at Romney to fear, I told myself, and thought, "Except murder, murder that lurked in the box for Rick." Then I stopped again, and backed a step, too frightened to turn and run.

Silently as a ghost, a man stepped out into the path, his face wild and haggard in the silver glow of the moon. And for an instant I thought it was a ghost, and the dreadful idea that we hadn't cheated death, Dan and I, struck my numbed mind . . . because I knew Alan Keane's body was under padlock and chain in the jail in Port Tobacco.

22

"Alan!" I gasped.

He drew a quick breath, almost a sob of relief. I knew then he hadn't been able to see who it was coming on him in the dark.

"What are you doing here?"

"Sam Dorsey let me out to see . . . my father. Purcell's in Baltimore. I've got to get right back.—Have you got those letters?"

"They're in my bag," I whispered. "Upstairs."

"Would you get them? I'll wait here. I've got to have them."

His face, and his voice, were desperately urgent.

I nodded.

He took a step toward me. "Look, Mrs. Latham—if I'm not here, burn them, will you?"

His hand on my arm was cold and trembling.

I nodded again, turned and hurried around the end of the kitchen. I could hear the clatter of pots and pans, and old Yarborough's voice quavering some incomprehensible dirge that had all the undertones of a tomtom beating in the African night. I ran, as quietly as I could in spike-heel sandals, across the white oyster-shell drive. Mr. Fellowes Dunthorne's car was still parked in it, and Major Tillyard's, and my own. I hurried up the steps. The screen door was unlocked, for a wonder, probably because the great white door was closed, I supposed. The hall was empty and silent. I paused a moment, listening. Romney was as still as the grave. I slipped upstairs. No one was there either, except Yarborough's undistinguished cat crouched at a mouse hole by a paneled cupboard under the third floor upstairs.

I went quickly along the hall to my room and opened the door, suddenly and quite inexplicably feeling something stealing open in my heart, the way a slow-motion camera shows a leaf or a petal uncurling, aware that when it was unfolded fear would lie there, as cold and intangible as a dark and terrifying bloom. I opened the dresser drawer and picked up my bag—it was white, made of wooden beads—and opened it. My knees were simply turned to water. Alan's four letters were gone. His pistol was gone too.

I steadied myself against the tall mahogany chest and looked slowly about the room. Who had taken them? Who knew what they were, except myself and Dan and Alan? Who knew even that they were in my bag? The scene at the Fountain Inn flashed into my mind. I saw all of us standing there, the Chews, Alan, Dan, Sam Dorsey the sheriff, Cheryl and Mara at the door, and Mr. Purcell with his gray eyes on me in the dingy fly-specked pier glass. And even then, who knew where I'd put my bag, beside myself, and Natalie? And Natalie didn't know about the letters.

Then another question seeped gradually into the center of my mind. Why was Alan Keane so desperately anxious to have the letters? What could conceivably be in them? What did it matter if his father, and the Chews, or even Mara, knew he'd been tottering on the brink of self-destruction? Then I remembered the fourth letter, under the others, the address of which I hadn't seen. Whom had it been written to? For a moment I just stood there, my mind the most awful chaos of suspicion and doubt . . . so that looking back on it now I wonder that God, who my cook Lilac says strikes colored people dead if they wash clothes on Sunday, didn't reduce me on the spot to my original atomic structure.

It seemed much longer to me, standing there dumbfounded, than it could have been, because when I snapped out of it and fled back through the empty halls Yarborough's cat was still at the mouse hole, and Yarborough was still in the pantry chanting his melancholy dirge. I hurried around the kitchen and into the path. I could see Alan, looming taller against the white trim of the dining room windows, and I ran quickly toward him.

"They're go—," I cried, and stopped dead. Smack in the middle of the path I saw two round live coals of fire, totally disembodied in the inky blackness of the box. For once I was smarter than the thieves in the old fairy tale. I didn't need light to tell me that supporting those live coals was the shaggy remainder of that unbelievable dog. And almost instantly I heard his master's voice:

"What's gone, Mrs. Latham?"

Since then I've thought of several quite bright things I could have said; but none of them occurred to me then, halted open-mouthed in the middle of the path. I just stood there, mute, wondering what could have become of Alan Keane, whether he'd got away in time to keep from being seen.

Dr. Birdsong disengaged his long frame from the side of the house—it was no wonder I'd thought a trick of the light

133

had elongated Alan Keane—and moved toward me, so that we stood facing each other in the silvery glow of the night.

"You don't have much confidence in me, do you, Mrs. Latham?" he asked quietly.

I moistened my perfectly parched lips and took a deep steadying breath. I was quite as surprised at that as I was at finding him there.

"No," I said. And if I'd been in complete possession of my senses I'd never have added as I did, "Is there any possible reason why I should?"

I could feel his body tense abruptly and his eyes sharpen, searching my face. Or perhaps it was those glowing eyes of his dog that I felt. I must say it was getting so I didn't in my own mind distinguish very clearly between them.

"Is there any conceivable reason why you shouldn't, Mrs. Latham?"

"You sound exactly like Irene," I retorted. "The iron claw in the velvet glove sort of thing."

The atmosphere around us was definitely electric for a moment. I heard that dog growl—very faintly but quite unmistakably—and then I heard his tail thump the walk, and the atmosphere cleared. Dr. Birdsong took his pipe and his oilskin pouch out of his pocket. Even without seeing him clearly I knew he had relaxed into his usual urbane self again.

"Don't you know, Mrs. Latham, that murder is one of the most dangerous games men play?" he asked casually. "And the dangerous thing about it is that it's only the first step that's hard? After that hump is cleared, a second one is pretty simple?"

"You mean," I said—and I suppose it was terribly foolish —"that it would be pretty simple for you to murder me?"

He jerked back as if I'd lashed him across the face, and I could feel the shaggy hair bristling along that immense dog's back. I was quite literally stunned. I meant chiefly to be—not exactly arch, but I suppose that sort of thing. And I was not only stunned, I was a little frightened. It wouldn't have surprised me in the least just then to have felt a knife between a couple of strategic ribs.

He recovered even before the dog—and much before I did. In fact, I haven't entirely recovered yet.

"I suppose it's Rick you're thinking of," he said quietly.

I stammered. "I . . . I didn't mean—"

"Perhaps you'll tell me what makes you think I killed Rick," he interrupted coolly. "Sit down, boy."

The boy sat down, but I could see those eyes fixed on me. If only I had sense enough, ever, to mind my own business, I thought. Those three glass nodules filched frim the State Road

134

Commission's sign were insignificant beside the two red gleaming nodules there that were ordinarily milky-blue and mild.

"Well, I don't know, actually," I said feebly. "It's just that looking back on it, it seemed odd that (a) you barged in at precisely the psychological moment, and that (b) after you left the scene of the crime a very important clue had left it too, and that (c) you went enormously out of your way to explain to me that without that very clue it would be impossible for anybody to shoot Rick, and that (d) it was you who pointed out to all and sundry that the tree was down and the road to Romney blocked so that Major Tillyard couldn't possibly have got back here, and incidentally established a similar alibi for yourself.—Though you haven't, of course, mentioned that."

"Since it would have been so simple to upset," he said quietly. "I had a car, even if Tillyard didn't, and even if the walk in from the tree wouldn't have been the least effort for my seven-league boots—which I happened so conveniently to be wearing last night—Tillyard's car was this side of the tree, with the keys even more conveniently in the ignition."

"I thought of that too," I said—a little angry at his tone, though I'm sure a man has a right to resent being accused of murder, whether he did it or didn't.

"I'm sure you did," he said coolly. "And what about the fact that I've admitted hunting game with a bow and arrow?"

"That too," I said, just as coolly.

"And my motive for killing Rick? Had you thought of that?"

"No. I'd not. Apart from the fact that you claim to have a sense of justice. But that doesn't prove you didn't have one."

"Certainly not. Just as the bit of yellow string caught in the splintered wood of the arrow that killed Rick doesn't prove that Mara used her glove to wipe off . . . even if the string does come from a blood-stained glove that does belong to her."

I caught my breath sharply. The scene on the terrace, at breakfast, before Irene and I found Rick's body, flashed into my mind . . . Mara coming in from her early canter, with muddy jodhpurs and muddy jodhpur boots, her shirt open at the neck, pale and excited, dropping a single string glove on the end of the table by her crop.

"You can't seriously—" I began.

He interrupted me so curtly that I couldn't believe we'd ever had an amusing friendly conversation. "Look, Mrs. Latham. Perhaps some day the simple fact will occur to you that there's not an animal in creation that—goaded far enough, and cruelly enough—won't turn on its tormentor and destroy it or be destroyed itself. Mara is a passionate, high-spirited human animal."

When he stopped short it was as if I'd had a blinding glare taken from my face. He went on, more casually, less intensely concerned.

"If you'd seen Mara as I saw her less than ten minutes ago, you'd know what I mean. I don't know what's happened to her, or when; but I don't think murder would be hard for her now. If last night she'd met Rick out there in the dark . . ."

He shrugged his big shoulders. I was aware suddenly of the heavy sweet fragrance of Latakia, and knew he was opening his oilskin pouch and burying his pipe bowl in the moist dark shreds. My mind raced desperately, trying to fit what he'd said into the pattern I knew. What could have happened, less than ten minutes before? Was it just a continuation of the scene in the hall, which he perhaps still knew nothing about? Could Irene possibly have seen her children in the library and instead of making peace with them, forged new bitterness? Did it mean that Mara now knew that while Dan was free to marry Cheryl, she was to be sent abroad to forget Alan Keane? Or had Irene reneged on Dan and Cheryl too?

Dr. Birdsong's voice interrupted my feeble surmises.

"Normal people don't kill without pretty overpowering cause, Mrs. Latham: love, hate, revenge, gain, fear. Rick's murderer was motivated, I haven't a doubt, by one of those five springs of human behavior. And Rick's sins were visited on a chosen few—personally, I didn't happen to be one of them."

In the pale moon glow above the boxwood I could see a faint smile light his eyes, and an ironic twist at the corner of his hard mouth. "Now if it had been Irene—"

He stopped utterly short and whirled around, and I caught at his arm with a terrified gasp. Splitting the silver silence of the night came the most appalling high-pitched scream of terror that I ever hope in all my life to hear. I stood there, clutching at him, petrified with fright . . . and I could just vaguely hear myself, hardly realizing what I was saying, my voice chilled and shaking:

"That . . . that's not a peacock . . ."

Before the words were out of my mouth it came again, unmistakably human, too awful to be heard.

Dr. Birdsong had jerked his arm away and was running at top speed toward the house, his long legs clearing the distance to the portico in a fraction of an instant. I ran after him, desperately. He tore at the bolted screen. It was too firmly hooked, any grip he could get on it too small, for him to rip it open; the door behind it was closed so that he couldn't kick it in. He tore a case knife out of his breeches pocket and slashed through the copper wire . . . just as that dreadful cry rose again, and then stopped quite abruptly, held for eternity at its highest note by the crack of a pistol shot.

Dr. Birdsong thrust his hand through the door and tore it open. I dashed after him, sick with fear, not daring to think, my heart pounding in my aching throat. He stopped for an instant at the hyphen door, and sprang forward again. I looked down there, when I got up to the door. A pair of dark legs and a white coat were stretched on the floor under an overturned chair.

"It's Fellowes Dunthorne!" I thought as I forced myself forward. Then I saw it wasn't. It was Yarborough. He lay motionless and limp, the blood oozing from a gash in his white head.

Dr. Birdsong was standing framed in the library door, the room dark beyond him. I crept up to him and looked past. On the grass carpet not five feet from where I was standing, glistening in the light from the game room, lay three bright pebbles. My eyes moved beyond them, slowly, as if weighted with lead, and then closed . . . but with dreadful futility. Printed in fire on my retina was still the image of Irene Winthrop lying across the hearth, unbearably motionless.

I felt Dr. Birdsong move, and opened my eyes as I heard the switch beside the door click, flooding the room with light. Irene still lay there, inert. But there was no arrow in her throat . . . just the mark made by the bullet that had gone through her heart, and in the room the heavy odor of cordite, grotesquely mingling with the smell of roses and spice pinks.

Dr. Birdsong's eyes were fixed not on Irene but on the floor, and as I followed them I saw a pearl-handled pistol lying on the thick grass carpet. It was Alan Keane's, the one he had held to his own forehead, the one that somebody had stolen from my white beaded bag in the top drawer of the mahogany dresser.

And that was not all. Backed motionless against the garden door, not three feet from that gun, was Mara Winthrop. Her dark eyes fixed on that pistol were so wide with horror that I thought she could never in all the world close them in peace again.

23

I have only the most confused picture of what went on after that. I know that as Mara slipped unconscious to the floor Dr. Birdsong cleared the room in two strides, picked her up and laid her on the sofa between the windows. And almost immediately—it seemed to me almost as if they'd been crowding the wings for some monstrous grand finale—everyone was there: Major Tillyard first, groping, desperately shaken, toward the figure huddled silently on the hearth. And Dr. Birdsong was back, keeping him from her, holding off all the others—Natalie, Mr. Dunthorne, the maid Anna and the old cook, and Dan, in the hyphen door, and in the garden door Mrs. Jellyby and the stable boy Jim and Mr. Keane.

He turned to me, his voice crackling. "Get Purcell on the phone.—Mrs. Jellyby, have Jim put Yarborough in the sofa and give him some aromatic spirits—he's in the hephen. Dan, you carry Mara upstairs and come back here. Mrs. Latham, you keep her quiet till I come up. The rest of you go in the living room and stay there."

There wasn't a sound or movement of protest as we all faded quietly out to do as we were told. No one dreamed of questioning his right to give orders, and if they had, I thought grotesquely, there was that huge crazy dog of his, ready to herd us the way they do the marked sheep in the trials in Hyde Park, his eyes, milk-blue now, alive with intelligence. And oddly it was Mara he chose—or perhaps was ordered, I'm sure I wouldn't know—to go along with. I saw him at Dan's heels as he carried the child up the old pine stairs. I saw Dan's face too, and I couldn't bear to look at it. I felt the scalding tears pouring down my face as I cranked the telephone and asked the operator for Mr. Purcell's house.

"He isn't there, ma'am," she said. "If you want him, he just went in the Fountain bar. Shall I ring him there?"

"Please do," I said. "And tell him to come out to Romney as quickly as he can. Tell him Dr. Birdsong wants him at once."

I hung up the receiver and wiped my face, and went up the third floor stairs to Mara's dormered chintz-hung room. Dan had laid her on the reeded applewood fourposter with its dotted swiss curtains and bright spread, which I saw had, with a kind of bitter irony, the old double wedding ring design the mountaineers in Tennessee use so much. He was standing beside her, rubbing her limp pale little hand, his lips pressed together, his head bent forward on his chest. The dog was sitting a little away, a dejected mirror of the man in front of him.

I crossed the room to the bed and stood there, saying nothing because there was nothing at all I could say that Dan didn't already know without my saying it. He turned away a moment. Then he said, so huskily that I could hardly hear him, "How did she get the gun?"

"It was in my bag with the letters," I said. "They're gone too."

"Then she found out he was trying to kill himself?"

I nodded. And that, of course, would be what had happened when Dr. Birdsong had seen her, less than ten minutes before.

He looked steadily at me. "We've got to keep it to ourselves, Grace. Nobody knows it but you and me and Alan. —Unless his fingerprints are on it. She wouldn't have tried to keep them off. Poor little devil."

His choked voice was almost inaudible.

He swung around abruptly and started for the door.

"I'll get hold of that gun."

"You let that gun alone!" I said sharply.

"And let those bastards hang her?" he asked, with dull fury.

"Better they than you," I retorted. "They'll never hang her anyway, and you can't tell what they might do to you. And by the way, where's Cheryl?"

He looked blank, almost stupid.

"The girl with eyes like hyacinths," I said. "Don't tell me you've forgotten her already."

He stared dumbly at me, turned and strode out. It may be entirely my disordered fancy, and heaven knows there was reason enough for it to be disordered, but I could almost swear that that impossible dog was laughing. But when I looked at him more closely he was sober again, his fringed eyes fixed anxiously on the bed.

Mara's lips were parted, and from them, inaudible if the dog hadn't pointed it out to me, came a low poignant moan, growing stronger and more heartbreaking momentarily as she toiled up out of the blessed abyss of unconsciousness. And suddenly there broke from her the most awful cry: "Mother! Alan, Alan!"

My blood froze as I grasped her struggling body and held it frantically. I'd never in my life thought I'd get to the all-time low of pleading with an animal, but I actually heard myself crying, "Oh, *won't* you get Dr. Birdsong?"

He got up immediately and trotted to the door, and I heard a sharp high-pitched bark, and another, and almost immediately there was the sound of running feet and Dr. Birdsong burst through the door.

"You've *got* to do something for her!" I said. "She'll go out of her mind—or I will! I simply can't bear it!"

He strode to the bathroom and came back in a minute drying his hands, his cuffs turned back. I watched his great sensitive fingers swab the pale flesh of her arm, sink the long needle and pump two c. c. of temporary oblivion into her writhing little body. It wasn't entirely the hypodermic that quieted her so quickly; it was also the healing power that flowed out of his rugged hands as he held her wrists in one of them, the other resting gently on her brow. We stood there on either side of the bed, waiting, until her breath came quietly again and her body relaxed gradually against the bright quilt. When I looked up from the pale mask of her pointed elfin little face his eyes, very level and compelling, were fixed on mine.

"Can you trust me now, Mrs. Latham?" he asked quietly.

I nodded.

"Were those glass buttons what you meant?"

I nodded again.

"There were three of them on the range that morning. There are six missing from the crossroad sign at the lane entrance on the county road. So there *was* a point-of-aim for whoever shot Rick. I thought you must know it."

He ignored that.

"And perhaps for somebody who was planning to shoot Irene," he said. "Until someone else barged in with the gun."

Neither of us let our eyes move to the girl on the bed.

"I hadn't thought of that," I said.

"Who did you expect to see when you came around the house, Mrs. Latham?" he asked abruptly. "And what was it that was gone?"

"I . . . can't tell you," I said. "It's not that I don't trust you—believe me. It's just that it's not my secret."

His gaze never left my face. I tried to meet it as unflinchingly as I could. Everything in me cried out that the best thing would be to tell him all I knew, from the very beginning—trust him implicitly. But there was Mara lying between us, as we stood facing each other across the white-curtained bed. And downstairs somewhere was Dan, who'd forgotten for her even his own loss of the girl with eyes like

140

faded hyacinths, the Holy Grail he'd spent two age-long years in finding only to lose again.

"I'm sorry!" I whispered.

He nodded. It had never occurred to me he'd be able to understand, but he seemed to.

"Will you stay here a while with her?" he said. "There's nobody but Mrs. Jellyby to stand by, and I'm afraid her heart won't do all these stairs."

"I'll stay," I said.

He let his fingers rest a moment on Mara's pulse, picked up a cotton blanket from the old chest at the foot of the bed and laid it over her. I watched him go toward the door, and took one impulsive step forward to call him back and tell him everything I had to tell. I caught myself just as he turned, gave me a very odd smile and went on out.

I stood there, quite still, for a long time. It wasn't only that smile that upset me. It was too intangible to mean much. It was the fact that the dog trotted out with him without so much as a backward glance or a wag of his tail. It gave me the uneasy feeling that I'd been neatly labeled—like Mrs. Jellyby's seeds—and then quietly deposited in the finished business basket. I tried to think back what it was I'd been saying.

I was still trying to, without the least success, when I heard a soft step on the stairs and then on the landing, and looked up sharply. Natalie Lane was standing in the door. She glanced around the room and took a step inside.

"Do you mind if I close this?" she asked.

I shook my head, though I did mind, really. I wanted to hear Mr. Purcell when he came, and I couldn't with the door closed.

She closed the door, came on in and looked around again.

"This is a nice room," she said calmly. "Did you ever see the horrible place Cheryl had? Full of the most god-awful late Empire monstrosities—perfectly mammoth things. It's a wonder she stuck it as long as she did. I would have taken an axe to them."

I looked at her, thinking she needn't have closed the door, if this was what she'd come up to say, especially now that Irene was dead. At the same time there floated through my mind a little scene at lunch at the Sulgrave Club one day in the early spring. Irene, looking too lovely in a pillbox hat made entirely of delphinium flowers enveloped in a veil with the most extravagant pink chenille dots all over it, had shrugged her slim elegant shoulders with that amused despair of hers and said, "It's simply that you've got to be brought up with old things to appreciate them. Poor child, she can't help it, I suppose—it

141

was silly of me to put so many of my best pieces in her room."

And Irene was dead, and Cheryl was gone.

Natalie came over to the bed, glanced down at Mara with a very perfunctory "Poor kid," moved over to one of the dormer windows and stood looking down at the gardens. After a moment she said, without turning, one hand holding to the glazed chintz curtain, the other resting on her elegantly minute waist: "Would you mind telling me what you told Fellowes Dunthorne about my father's debts, and his insurance?"

"Oh, dear!" I thought. "Does one have to go into that."

Aloud I said, "Not at all. I told him what Irene told me—that you used your father's insurance to pay back unsecured loans he'd had from friends, when you weren't legally obliged to."

She turned then, the most extraordinary smile in her really lovely hazel-green eyes.

"Did Irene tell you that?"

She laughed, a curious laugh compounded of more sardonic disillusionment than it had occurred to me could be got into one short sound.

I nodded. I was also a little annoyed.

"She didn't, I suppose, tell you it was Mr. Winthrop loaned Dad the money—and that neither of them ever thought of it as a loan, but just an additional part of my mother's share of their parents' estate . . . which she hadn't taken originally because my father was so much better off than Mr. Winthrop and didn't need it?"

I shook my head. She certainly had not.

"Or that it was Irene herself who demanded the money as soon as she came into the estate? And that I was only eighteen, and pretty broken up by Dad's . . . suicide, and didn't realize he'd only done it so I could have his insurance—and didn't know I wasn't required to pay it, legally? And didn't know it for several years?"

"Oh dear!" I said.

She came over from the window.

"Not that it mattters now. In fact it taught me more about . . . things than I'd probably ever have had sense enough to learn by myself."

She moved gracefully across the room to the door, and turned back to me. She laughed again, this time as if she was genuinely amused.

"But thanks just the same!"

"You're very welcome," I said. "Delighted to oblige at any time."

She put her hand on the old black iron latch and pressed it

down. She didn't pull the door open, but just stood there for a moment. And I was surprised to hear myself remarking in the most astonishingly casual fashion, "I take it you're planning to marry Mr. Dunthorne?"

She nodded. Then she nodded again, not emphatically exactly, but certainly not dubiously at all.

"Why?" I asked. "Because he's filthy with money?"

"Not entirely."

She smiled ironically.

"I suppose that surprises you?"

"It does, rather."

"I wonder," she said, looking at me appraisingly. "You see, Mrs. Latham, the only trouble with Fellowes Dunthorne is friends like Rick, for one thing, and for another, he actually *believes* men wear what he sees in magazines about what the well-dressed man will wear. Some day he'll learn they don't, not unless they want to be funny."

She went over to the mantel, picked up a cigarette and lighted it.

"The point about his money is first, he made it himself, and second, he's hung on to it. Furthermore, he knows how much he can drink, and he doesn't drink any more—and he's arrived at the age of forty-one without falling into one of the many matrimonial venus fly traps set for him—including my own."

"Is it just another of Irene's stories," I asked, "or could you have married Rick?"

"I didn't know she knew it," Natalie said calmly. "As a matter of fact, Rick was too like his mother to fool me. I don't want to be on the toboggan to the divorce court the minute I marry a man. Furthermore Rick drank like a fish, he'd bet on a dry leaf blowing across the street, and—if you'll let me be contemporary—he was a sucker for every blue-eyed glamour gal on Broadway."

She shook her head.

"Call me a materialist—or worse if you like—but Fellowes Dunthorne can learn everything Rick knew . . . and I can help him. Rick couldn't learn the things *he* knows, because he wasn't born with them. Fellowes thinks all this is what counts."

She waved her hand over all Romney.

"Rick thought it was eyewash. I don't think it's all that counts, but it's important, because it's decent, and . . . well, laugh if you want to, but it's—American. And I want my children to think so too. It doesn't have to make people like Irene and Rick. They can be like Dan and Cheryl."

She nodded down at the bed. "And that brat—when she finds herself."

I looked at her grinding her cigarette out on the fireplace with the tip of her gold evening sandal.

"Sermons in stones," she said with a quick smile—to my surprise. "And good in everything—a little anyway."

She opened the door, stopped abruptly and shot an alarmed backward glance at me. I'd risen, my heart standing perfectly still before it gave a cold nauseating lurch. I ran across the room, pushed her out into the hall and pulled the door firmly shut behind me. Then I rushed to the stair rail. Below me, at the bottom of the long well, focused in a square of bright light like a theater stage, was a crowd of people . . . Dr. Birdsong and Mrs. Jellyby, Mr. Keane, Major Tillyard and Dan. And suddenly, excited, strident and noisy, Mr. Purcell bolted in among them, almost dragging Alan Keane after him. The boy's white shirt was ripped half off his back, his face was ashen, his hair damp and disheveled.

Up the dark stair well came the State's Attorney's voice, harsh and contemptuous and triumphant:

"Here's your murderer. And what's more, Tillyard—and you, Birdsong—I've got the hot bonds you all insisted he never stole . . . right in the map pocket of that heap of junk he drives around in. All stowed away ready to scuttle!"

My fingers gripping the pine satin-smooth stair rail were like icicles. I turned quickly. Behind me, so quietly that I felt rather than heard it, the door had opened. Mara Keane stood in it, as silent and rigid as a pillar of stone.

24

I'm not sure, looking back on it, how we got through the rest
of that night without at least five additional unpremeditated
homicides—or at least homicide committed wilfully and without premeditation on one man by at least five others. It was
extraordinary how Mr. Purcell managed to antagonize practically everybody at Romney to a point of frenzy. It amounted
almost to a genius, some way, or so I thought until I realized
—and I don't think there's any doubt of it now, though none
of us so much as thought of it at the moment—that what he
said and did, and his whole manner and conduct, was simply
because he was more genuinely upset by Irene's death than
anyone else on the place, not even excepting Major Tillyard.
It wasn't only because Irene—as several people suggested—
had loaned him considerable amounts of money from time to
time. The local gossip that had had him in love with her for
years undoubtedly had the sharp kernel of truth in it that
gossip, no matter how little one likes to admit it, usually has.
It could hardly have been anything but the fact that he had an
almost idolatrous devotion to Romney's lovely mistress that
made him lose all his politician's suavity and lash out bitterly
at the people he thought were trying to protect her murderer.

And the first to be lashed at was poor Mr. Sam Dorsey the
sheriff. Mr. Dorsey, it appeared, having been born and
brought up in Port Tobacco, had a deep-seated sectional conviction that crime, whether chicken-stealing or homicide, unless the latter was plainly mandatory—as for instance when a
boundary or a woman's virtue was involved—was naturally
and inevitably committed by a negro. That was why he had
let Alan Keane out of jail, it was why he had watched with
slow good-natured tolerance all the crackpot business of
fingerprints and arcs and inductions that his deputy Dr.
Birdsong had prosecuted with amiable idiocy—and small success.

It was, of course, extremely unfortunate that in the first
place, Irene was murdered while he thought Mr. Purcell was
in Baltimore and while Alan was out of the jail, and in the
second place, he had been impelled to arrest Jim, the stable
boy with white buck teeth and bulging thyroid eyes, at the
very moment that Mr. Purcell was stopping Alan in his mad

flight from Romney. For Mr. Dorsey, pursuing his long-established line of reasoning, had found a lot of peacock feathers under the corn-husk mattress in Jim's room over the stable, and the plump exotic carcass of the bird itself stewing in the iron pot in the fireplace. Two and two make four, and a negro and a fifty-dollar peacock made murder, especially when the terrified boy confessed that Rick Winthrop had caught him wringing the cock's neck.

The veins stood out on Mr. Purcell's forehead like mountain ranges on a relief map.

"And he was eating its tongue on Melba toast, I suppose?" he roared.

"No, *suh!*" Jim's face was the color of a sick oyster, his eyes stood out like skinned grapes.

"Get him out of here!" Mr. Purcell bellowed. "Or I'll—"

"Or you'll have apoplexy," Mrs. Jellyby said calmly. "Go back to bed, Jim."

It was Mrs. Jellyby who had taken over Romney; and it was when that fact first struck me that I was also aware of the very curious fact that whereas Rick's death had relieved the tension in the house for a few moments, it had become infinitely more menacing as the hours went on, Irene's death on the other hand had snapped all tension completely. It was as if some extraordinary elastic that we'd all been pulling at in an unseen but desperate tug of war had suddenly been released at the other end. And it was strange that I didn't for some time realize it wasn't Irene's death alone that had released it. It was just as much, or perhaps more, the finding of that fifty thousand dollars' worth of stolen bonds in Alan's car that had done it. That, and Mara's death—for say what you please, she had died a kind of death as she stood there hearing Mr. Purcell shout that he'd found the bonds in that car.

She'd just stood there a long time, so long and so motionless that Natalie Lane, with a tact I'd not thought of her as having, had crept away out of sight, not downstairs but into one of the rooms up there, and closed the door. Mara hadn't made the least resistance as I led her back to her bed. She lay down on it, staring dry-eyed and silent up at the white muslin-covered tester. It seems to me that lately I seldom pick up a magazine without an article pointing out that doctors and clergymen say when death finally comes it's painless, that only in the struggle against it, which is still life, is there agony. That seemed to me what had happened to Mara. Everything up to now had been agony, with love struggling to believe and to live. Now that she knew, there was no longer any pain, only anesthesia, and then sleep.

146

I turned out all the lights except the one on the night table and closed the door. I knew if I were the one I should rather have been alone.

I hadn't, of course, heard what had gone on downstairs after Mr. Purcell's bomb had dropped. When I got down they were all there, and all still terribly shattered. Alan Keane stood white-faced and defiant, his eyes searching the stairs and doorways for the one dark pointed little face that even if he had been Dillinger himself he must have dreaded to see. And I was the only person there, I think, who realized that. The rest of them put it down to fear, and Mr. Purcell to natural shiftiness. Then they showed him his gun, and he cracked, and buried his face in his hands. I didn't stay. It wasn't only he that made it all too harrowing to be endured. It was his father, his face ashen, his lips drawn to a tight gray line, his hands shaking like aspens. And the others, too, who had tried so long and desperately to believe in him—Major Tillyard and Dr. Birdsong. I don't know about Mrs. Jellyby. She gave the impression that if the universe turned to spun sugar it wouldn't have altered her monumental plastic calm. Her snow-white cropped hair and her sunburned weather-beaten face above her square body were still solid and practical and invulnerable.

I went out on the porch and stood for a few moments, leaning against one of Romney's white fluted columns, look-ing down over the gardens to the Potomac. Then I wandered down to the white marble balustrade and sat there, feeling as if I'd felt the last drop of emotion that I would ever be capable of again. I looked back at Romney. It was incredible that such things could happen there, yet not change one brick or one leaf of all its beauty and all its glamour. I looked back over the dark water. A boat was going downstream. People watching from its decks, seeing Romney lighted from wing to wing and cellar to garret, would not know till they saw the morning papers that it was a dance of death going on there.

Quite abruptly Dan was standing beside me.

"Well, I guess that's that," he said, after a long time.

He was silent again.

After a few moments I said, "Dan, did you see your mother, before . . ."

He nodded. "Mara, too."

"What did she say?"

"She'd decided to divide the estate, into four parts—keep one, give me one, put one in trust for Mara as long as she didn't marry Alan. The other to go to Natalie and your kids. —She said she was tired of all this bickering."

147

"It was all right . . . about Cheryl, then?"

He shook his head.

"She wanted me to promise not to try to see her, or get in touch with her, for a year. Then, if I . . ."

He stopped.

"Did you promise?"

"A year, or ten years, won't make any difference."

I caught my breath.

"You mean you're . . . going to let her—"

"I didn't promise," he said. "That's what makes it . . . binding, now."

"I think you're crazy," I said.

"You don't understand."

"I certainly don't. You probably wouldn't marry her for a year anyway. But just letting her wander off . . . It'll serve you jolly well right if she marries on another rebound, the way she did Rick. Your mother was a whole lot smarter than you are.—I'll be glad to shut up if you'd like me to."

"No, go on," he said. "Everybody needs one salt hair shirt."

"That's exactly the trouble with you," I remarked. "Personally, I've always approved the practice of keeping the martyrs on pillars and sending their food up in baskets twice a week. —Meanwhile, if I were you, I'd go and see Mara. She knows what's happened."

"Oh, God!" he said. "Who told her?"

"It's just as well she heard it while she's still doped. If she can talk about it, that'll help too."

I stood there a little while after he'd gone, then wandered over to the terrace and sat down, leaned my head back against the green and white cushions of the long chair that Natalie had spent the hot afternoon in, and closed my eyes. I opened them again almost immediately, hearing voices.

"It isn't possible," Major Tillyard was saying. "It simply isn't possible. I think I can understand his killing Rick. After all, Rick was asking for it. He was putting the boy's father out of his living, he was spying on him and Mara. He was in the bank when the bonds were stolen. He may even have known Alan had them. It's a hard thing to say, Tom, but I don't mind telling you it was always my idea that Rick had those bonds. I've always felt guilty about not having said so. But there was Irene, and I couldn't make her suffer. That's why I tried to do as much for Alan as I could. I thought it was pride that kept him from taking help. I didn't know he was—"

He interrupted himself. "But even so . . . that poor girl! She was more like a child than a woman!"

They came onto the flagged terrace. I straightened up. They nodded to me and sat down, not seeming to mind my being there particularly.

"What will they do to him?" I asked.

"Hang him," Dr. Birdsong said laconically.

After that nobody said anything for a long time. Then Dr. Birdsong spoke.

"I still can't see Alan murdering Irene," he said. "Even granting the business of the bonds. Not unless she knew about them—and if she did, why didn't she use her knowledge, a long time ago? I think you're right about her being a child, and a child wouldn't have kept a trump like that up its sleeve."

He turned to me.

"What happened at the Fountain?" he asked quietly. "You know there's nothing to be saved anyone now."

"Alan was on the point of putting a bullet in his head," I answered. "Dan stopped him. He was going to bring him back here, but Mr. Purcell had him arrested before we got to the door."

"Is that all?"

"Except for the letters."

"What letters?"

I told him about them.

"He'd written four, when he was going to kill himself. One was to the Chews, one to his father, one to Mara. I didn't see the fourth."

He looked at me inquiringly. "Were those . . . ?"

I nodded.

"I had them. I got them from him before they took him to jail, and put them in my bag with the gun. Dan took it away from him, and I took it away from Dan—thinking it would be safer."

"You didn't see who that fourth letter was to?"

"No. I just stuffed them in my bag. When I went to get them they were gone. So was the gun. The next time I saw it was there on the library floor."

"And who were you getting them for?"

"For Alan. He said Mr. Dorsey let him out of jail to come and see his father. I suppose it was Mara, really."

Major Tillyard smiled dryly.

"I doubt if Sam Dorsey let him out. He's too scared of Purcell. Nobody would have much trouble getting out of Port

Tobacco jail. Most people they put in it are glad enough to sleep till morning."

"You don't think he just came for those letters?" Dr. Birdsong went on.

"I wouldn't know," I said. "Didn't you see him when you came out?"

He shook his head.

"I was talking to Yarborough in the kitchen."

"How is he, by the way?"

"He'll be all right if he didn't burst out all the stitches in his scalp when he came to. I don't know whether he thought Mrs. Jellyby was a ghost or what, but he about had a fit."

"Did he fall over something?" I asked.

Dr. Birdsong shook his head. "He was hit with a book end. If he didn't have the skull of a rhinoceros, he'd have been done for."

"And he doesn't know who hit him, I suppose."

"Neither who nor what. All he knows is he was in the hall locking the screen door when he heard Irene scream. He ran in as fast as he could, he says, and as he got to the middle of the hyphen he heard her scream again, and the shot. The door opened and something hit him. Purcell asked if he wasn't wearing his glasses, and he said he was. Purcell thinks, of course, that he's trying to shield Alan. It seems he's been not seeing an awful lot around here lately."

He drew a deep breath and shook his head slowly.

"And there's an odd point about that. What Purcell won't see until he gets the blood out of his eyes is that nobody could see through those glasses Yarborough wears unless he had a refraction of six point two. But they're gold-rimmed, and they once belonged to a baron. The baron also left a bottle of sleeping medicine here that almost put Yarborough and the cook to sleep permanently. Yarborough's the only one can wear the spectacles, fortunately."

I tried to think what that odd vanity of the old darky could mean.

"You really think he couldn't see who it was?" Major Tillyard asked.

"I'm sure he couldn't," Dr. Birdsong said. He smiled. "Except that he or she looked vaguely like Mrs. Jellyby. I think you can assume that from his reaction when he woke up and saw her standing by him."

He got up.

"It's those letters I want. I want to know who that fourth one was written to.—You'd better come inside Mrs. Latham. It's not too healthy out here. You know about the miasma rising from marshes? Romney has a pretty lethal brand."

150

Mr. Purcell came to the door as we started up to the house. "Oh, Tillyard!" he shouted.

Major Tillyard took a deep breath.

"I guess the wheels are turning," he said. He quickened his pace across the grass.

25

Dr. Birdsong and I went in.

"I don't see how it *can* be like this," I said hopelessly.

"Who knew about those letters, Mrs. Latham?" he asked.

"Just Dan and me and Alan. I mean, we're the only ones who knew what they were, or knew he'd tried to kill himself."

"You haven't told anybody about that?"

"Of course not."

"And who saw you take them from him?—I suppose you pretended you'd given them to him to mail."

I nodded, and tried to think.

"The Chews, Mr. Purcell, Dan, Mara, Cheryl—not Major Tillyard, he didn't come in till later—and Mr. Dorsey."

He thought a moment. "Then the only people who *didn't* know are Natalie, Dunthorne, the major, and Keane."

I nodded again.

"I wish you'd told me about that point-of-aim business," he said abruptly.

"I thought you knew. Anyway, would it have made any difference if I had?"

He shrugged. "Considerable."

"The only difference I can see is that the implication would have been stronger in your mind that Irene and Mara and Cheryl were involved."

He nodded, rather grimly.

"Just what we were meant to think from the beginning."

I don't know what there was about the way he said that, but I stopped for an instant and stared up at him, a kind of hope beginning to swell in my heart.

"And . . . the three in the library?" I asked.

He didn't answer for a moment. Then he said, slowly, "This whole point-of-aim business is a pretty tricky one. There are several possible explanations for those discs in the library. One: somebody was getting ready to kill Irene just the way Rick was killed, and changed horses in mid-stream when the gun turned up. Or two: somebody else turned up with the gun and did the job instead."

He hesitated a moment, and then looked down at me rather strangely.

"Or what would you think, Mrs. Latham, of Number

Three: they were put there solely to point out that we hadn't paid enough attention to them in the first murder?"

I tried to think something about that, and couldn't. "I . . I wouldn't know at all," I said. "—You think there were two people who would have killed Irene."

He nodded, very sardonically.

"I could name half a dozen without the least trouble—and so could you. And with motives not many people would resist forever. Alan, Mara, Dan, Mr. Keane, Natalie—"

"Natalie?"

"She's been living on bread and rat cheese a long time, Mrs. Latham. She comes into quite a bit of money now Irene's dead. If Irene had lived, she'd have spent Natalie's share under the guise of gifts, and probably billed her for a few hundred over, if she'd ever got around to dividing the estate. Natalie could do with some hard cash. Furthermore, Yarborough tells me they staged a fight shortly after Irene came back from town this afternoon in which even Irene lost her emper."

I wondered about that, knowing a good deal more about it, possibly, than he did.

"Do you know where Cheryl is?" I asked suddenly.

"She went out to the county road with the milk truck this evening. They left her there. She probably got a lift to Port Tobacco, and took a bus to Washington. She wouldn't let Jim take her in. Purcell will get around to that soon enough. I'm surprised he hasn't already."

We were almost to the porch.

"Dr. Birdsong," I said, "—Rick wrote a letter to Mr. Dunhorne the night before he came, telling him not to come."

"No, he didn't," he answered quietly. "That's the letter Tillyard posted. I got in touch with the District Attorney in New York, and his office collected the letter. There wasn't a message of any kind in it—just a check for five hundred, made out to Rick by Irene and endorsed to Dunthorne."

"But he came out as far as the tree, that night, and Dan ound a letter half-written . . ."

"I know," he said. "He admits he came out to the tree. Which was helpful, because I had some idea that another person might have borrowed his car. And I saw that letter in Rick's room. I wondered if you and Dan had picked it up. Also the charred remains of another in the fireplace. Where was the half-written one when you saw it?"

"Under the desk pad."

He smiled. "It was in the waste basket, early this morning." I stopped on the stone steps.

"Look, Dr. Birdsong," I said. "Are you being mysterious,

153

by any chance? Alan Keane couldn't possibly have done that, if that's what you mean—he hardly dared set foot in the house."

He stopped too, looking down at me.

"My dear Mrs. Latham, your trouble is the trouble with all women. Your emotions are like Yarborough's glasses—they blind you, and it isn't until evidence hits you a blow on the skull that you're willing to see it. Just because Alan Keane stole some bonds from the Port Tobacco bank three years ago doesn't prove that he killed Rick and Irene."

He smiled that very grim smile of his.

"I've given you one very definite clue. There's another one —a kind of clue—that's been steadily under your nose . . . right down there in the dining room . . . all this time; and you won't as much as look at it."

I couldn't, of course, try as I might, get the shadowiest idea of what he meant. I did think of something else.

"You know," I said, "there's one other piece of information. I got it by eavesdropping. It will have to come out sooner or later. If I tell it to you, will you promise, on your honor as a doctor, not to use it unless you can use it *for* the persons it chiefly affects?"

He looked at me a moment.

"I promise you that."

"Mara and Alan are married.—Or did you know it?"

He didn't answer for a little.

"You're quite sure of that? I mean, legally?"

I nodded.

"Mara told Alan that Rick's threatening to tell Irene about it was what made Cheryl come back that night. I don't know whether it was after Rick's quarrel with Mr. Keane and Alan, or before. I suppose you know about that, at any rate."

"I do, but Purcell doesn't," Dr. Birdsong said. He stood there filling his pipe.

"If you would look back, Mrs. Latham, and see what happened before each of these people was murdered, I think you'd see something. I think also that if I were you, I'd keep my mouth shut. And furthermore, I think if I were you I'd go to bed. And take a couple of these."

He smiled. "Afraid?"

I'm not sure that my knees weren't a little weak, actually.

He opened the torn screen door, not hooked now that old Yarborough was lying on his cornhusk mattress like a white turbanned mummy. I remember wondering suddenly if the pantry had got full of flies and wasps.

"Thanks for telling me about Mara," he said quietly. The

154

last I saw of him that night he was going slowly up the third floor stairs.

I was glad to find I did wake up, the next morning, because I took the two pills, and it would have been mortifying to discover—or not to discover—that I'd been too trusting. As I went down to breakfast I glanced out of the Palladian window and saw the dog sitting on his haunches in the drive. I raised the window quietly and pressed my nose against the screen. There on the grassy range was Dr. Birdsong. He was down on his knees, acting very much as if he were Nebuchadnezzar.

I went downstairs and out onto the porch.

"What are you doing?" I called.

"Testing your observations," he said with a grin. He got up and came back to the porch, and held out his cupped hand for me to look into. There were several minute white specks on his palm.

"Dried paint," he said in an undertone. He glanced inside the cool quiet hall. "—Will you do one more thing for me?"

I nodded.

"Try and remember what everybody had on the night Rick was killed. Do you think you can?"

"Oh, dear," I said. "It isn't just to test my I. Q.? Because it's lower than most people think."

He shook his head.

"By no means. I'm going to do a little scientific vacuum cleaning. Somebody carried those glass pellets around in something before he deposited them. You'd be surprised at how many people have been hanged for a bit of fluff from a pocket or a trouser-cuff."

"Do we have to hang somebody?" I asked. It sounds, I suppose, much more flippant than I felt.

He nodded coolly: his hard lean corrugated face was set like iron.

"We have to hang somebody," he said quietly. "And not so much for the murder of those two people—which I gather you've noted doesn't distress me very much—as for . . . something else. Including one simple little act that took place during your scene at the Fountain yesterday. It was about as devilish as anything I've ever heard of."

His voice was icy spray against my face.

"I think I would like a cup of coffee," I said.

He followed me into the hall and out to the terrace. Mara was sitting at the table, a cup of coffee and a golden juicy melon in front of her, both untouched. Her face under her dusky hair had shrunk so that there was almost nothing to it

155

except two enormous dark eyes, staring, fixed and unseeing, in front of her.

Dr. Birdsong lifted her hand lying limp on the table and held his fingers to her pulse. Then he stood there, holding it in his own hands until some of his electric energy seemed to communicate itself to her. She looked up and smiled wanly.

"Where's Cheryl?" she asked suddenly. "Can't somebody bring her back?"

She picked up her spoon.

"Though I don't suppose she'll ever want to come back to this terrible place."

"Where is her home?" Dr. Birdsong asked. He took the cup of fragrant coffee I handed him.

"She hasn't got one," Mara said. "She was brought up by a bank, in New York, in boarding school and summer camps. When she was twenty-one they sent her a check for $1742.38. She went abroad on it—she thought it would be fun to start from scratch. She got back to New York with some French clothes and the $2.38, I guess."

She lifted her spoon to her lips and put it down again, the melon untasted.

"I don't think she's got that much, now," she said bitterly. "I know she hasn't any clothes, except the ones she brought here, and just enough to keep the authorities from arresting us for running a nudist camp. So I suppose she's gone wherever it's easiest to start from scratch again.—Oh, it's beastly the way everybody treated her!"

And then she put her head suddenly down on the table and broke into a torrent of tears. I got up. Dr. Birdsong, I was sure, was much better at that sort of thing than I was. I took my coffee and a piece of toast out on the terrace steps. The peacocks out there in the sunlit gardens, training up and down with their scurrying entourage of hens and chickens, seemed to me a curiously enviable tribe. At the end of the garden I saw Mrs. Jellyby's peaked sombrero, and heard her calling the flock to their feeding ground.

Suddenly Mara's voice rose clear and passionate: "I don't believe it, I'll never believe it till he tells me with his own lips! How could he have gone to Grace's room to get the gun?"

"Natalie says she saw him upstairs, Mara," Dr. Birdsong's calm voice said. "He wanted those letters—he had to get them. He had to take the risk, to keep—"

The door banged shut again. I got up, wondering if that was the evidence that was under my nose and that I couldn't see because I was blinded by emotion.

At the end of the garden I saw Mrs. Jellyby setting back toward her cabin under the weeping willow, and almost unconsciously I set out toward it myself. I opened the little gate into her garden and walked down the herringbone path to the door. It was open, and I stopped abruptly as I came up to it, staring in. Mrs. Jellyby was seated on her stool at the end of the table. Mr. Keane was there too, and—of all people under the sun—the elegant Mr. Dunthorne, done up in white linen plus fours and the loudest checked jacket I've ever had the pleasure of seeing off Epsom Downs. They each had a little tin of seeds, and a little stack of white cotton sacks, and a pile of labels. And I stood there speechless for a minute, watching them put a spoonful of seeds in a little bag, pull the string tight, tag it, put it in the osier basket, and pick up the spoon and another little sack.

Mrs. Jellyby looked up at me.

"Has Mara come down?" she asked brusquely.

I nodded.

She pushed her stool back, got down from it and picked up her sombrero.

"I'll be back," she said.

Mr. Keane's eyes moved up from his tray of seeds and followed her, like an injured dog's. He got up too, put on his hat and went out after her.

26

Mr. Dunthorne scratched his head. I sat down on Mrs. Jellyby's stool, picked up her spoon, filled a sack, labeled it with a tag on which was written, in her extraordinary copper-plate script, "Cypress Vine from Romney," and put it with the others.

"This old lady's the only person I ever heard of that Rick had any real respect for," Mr. Dunthorne said abruptly. He put a spoonful of larkspur seeds into a bag and labeled it. "Rick said they liked her best when their mother used to go down to Aiken or up to Bar Harbor, and she used to eat up at the house. They'd sit around and play rummy, or talk—"

He stopped suddenly. "Hey, what's that?"

He got up and leaned across the table.

"What?" I said.

"In the bottom of your basket."

He thrust his spoon down in the millions of tiny black seeds in my wooden grain measure and stirred it around.

"There," he said. "Looks like a diamond, but it's just glass. I guess she puts prizes in some bags."

He sat down again. I couldn't say a single word, for some time. All I could do was sit staring helplessly at the two glass nodules that Mr. Dunthorne's inquisitive spoon had turned up —knowing that in the bottom there was another one, knowing too that Mrs. Jellyby had thought they were very safe at the bottom of the measure she herself was working on.

Mr. Dunthorne fortunately wasn't looking at me. He was plainly fascinated by the job of putting a teaspoonful of larkspur seeds into a little cotton bag.

I covered the discs over again.

"Probably came up from the barn in the measure," I said, when I'd found my voice. In my mind I could see that young cop sitting on the running board of the car Mr. Purcell had come in, and at the end of the range Rick's body cold and stiff, covered with a tarpaulin, and Mrs. Jellyby down there, by the box alleys. I wondered what had she known? Which of the children she had raised was she now struggling to protect? What—above all—did she think now, when three more glass pebbles had appeared with yet another murder?

Out the door I could see her heavy tweed figure with that straw sombrero coming slowly back to the cabin through the lanes of bright flowers—scarlet poppies, zinnias, marigolds. I got off her stool and sat down at the shallow pan Mr. Keane had been working on, trying to still the ache in his heart. And suddenly it occurred to me—was all of this for that purpose I'd been thinking of? Or had Mrs. Jellyby herself for many years been stilling an ache in her own heart, with her bags of seeds and her mothering of the little brood in the great house, whose own mother had no gift for the whole business of mothering?

I glanced at Mr. Fellowes Dunthorne. There was certainly no ache in his heart—just puzzlement. "If she *sold* these damn seeds, I could figure it out," he said. "But she just *gives* them away."

"I know," I said. "And without being asked, either."

Mrs. Jellyby came down the path, more slowly than I'd ever seen her walk before. She hung her hat on the door. I felt her eyes move from the wooden measure to her spoon to Fellowes Dunthorne to me.

"They're asking for you at the house, Mr. Dunthorne," she said. And when he'd left she sat down on her stool and went back to her task.

"What did you think of Irene, Mrs. Jellyby?" I asked suddenly. I hadn't meant to, and I was sorry the instant the words were out of my mouth. Her face was drawn in a little spasm of pain.

"I'm sorry!" I said.

A pair of yellow butterflies flew in the door and out again. Great black and gold bumblebees lighted on the larkspur, bending their blue spears almost to the ground.

"She was wilful and capricious even when she was a baby," Mrs. Jellyby said slowly.

Then her eyes, so patient and so full of old pain, met mine.

"I was her mother, Grace.—And no better at the job than she's been. Except that I was very young then . . . and very ignorant."

I sat there staring at her, quite speechless, I should have thought, if I hadn't heard my own voice, barely audible, saying, "Mr. Winthrop . . . did he . . . ?"

"Irene never knew he knew," she said quietly. "None of the children must ever know."

Her hands gave up their mechanical dipping and tying, and lay still on the table. She sat there, her face as impassive as a square of rawhide. Only her eyes lived, gazing down the years. After a long time she said, "Go tell Tom Birdsong I want to see him."

I went out, but I didn't, as a matter of fact, have a chance to tell him just then. I realized even before I opened the big door of Romney that something was happening. Mr. Purcell's

159

car was in the drive, the motor still running, and inside I could hear his voice. He wasn't shouting now, and the effect was rather more disturbing. I hurried through the hall to the sitting room, almost as frightened, I think, as I'd been the night before, waiting for Dr. Birdsong to crash through that hooked screen door.

Mara was standing in the middle of the room, steadying herself against a mahogany Pembroke table. Dan beside her had his arm around her shoulders, his face almost as bloodless as hers. The State's Attorney, his hands in his white linen pockets, rocking back and forth on his brown and white brogues on the hearth, had a look on his face that I couldn't even attempt to describe. It wasn't only anger, and triumph, but more impersonal, in some way, than either. It made me think of the way a man would look who'd thrown every possession he had in the world into the pot, and won.

Major Tillyard was beside him, his face still gray from his sleepless vigil beside Irene's body. Dr. Birdsong looked on, casual and inscrutable and detached. And at the end of the room Natalie and Mr. Dunthorne were standing, not, I thought, unlike a couple of people who in all likelihood had got something for nothing, and were just waiting to take over as soon as the messy procedure of eviction was over.

"I understand your feelings, all right, Dan," Mr. Purcell was saying, not unkindly. "But I've got my job to do. Friendship doesn't change the picture."

"But you're crazy, Purcell!" Dan said angrily.

"That's for the grand jury to say. You just don't know what's been going on around here for the last three years. There's not a shadow of doubt Mara's known all along that Alan had those bonds. She was getting ready to run away with him last night. Her bag was in the back of his car and the bonds were in the map pocket."

The table scraped along the wide boards of the old floor as Mara swayed. Dan's arm tightened around her shoulders.

"And this gun. It's got her name on it too, like that bag— only she tried to wipe these off. Her fingerprints—all over it, smudged on the grip. Oh, I don't say she planned to kill your mother.—Mara, the smart thing for you to do is come clean, and admit that when your mother put it to you that it was either giving up Alan Keane or giving up your share of the estate, you saw red."

"That's a lie!" Dan said hotly. "I was there when Mother told her that. She didn't do a damn thing but walk out."

"All right, Dan—she walked out. But both she and Alan walked in again. His prints are on the library mantel and on

160

the table.—You don't deny he was in the library, do you, Mara?"

Her "No" was hardly audible, her lips scarcely moving.

Purcell took a step toward her.

"And you thought if you told your mother you were married, it might change things—didn't you?"

She nodded slowly, her eyes closed, tears crowding under her short thick black lashes. Dan stared at her, his face blank, his arm around her shoulders loosening. She didn't look at him, or move a muscle to indicate she hadn't known that Mr. Purcell or any of us had known. Major Tillyard drew his hand slowly across his forehead. I couldn't tell whether he'd known too, or whether he hadn't.

"So that when it was a question of your husband or your mother—"

Mara threw back her dark little head suddenly, desperately.

"I don't care what you do with me," she cried, "only quit *talking!* Quit, I say! I didn't do it, I tell you! I didn't do it! But *quit* talking about it!"

"All right," Mr. Purcell said quietly. "If you didn't, Alan did. And you know he did do it—you knew he had the money! I think you'd better come along with me."

"You haven't got any place in that stinking jail for a woman," Dr. Birdsong said abruptly. "You can leave the girl here."

"She can stay here till somebody takes her to Baltimore," Mr. Purcell said. "And now I want you to tell me where Cheryl is."

"I've told you I don't know!" Mara cried; and Dan, who'd gone to the table in the corner and picked up the telephone, put it down and strode back.

"What do you want Cheryl for?" he said.

"You seem awfully interested in the young lady, Dan," Mr. Purcell snapped.

"I am. So what?"

"So how many of you are accessories—before and after the fact—to the murder of your brother Rick and your mother? —And perhaps *you* know where she is?"

Dan was quite white, but I thanked heaven he'd got control of himself again.

"It just happens that I don't," he said quietly.

Mr. Purcell's eyebrows raised. "The Department of Justice will find her quick enough."

Dan's face turned a dark unpleasant red. I had the feeling that if Mr. Purcell were smart he'd use a little less of the mailed fist—his suit was so beautifully white and pressed, his gray hair so perfectly in place. I take it Dr. Birdsong may have had much the same idea. At any rate it was he who brought this scene to an end.

"Don't you think, Purcell," he said, with a kind of unusual amiability, and even suavity, "you're making a mistake in assuming that because Alan stole those bonds, he necessarily committed murder? It's my guess you can settle it all quite simply . . ."

"Yes?" Mr. Purcell said. His voice had a very heavy ironic politeness.

"I think so."

Dr. Birdsong's voice was imperturbable.

"You can settle it by simply reading the confession Alan wrote yesterday—before Mrs. Latham and Dan stopped him from killing himself, at the Fountain."

I may be mistaken, but I certainly thought Mr. Purcell gave a violent start.

"What's that?" he said harshly.

"He wrote several letters. It was the desperate necessity of getting them back—from Mrs. Latham's bag—that brought him out here last night. Unfortunately . . . he didn't get them. Someone else had got them."

Mr. Purcell the State's Attorney gave me what I can only describe as a very dirty look, and turned back.

"What's in them?"

"I don't know," Dr. Birdsong said calmly. "I haven't read them. They aren't addressed to me. One of them is addressed to you, and it's quite thick. My guess would be that it confirms the belief Tillyard and I have had for a long time, as you know—that he wasn't alone in taking that money. There's no doubt he was protecting somebody else. That ought to come out. . . ."

He stopped for a moment, and went on slowly:

"Unless, of course, Tillyard is right in thinking the motive behind Rick's murder was to get the entire possession of the bonds."

The only sound in the room was the silvery tickety-tock of the French clock in the hanging corner cupboard.

"Where are those letters?" Mr. Purcell demanded. His face was flushed, and he spoke with a restrained violence.

"I . . . they're coming along later," Dr. Birdsong said. He looked at his watch with great deliberation.

27

The next shock I got came only a little while after that. Dr. Birdsong had gone down to Mrs. Jellyby's. I saw his great figure disappear through the arborvitae, his dog padding along at his heels. Major Tillyard was standing with his foot on the running board of Mr. Purcell's car, talking to him very vigorously. Mr. Purcell, one hand on the gear shift and his clutch just enough engaged so that his car kept inching forward, was obviously impatient to be gone, and I supposed annoyed at what he thought was an attempt to apply family pressure. Natalie had disappeared, and Mr. Fellowes Dunthorne had set out somewhere, with a sort of paddocky look about him—though I never did find out if he could keep his seat if he once actually got on a horse.

As I started back into the house I saw Dan barge out of the sitting room and out the front door, giving the screen a bang that would have shaken an ordinary house to its roots, and stride down toward the river through the long alley of green box. A peacock strutting in the sun quickened his pace, and then folded his glittering fan and scuttled off in alarm. I looked in the sitting-room door. Mara was still standing in the middle of the room, her hands hanging at her sides. She turned her dark little face wretchedly as I came in.

"Dan being the heavy brother?" I inquired casually.

She nodded. Then she came over and sat down on the edge of the love seat, where I'd sat when I first saw Dr. Birdsong and that fantastic dog.

"Grace," she said. "Is it true they can't make me . . . give evidence about Alan, because we're . . . married?"

"It is," I said.

"But they'll let me—I mean, they won't make me not, will they?"

"Oh, *dear!*" I thought. I stared at her open-mouthed. "Why?" I asked. "Do you want to?"

When she nodded I really thought I was definitely losing my mind.

"You see—I *did* tell Mother I'd married him. I was angry, and I didn't care what I said."

She caught her lower lip in her white teeth and looked away.

"But . . . oh, Grace, I know Dan doesn't believe it, and

163

nobody else will, but it's true . . . Mother just stopped saying all the things she'd been saying, and stood looking at me, and then all of a sudden she put her arms around me, and kept saying, 'My poor lamb, why didn't you tell me!' She was marvelous, Grace—she really was! Just like she used to be. I went to find Alan, but . . . he wasn't there, and when I got almost back I heard . . . I heard her scream, and just as I got to the door I heard that shot, and the lights went out. . . ."

Her fingers gripping my hand were like cold ribbons of steel.

"It couldn't have been Alan, Grace, it couldn't! Because Mother was going to help us—you've got to believe me, Grace!"

"Then you weren't going away with him?" I asked.

"Oh, no, no! Those were Cheryl's clothes in his car. Her bags were down in the storeroom. She borrowed one of mine. Alan was going to take her to Washington. We put it in the car before we went to the Fountain, just before they arrested him. And she had to come back here. But if I told Mr. Purcell that, he'd think she—"

"And those fingerprints on the gun?"

She nodded.

"They're mine. Oh, Grace, I did an awful thing! Don't be cross, please—but I saw those letters when Alan gave them to you. It was his handwriting on them. I . . . I had to see them, so I took them. I'd been so afraid that was what he'd do. And I knew the gun was his too. I did pick it up, but I didn't take it. I only took the letters."

"Have you got them now?"

She shook her head.

"Where are they?"

"I don't know," she said. "Oh, Grace—I'm so afraid."

She buried her dusky head in my lap and lay there, perfectly still, for a long time. Then she raised her head. "Grace —go talk to Dan. He didn't mean to be so beastly. It's just because he really cared a lot about Mother, and because he's almost out of his mind about Cheryl.—What if they should take her to prison?"

"Don't be silly," I said. "She wasn't even on the place last night."

"Yes, she was. Alan picked her up in the road and brought her back. He left her in the car just in the drive. He was going to take her back. I don't know what happened, because she couldn't have been in the car when Mr. Purcell stopped Alan, or he'd have said so."

I gave up trying to think about anything, with that, and

164

went out. Dan was sitting on the float, in exactly the same spot and in exactly the same attitude that I'd found him in the morning Dr. Birdsong had quietly wiped the brand of Cain off his forehead.

"If there was only something anybody could do, Grace," he groaned.

"In a year you can start hunting for Cheryl again," I said, rather callously, probably.

He shook his head.

"I'd never have the crust to look her in the face again," he said despondently. "Look—do you think Mara knew the kid had those bonds?"

"I think the less we speculate about what Mara knows, the happier we'll all be, Dan," I said. "I also think if you got it into your head that she's grown up a lot further and a lot faster than anybody else around here, you'll make a lot more sense than you're doing now. Just think of a few of the things you've heard about a woman in love, and remember that there's nothing Mara won't do to save Alan, or try to—even if he'd left the place a complete shambles."

That was the first time I'd realized how little I myself believed of the story Mara had just been telling me.

It seemed to me that many years got mixed up in the time span of Romney that afternoon. It was like watching a never-ending slow-motion moving picture of a day in the country, where nothing ever happens but you don't dare take your eyes off it, because you know something is going to happen, suddenly and inexorably, that will immeasurably change all the rest of your life.

People kept coming and going. Mr. Dunthorne kept coming and going in different sets of extraordinary clothes, as if he thought that if he'd just the right combination of plaids and checks, everything would be all right again. Dr. Birdsong and Major Tillyard kept coming and going, or staying closeted with Dan and a man who'd come down from New York who had been in charge of Irene's affairs. Natalie sat in the long chair under the mimosa tree with her white-rimmed sun glasses. Mr. Keane chugged monotonously up and down between the rows of corn with the yellow cultivator, and Mrs. Jellyby went around untying all the little red strings she'd tied on the sweet peas she'd intended saving for seed. Mara sat all afternoon beside Yarborough's bed in the stuffy room over the kitchen, putting witch hazel fomentations on his splitting old head.

Once just before supper Dr. Birdsong and I were alone on

165

the front porch. He was filling his pipe from the old mended oilskin pouch.

"Mrs. Jellyby told me she'd told you," he said quietly, without looking up.

I didn't say anything. He glanced around at me and smiled a little. "And now it's in the limbo of forgotten things?"

I nodded as the supper gong rang.

Then the sun went down behind the blue Virginia hills beyond the Potomac, and the fireflies rose out of the dark box and along the smooth lawns. The peacocks quit training up and down and took to the branches of Romney Oak, and roosted there like great black birds of prey. And it seemed to me that an ominous muted sense of culmination settled over Romney Marsh.

I don't know just how it had occurred to any of us that those letters were going to come into Dr. Birdsong's possession . . . whether they were going to drop from the sky, or whether there'd be a sudden materializing of trumpets from the spirit world and when the lights went on there they'd be on the dining room table. He and Major Tillyard sat out in the hall all evening, just waiting. At ten o'clock, when Jim came for the mail pouch and brought Major Tillyard's car for him to go and get Mr. Purcell, I for one was on the point of nervous prostration. Dr. Birdsong came out onto the portico where Dan and I were sitting, and glanced at his watch.

"Would you like to go down to Mr. Keane's with me?" he asked.

We got up. I could see from the look on Dan's face that he was as taken aback as I was. Neither of us said anything. We followed Dr. Birdsong around the house and down the lane to the tenant house.

It was dark except for a single unshaded bulb in the kitchen, and that had just been turned on, because it was still swinging back and forth across the window when we came into the fenced yard and Mr. Keane's little rabbit hound bitch wriggled forward on her belly to greet us. Dr. Birdsong went quietly into the hall, with Dan and me on his heels. His dog had stopped outside the gate, as if his personal ethic precluded late calls on rabbit dogs. Farther along the lane the white barn loomed like a great pale ghost. Beyond it, in the paddock, a horse whinnied and stamped. Except for all farm odors and sounds the place was like a deserted ranch on a painted desert. I'd never realized how far away the big house was, or how secluded in its vines and trees and boxwood gardens. Its two broad flat chimneys were lost in the leaves.

I saw Dr. Birdsong feel along the side of the door for the light switch, and waited for him to turn on the light. But he didn't. He just motioned us in, and stood there, in the dark doorway. We stood there too, until Dan, outlined in the window, turned suddenly.

"Look," he said, "what *is* this? If you know who killed my mother and Rick, why in God's name don't you say so, and cut out all this Fu Manchu.—Or do you know?"

"I do know," Dr. Birdsong said gravely. "I have known for some time. In a sense I'm . . . responsible for your mother's death, even though it was something I couldn't possibly have foreseen. And it happened because I've been trying to save your sister—and I'm still doing it . . . and trying to save Cheryl."

The silence in the room was as profound as the darkness that hid our faces from each other.

28

It seemed an age before he spoke again.

"Three years ago," he said then, very quietly, "—just two weeks before you went abroad, Dan—fifty thousand dollars' worth of bonds were stolen from the Merchant's Bank in Port Tobacco. Alan Keane was sent to prison. He was let out after thirteen months of his sentence because some of us didn't think he stole those bonds. For three years the bonds have been missing. Several people have thought Alan Keane has known a lot he's never said, because he didn't dare say it, without proof he didn't have. And for the simple reason that no one in the world would have believed him."

As he paused I could feel him looking steadily from one to the other of us.

"But he wrote a letter to Purcell, just before he put a gun to his head, knowing, I suppose, that a dying man's word has a special truth—even a special legal truth. And that letter's out there now, in the mail bag Jim collected from the hall this evening at ten o'clock. It's in the mail, going to Purcell. And the person who can't let that letter get to Purcell is the one who murdered Rick because Rick had persuaded his mother to divide the estate, and who murdered Irene because after Rick's death she'd decided again to divide the estate so you could each find salvation in your own way—herself and Tillyard, you and Cheryl, Mara and Alan, and Natalie. She had to die because she made that decision—for if she did that, that fifty thousand dollars' worth of bonds that she herself had been holding, in complete ignorance of their origin, for nearly three whole years, would come to light.

"Alan Keane didn't put those bonds in his car. His hand was not the hand that held and drove that hunting arrow into Rick's throat, and left three bright pebbles in the grass to make us think your mother, or your sister, or Cheryl, had *shot* Rick, and put the lighter under him to make us think he could be shot at night. Nor was it Alan Keane who slipped into Mrs. Latham's room to get the letters, having seen her put them in her bag at the Fountain Inn, and found the letters gone but the pistol still there, with Alan's fingerprints still on it.—And that person knows those letters are in the mail sack, hanging in there, in the tack room in the barn."

The room was very still. I peered into the darkness, my

eyes aching, trying to see their faces. Somewhere—like a door close at hand shutting quietly, or one at a distance opening— there came a sound. We waited. I could hear my own heart pounding, and the clock on the wall ticking. Then I heard Dr. Birdsong whistle softly, and through the open door I saw that dog of his get to his feet, hesitate, and set off toward the barn. Then, as sharp and urgent as a fire bell in a house filled with smoke, an alarm above the door clanged, and I saw Dr. Birdsong's arm shoot out and jerk down a switch, and suddenly the whole world, it seemed to me, was filled with white light.

I turned quickly. Dan wasn't in the room. I stood, it seemed to me for ages, leaden-footed, immovable. Dr. Birdsong went deliberately to the door. I ran up to him and peered out, almost blinded, across the barnyard as brilliantly white as noonday in the desert. The dog gave a high-pitched bark and dashed forward to the barn door, and stopped, his head thrust through the door, open just enough for a man's body to slip through. He dropped back, barking frantically, jumped forward, and back again. Dr. Birdsong went out, walking slowly toward the door, and I went after him, with a confused and frightened sense of other people coming behind me. He came to a halt at the edge of the whitewashed enclosure, hesitated a moment, and whistled. The dog, every hair on his back bristling, his long pinkish tongue dripping, his eyes glittering through their gray fringe, came back reluctantly.

Dr. Birdsong went forward slowly toward the door, cautiously and steadily, his right hand in his jacket pocket.

On the threshold he stopped, and went on again. I saw him roll the white broad door back on its oiled runners, take one step into the barn, and stop abruptly.

He stood there without moving for so long a time that I ran across that flood-lit yard and came up by his side. And I caught at his arm again, just as I'd done when I'd heard that cry that was not the cry of a peacock . . . catching my breath and trying to stop the beating of my heart, and wishing I'd stayed back there in the tenant house, or anywhere.

The body of a man was hanging motionless from the hay trap above the broad center aisle—motionless, except that it was still swinging slowly around. I stared at it in a kind of dreadful fascination, seeing the leather straps of the mail pouch fixed over the old oak beam, and suspended from it by them . . . and still, it came to me with an incredible grotesqueness, rather prosperous and self-satisfied . . . the body of Sidney Tillyard.

I closed my eyes just as I saw Dan come around the side of

169

the barn, and opened them again to see him and Dr. Birdsong mercifully rolling the great white door shut.

It was the next morning in Mr. Purcell's office across from the Fountain Inn in Port Tobacco that Dr. Birdsong, Dan and I stayed on after the State's Attorney had formally released Alan Keane, and he and his father had gone back to Romney together. Mr. Purcell was still pretty dazed. For three years he had talked over every phase of Alan's affair with Major Tillyard; and you could see by looking at him that he'd spent a sleepless night just now, going back over it, trying to see how much and in what ways he'd been misled.

"There were two interesting initial fallacies about this affair," Dr. Birdsong said. "That a man who defalcates inevitably loses money, and that he doesn't take more than he needs. Three years ago Tillyard's affairs were in perfect order. He opened all his private books to the Department of Justice. There was no evidence he'd need money, until much later, and then only a few thousands. The first time he put up collateral in bonds registered in Irene's name, you looked into it, Purcell, you remember; but Irene said it was all quite regular, and you knew she loaned money to her friends— she'd loaned money to you. Tillyard knew Irene was a complete miser—he told me so, in fact. It was perfectly simple to trade her bonds, a few thousands at a time, have her send him the coupons, which he took up out of his own pocket and destroyed. Irene, who knew all about keeping money and nothing about finance, never questioned, I imagine, that his interest in helping her was because he was going to marry her. Which in a sense was true."

He took out his oilskin pouch mended with adhesive tape and unrolled it thoughtfully.

"If after he'd doubled that fifty thousand—and he never had a loss—he'd been content to stop, trade back good bonds for the hot bonds, destroy them or have them turn up in an ash can in Baltimore, everything would have been invulnerable; but he couldn't bring himself to it . . . until it was too late.

"When Rick forced himself into the picture then, Tillyard jumped at what looked like a perfectly simple and permanent way out. That tree going down was like a sign from heaven: it gave him a stunning alibi. Well, every day we sat out there looking at the river, and every day we saw that painting of General Washington waving good-bye from his barge. It never occurred to anybody—not to me until Cheryl brought out that perfectly damning and conclusive fact about the gold lighter—that from Tillyard's place across Potobac Creek,

Romney is eight miles distant by car, and three-quarters of a mile by water. Tillyard didn't have a car, but he did have a boat. He came to Romney in it, stabbed Rick with a hunting arrow he'd probably had for years, and left the same way. He didn't need the tree, in fact; he could have left his car in a garage to be serviced. That Rick had started chopping the tree down was a bit of superfluous luck. And Rick was doing it for the quite simple reason that half the trees along the lane are over a hundred years old and most of them rotten. He'd been talking about doing it for days, and he gave up on that one when the storm was coming along, planning to go back to it.

"And using me for his alibi was just more of the same. I'd guess that when he said he was going back to see Rick, he gave him the note we found burned in the fireplace, making an appointment. He could have offered any number of things as bait. Rick's letter to Dunthorne, that Tillyard said Rick asked him to mail, was the one Dan found on the desk. Rick wasn't sending it, because he knew Dunthorne would be down in the morning; he'd called him in New York, he'd told Natalie he was coming. It was too late to try to head him off. He'd got the check from Irene that Tillyard did mail, but there was no use sending it.

"That part was opportunist, but the whole thing had been deliberately planned. Mara's glove, that I've seen a thousand times lying on the sofa in the hall with her riding crop and hat, the lighter, the alibi, the arrow. Then came the letters."

Dr. Birdsong turned to me with an amused smile.

"You told me Tillyard came in, at the Fountain, *after* you'd got those letters from Alan. If you'll think back—as I found out by interviewing the Chews—you'll recall he *spoke up* after that. He was already there before anyone noticed him. There's no doubt he saw you put them in your bag.

"Those letters, of course, were mixed up with the whole business of Rick and Alan. There's no doubt Rick honestly believed Alan had stolen the bonds, added to which there was all the business of Alan and Mara. Alan now admits he always thought Rick stole them. You'll recall it was just after their disappearance that Rick left the bank and started the gay life in New York. But Rick was a Winthrop and wealthy, and because of Mara, and his father's job, Alan couldn't say anything and didn't. So while each of them suspected the other, neither suspected Tillyard. In that letter Alan wrote to you, Purcell, all he did was assert again—with all the solemnity that even the law admits to dying testimony—that he did not steal the bonds.

"Well, Tillyard didn't know that—which is the beautiful irony of the thing, and shows, if it needed to be shown again,

171

that the guilty soul is never a free soul. But he knew one thing very well: he knew Alan hadn't confessed a crime that he himself had committed. And he was bound, as the guilty person, to fear that Alan might have pointed to him. The idea that he was suspected may have been growing in his soul for months, perhaps—built up out of a word, a look, or a gesture of Alan's that was actually meaningless. Hence undoubtedly his planning of his new crimes to hang the boy. His eminent respectability and integrity was his protection, he couldn't bear the shadow of a real suspicion. So he had to know what was in that so-called confession."

He turned to me.

"Then you told me, Mrs. Latham—in Tillyard's presence—that you'd got the letters from Alan when he was on the point of killing himself. Tillyard must have suspected even earlier that they were important—when he saw the relief on the boy's face as he gave them to you. He tried to get them as soon as he could, to make sure, found they were gone and took the pistol. But until you told us then, he hadn't known they were written in the shadow of death, when Alan would be released from any fear of saying what Tillyard, being guilty, thought he must suspect. At that point the necessity of getting those letters became desperate.

"The other person beside Alan to whom those letters would mean something would be Mara. I saw her, and persuaded her to give them to me. I read them. I was certain before who'd done all this and why—I've been thinking about it a long time, for three years in fact. So I confided to Tillyard, and no one else, that I'd got them—thus letting Mara out; she'd have been in pretty grave danger after it had come out that her prints were on the gun and it was plain she'd taken the letters. I told him I'd put them in the mail pouch to go to you, Purcell, for two reasons: first that I had no right to read them, and second because I didn't want to risk carrying them around so Alan and his father could do away with me and get them.

"Well, Tillyard must have been in a dreadful quandary. Either I'd read that letter, or—as I told everybody—I hadn't. If I had, either it said he was guilty or it was a confession or it said nothing about all this. But he knew it wasn't a confession, and if it said nothing there was no reason in the world why I shouldn't tell him so, and if it said he was guilty it was hardly likely I'd be talking to him as I was. So, with the fact that I really had no right to read it—morally, anyway—while the State's Attorney had, his assumption of course had to be that I really hadn't read it.

"He and I didn't leave the hall until Jim took the mail. He

172

knew, of course, that the pouch would stay in the barn until the milk truck picked it up. He went after it, and he forgot the alarm put in there last year when there was an epidemic of barnyard thievery. And when he heard that bell and saw those lights, of course he knew the devil had caught up with him—even if he had time to see that the letters were not in the bag. There was no reason in God's world for an innocent man to be down there. It would instantly occur to him that I'd set a trap for him, that I consequently must know other things, and that many small things out of the past would take meaning in Purcell's mind when he once started looking back."

Dr. Birdsong studied the bowl of his pipe for a moment.

"I wish I'd left a gun there. He'd have preferred that, and so would all of us. He didn't have one, because you can't conceal a gun in a linen suit. He really couldn't afford to have one on him anyway, or carry one in his car."

He looked at me again.

"I asked you to think what had happened before each of these killings. Irene had announced her decision to divide the estate, of course.—Anything else?"

"Yes," I said. "Irene's saying Rick had the lighter when he came to her room; and the one simple act at the Fountain that you thought was worse than killing two human beings."

He nodded.

"Irene's story was a complete fabrication. She didn't dream Tillyard had actually killed Rick, she was just defending him from what she thought was a horrible accusation Cheryl had made against him, and taking out a little spite against Cheryl. She hadn't the faintest suspicion that Tillyard hadn't given the lighter back to Rick, just as he'd said. Yarborough's testimony was absolutely meaningless, of course. Even if he really had wanted to burn something, Rick would have had matches with him.—And the second point."

His face hardened again.

"Tillyard asking you to come to Romney in his car—deliberately throwing Dan and Cheryl together just when it would infuriate Irene beyond endurance . . . and ruin for both of them something that I should think is pretty important."

He didn't look at Dan, but I did, and Dan was looking down at the floor between his feet.

173

29

It seemed odd, coming back to Romney, Dan and I, after we left Mr. Purcell's office. He and Dr. Birdsong had disappeared into the Fountain bar. I think Dan would have liked to go with them, and I'm not sure I wouldn't myself. But it wouldn't have looked well, and in Port Tobacco that's still important.

The State Roads Commission, I noticed, had put the glass pebbles back in the sign at the entrance to the cedar-lined drive. Mara was alone in the sitting room when we came in. I think we both expected to see Alan there, but he wasn't. I saw Dan go to the window and look out. Natalie Lane, in her white-rimmed sun glasses, was sitting under the mimosa tree, and so, not much to my surprise, was Mr. Fellowes Dunthorne, in his. Dan cleared his throat, came over to Mara, sat down beside her, twined his big bronzed fingers in her small delicate ones.

"Where's Alan?" he asked.

"He's at his father's," she said. "He won't come here—not unless you ask him.—If you'd rather not, we'll wait till we can go away together."

Dan got up without a word. I saw his blond head disappearing over the box toward the tenant house; and it seemed to me less than a moment before he was back again, and Alan Keane and Mara were lost in each other's arms, and Dan and I were definitely superfluous.

We went out into the hall, but at the door we stopped. Dan grinned. "I guess we'd better leave Natalie the farm girl to her haying," he said, and we went out the other way and down the path through the arborvitae to Mrs. Jellyby's.

I felt sorrier for him that I'd ever felt for anybody, I think, in all my life. He hadn't mentioned Cheryl, not once, and every time Dr. Birdsong had spoken her name I'd seen one more drop of barren longing distilled behind his blue eyes. Yet he didn't ask if Dr. Birdsong had found her, or if anyone had found her. I thought in a way it was keeping his last unspoken promise to his mother, a sort of penance for the doubt he'd had of her . . . for I think he hadn't been sure at first, nor had he believed, just as I'm not sure I believed, that Irene had at last relented about Mara and Alan. Just once while Dr. Birdsong had been talking, he'd looked at me with a twisted smile and a shrug; but I knew he'd go on, as he'd said in my Georgetown garden, not seeing a plane in the air, or blossoms on a branch, or ice on a brook's edge in the woods, without thinking about her.

Or certainly not a weeping willow on the river's edge, I thought as we came down Mrs. Jellyby's walk. She looked up from her wooden measure of columbine seeds, her clear level eyes serene and understanding.

"What's the trouble with you?" she said.

"Nothing," Dan said. "I just came to say good-bye. I'm going back to Paris."

I blinked. I don't think he knew himself that that's what he'd decided to do.

"Nonsense," Mrs. Jellyby said. "You can't keep running away from yourself. Sit down. Not there—that's Cheryl's seat."

He stopped, balanced and suspended in mid-air, staring at her.

"Cheryl . . . ?"

"Would I let her go barging off by herself?" Mrs. Jellyby asked curtly. "Cheryl!"

And in the little door that led to Mrs. Jellyby's bedroom I saw the girl with the golden hair and the eyes like faded hyacinths.

Dan looked at her for a long time, and neither of them spoke. Then his face broke into his old irresistible grin.

"And you can both of you get to work," Mrs. Jellyby said. "And no nonsense. Bring those strings, Grace. I need somebody tall to help with the trumpet vine."

In the garden she took the red string, and handed me a tin measure full of bright yellow corn.

"You go and feed the peacocks—the trumpet vines are all done."

Mrs. Jellyby smiled.

"She's the kind of mistress I've always wanted for Romney," she said.

I couldn't make the sort of noise she made to call the peacocks, but as the first grain of corn hit the ground they started for me. And behind them—and not entirely out of place, I thought—came Mr. Dunthorne.

"You know, I've got to thank you," he said.

"Really?"

"I've decided to marry Natalie."

"That's grand," I said.

"I never could make up my mind," he went on, "until you told me about that business of the insurance."

"Really?"

"A girl's got something who'd do that and never talk about it."

"Natalie's got plenty," I said.

He burrowed around inside his bright plaid jacket, and fished out a leather billfold. "And here's this," he said.

He held his hand out, and I held out mine, and saw in it two five hundred dollar bills.

"What's that?" I inquired. "The marriage broker's fee?"

"No," he said. "But you bet they'd hang the guy, and I bet they wouldn't. Just a sporting proposition, and I always like to pay up on the line."

I've never, I may say, been quite sure about that bet . . . and I don't really know what I'll do when Cheryl pays me back.—I do know, however, that I never see a bright pebble out of a roadside sign that my heart doesn't miss a beat.